LIVE

AND LET

BEE

D S NELSON

Black Hat Books

LIVE AND LET BEE

First published 2016 by Black Hat Books

ISBN: 978-0-9928480-2-6

Copyright © D S Nelson 2016

www.dsnelson.co.uk

info@dsnelson.co.uk

Cover art by Kathryn Ellis-Blandford
krizena@hotmail.co.uk.

'Honey is sweet, but the bee stings.'

Old English proverb

1.
Drifting

Drifting refers to the movement of a bee that has become lost and entered a different hive. This can often happen when hives are placed close together in straight lines.

There were two bodies on the beach that morning: two bodies and one soul. The sea dragged itself away from the shore, white froth hissing at the sand and clinging to stray shingle that peppered the beach. Above, the moon and the sun occupied the same hazy blue-grey sky. At the edge of the world, the sky and sea merged, gulls and guillemots moving easily between the two, plunging into the water from the surrounding cliffs.

It was six-thirty; I was alone, and free to commune with nature, to greet the day. Without a hat, the wind pulled at what hair I had left and my ears ached from its icy bite. This was bliss. In the dark days of winter, the long days of summer were something I looked forward to and this year's summer held particular joy for me. I was attending the wedding of my oldest friend, Lord Rufus Blackwood.

When the Isle of Salderk was first mentioned as the location for Rufus' nuptials, I had raised an eyebrow. To me the more obvious venue would have been the Blackwood's own estate. However, his normal residence, the manor and surrounding fields back home in Tuesbury, appeared not to be enough for Rufus' high maintenance Russian fiancée. Matilda had insisted they marry on the Isle of Salderk, which boasted a castle with palatial grounds. I had learnt over the last four months, as preparations for the wedding commenced, that what Matilda wanted, Matilda got.

'Why Salderk?' I had asked. Rufus had informed me that Dame Albrecht De Vries, matriarch of Salderk, was Matilda's family and the castle was special to Matilda. I had never heard Matilda mention the Dame before, but now, standing on the beach, with the fresh salt air pounding my eyes and ears, invigorated by the life spilling forth from the ocean, it didn't matter. I could see why this isle was special. Eleanor, my late wife, would have loved it.

Perhaps Matilda was not the cold-hearted, money-orientated woman I suspected she was. She had shown me several times now that she had a heart. However, for my friend's sake, I remained concerned, as to where that heart truly lay.

Rufus and Matilda were staying in a small cottage on the edge of the castle estate, aptly named *'Bumblebee Cottage'* in reference to the Dame's honey farm. Rufus had wanted me to stay in the castle with the family but this time it was my turn to insist. A bed and breakfast just fifteen minutes up the road would do me fine.

Salderk is still a feudal isle and the Dame is very much in control. From what I have been told, Dame Albrecht De Vries is benevolent in her reign and likes to think she has allowed the residents freedom to work for themselves, releasing them from any ancient obligation to work on her estate or any of her connected businesses. According to Rufus, she has even allowed an ex-employee to set up his own organic apiary just a mile down the road.

Six miles long and four miles wide, the Isle of Salderk has a population of just over nine-hundred; fewer than

Tuesbury and definitely fewer than the seabirds that migrate here. From Tuesbury the island can be reached only by a four-hundred and fifty mile car journey, to the ferry at Oban, a four hour ferry ride to the larger island of Calner, where, with no cars allowed on Salderk, we parted with our hire car and boarded a smaller ferry for an hour long trip to complete our journey.

Unsurprisingly, the isle was not somewhere I'd had the pleasure of visiting before. The journey had proved a logistical nightmare for transporting three of my finest hand made top hats and of course the bride's bespoke order. I prayed they would survive, as I had no tools to carry out repairs. Whilst it was perfectly possible to reshape the sinamay adornments on Matilda's hat with only a kettle, the top hats would prove much more tricky to repair should they become damaged.

In the end, the trials and tribulations of the journey were insignificant. I was honoured to be Rufus' best man, here to support my friend in any way I could, even if it meant sixteen-hours travel across land and sea. Despite his reputation as a ladies man, Rufus was trying to make up for past mistakes. This marriage, he said, would be his last and he wanted to celebrate a new chapter in his life. With the discovery of his two sons, previously unknown to him, he was determined this should be a festival of love, family and unity.

The wedding had been moved forward at Matilda's insistence. She wanted to show support for Rufus after the events of the spring. I hoped this was the case and that it wasn't Rufus' discovery that he had two sons that had ignited her enthusiasm for matrimony. Rivalry for the Blackwood fortune had already caused enough heartbreak.

In the time that I had been acquainted with the soon-to-be Lady Blackwood, I had found that Rufus and Matilda could not be more different and yet in some ways so alike. With classic alpha male looks: dark eyes, silvering hair, a furrowed brow, swarthy, weather-beaten skin and, despite being in his sixties, a well toned triangular upper body, Rufus had outdone me with women in the past and was certainly outdoing his peers now. Although a Lord, and sole heir to the Blackwood estate, Rufus would never have let you know he had aristocratic roots. Proud but not pompous, his privileges were something he bore with neither arrogance nor strain. He was ambivalent to his situation in life, taking each day as it came.

Matilda, twenty years his junior, was sophisticated, tall and delicate. I would wager not a pound above eight stone. She was the sort of woman who slept on silk bed sheets and only ate organic yogurt and blueberries for breakfast. Of Russian descent, Mrs Matilda Darensky had also been married before. To all intents and purposes she was the archetypal gold digger, but Rufus was sure of her loyalty and very much in love. Their union had been a complete surprise to me but then again, in the years between childhood and retirement, Rufus and I had grown apart. A fortuitous side effect of recent, less fortunate, events had been the rekindling our friendship.

There were still three weeks to go until the wedding itself. After I declined to stay in the castle, Rufus had insisted on paying for my accommodation on the island so that I could be a part of the preparation. I did not relish the thought of three weeks of wedding preparations; however, Rufus and I had grown apart for no other reason than lack of effort, on both parts, and I was determined I was going to put this right. And so it was that I found myself on east side of Salderk, walking the flotsam-strewn beach and contemplating the delights of summer.

An almighty storm last night had rattled the sash windows of the little bed and breakfast. The rain pounded on the window and Prince, my recently adopted Spaniel, had been persistent in his plight to burrow under the duvet, defying my objections. I discovered, on listening to the radio this morning, that the freak weather was the back end of Hurricane Bertha. I thanked my lucky stars we had not still been on the ferry.

The beach was littered with the paraphernalia of human existence. A plastic drinks bottle, a polystyrene cup, splintered wood, old fishing nets and a marker buoy were just a few of the things I could actually define. A herring gull screamed its disgust as I disturbed its scavenge through the debris. I looked down at my feet. My shoes were salt stained and laced with seaweed. Inside my shoes my socks were damp. Perhaps brogues had not been the best choice of footwear. I had brought with me another pair of dress shoes, saved for the wedding itself, but I had made the grave omission of wellies from my luggage. I would have to walk down to the small row of shops at the heart of the island and hope they had a suitable pair of Hunters.

Something caught my eye to the left of me. In the surf, about three feet away, lay a battered Breton hat. I stepped forward and picked it up with my thumb and forefinger, hopping back quickly as the sea came up to meet me. The wool hat was soaked through, akin to being washed up on the shore rather than blown off a passing fisherman's head. A traditional Breton, worn by both fishermen and moneyed yachting folk, was not an entirely strange thing to find on a shoreline.

Looking inside I found the maker's label was not known to me. I pride myself in knowing milliners labels; my only excuse is this one definitely wasn't English. If it had been French, as you might expect for this eponymous hat, I would stand a chance, but this one wasn't even European. Unwilling to return it to its resting place in the surf, I lay it on a rock to dry in the sun. Perhaps its owner would return for it?

A solitary bark from Prince indicated a find. I assumed the singularity of Prince's bark told me he had not yet forgiven me for the extended car journey and long ferry trip over. There was no explaining travel sickness to a cocker spaniel. In his view, my actions were heinous. The ensuing overnight storm had only proved to him that wherever I had taken him, it was far from the beloved sanctuary of Tuesbury and our home. No amount of Bonio was talking him down from this sulk.

Picking my way through the bladder-wrack and tiny rock pools stuffed with anemones, I looked up to where Prince was waiting. Tugging at the object with all his might, the tide receding around him, it became clear that what Prince had found was not at all aquatic but, in fact, very human. I broke into a precarious jog, trying hard not to become entangled in the surrounding seaweed or slip on the wet rocks.

Out of breath, my face stinging from the wind, I looked down at the mass beside Prince. It was clearly identifiable as a man. Still retaining a checked shirt, heavy donkey jacket, jeans and one, pure white sock. His face was grey, his beard heavy with seawater and his lips bloated and blue. Was this the owner of the Breton? I'd unfortunately seen enough dead bodies to know he had no need for it now.

I bent down to pull Prince away, praising him for alerting me to the plight of a fellow human. He wasn't easily dissuaded and as I tried to reassure him, the sun glinted off a piece of metal beside the body. I reached forward and as I did a gull plummeted from the sky to fight me for the prize. Instinctively I withdrew my hand but a sharp bark from Prince had the gull flinging itself back towards the sun.

Free to pick up the metal object without fear of attack, I found it was a pocket watch made of heavy silver, embossed with navy blue enamel. I lifted it up to take a closer look only to discover it was attached to the inside of the man's donkey jacket. The cold silver case displayed two eagles standing proudly either side of an enamelled shield and as I popped the case open, the time read one fifteen; I assumed in the morning. The same time the storm had been at its peak.

There was no point in using my mobile - I hadn't even brought it with me - I knew there would be no reception. There'd been none since I arrived on the island. I looked up and around me and saw a lone figure walking on the cliffs above with, what I could just about make out, was an Old English sheep dog. I shouted and waved my arms. The wind carried my voice away from the cliffs and out to sea, but the figure stopped momentarily and waved back. For a second I had a faint hope I would have some help, but my shoulders sagged as the figure set off on their way once more.

Could they not see what I was stood next to? Were dead bodies normal in these parts? Did they really think someone was sunbathing at six-thirty in the morning in full attire? Either way, no help was coming from the cliff above. Prince barked once more, impatient at my lack of action.

'We're going to have to walk back to the bed and breakfast, old boy,' I said.

He replied by heading back along the beach and stopping a few feet on to see if I was following. I was reluctant to leave the man in his supine and undignified state but I knew there was little to be done. The ocean had his soul and now I had to be the one to tell the authorities. I'd had many blissful years without a gruesome find, shocking occurrence or even a broken bone and now in the last two years I'd seen more corpses than I could shake a stick at. I pulled my coat closer and resigned myself to the inevitable. I yet again found myself in the uncomfortable yet familiar position of having to report the discovery of a dead body.

2.
The Drone

A drone is a male honeybee that is produced from an unfertilised egg, laid by the queen. Drones have little to worry about in life as they are fed and tended to by the worker bees. Their only purpose is to mate with a new queen when she appears.

My discovery created quite a stir at the bed and breakfast. With only one policeman on the whole island, it was easy to establish who should be informed of the body on the beach. The problem was convincing my hosts and owners of the bed and breakfast, the Naismiths, that it was a police matter.

Situated in an old water tower, the bed and breakfast had two large double rooms, a shared bathroom and a breakfast room. I had chosen this quaint if not quixotic little bed and breakfast as the owners had no qualms about Prince and in fact welcomed pets. On hand for breakfast and indeed dinner should you require it, Mr and Mrs Naismith lived in a purpose built extension adjoining the tower. On the discovery of dog friendly accommodation, it wasn't long before Delilah, Rob and of course Delilah's Jack Russell Bertie, booked the other room for their arrival in a week's time.

Since she and Bertie had entered my shop two years ago, murder and intrigue had following them and Delilah had a nasty habit of dragging me right into the middle of it. So much so, that now I am retired it has been suggested, by more than one person, that I set up my own investigative services. I'm not so keen. It is one thing to have a passing interest in how someone you know has met an early demise; it's another to positively invite the speculation into your living room. However, I could not blame Delilah for the current situation; she hadn't even arrived on the island yet.

Delilah and I are polar opposites. I prefer to be able to withdraw from the fray should it be necessary, especially after my near miss earlier this year and I enjoy the shelter of my hat-making shed on my allotment back home. In contrast, Delilah is never one to miss out on a social gathering and loves a good wedding. She had been ridiculously excited when she and Rob had been invited.

My first meeting with Rob had not been altogether auspicious but he had grown on me. Once I'd chipped away at the policeman's veneer of detached observation, I'd discovered a warm heart, with a clear affection for Delilah and a strong sense of justice and duty. My only concern was Delilah's propensity for finding trouble. I like to think I temper her enthusiasm for murder and I was in some respects pleased she had not yet arrived. Nonetheless, I would have been grateful of some moral support from her and her young sergeant, as I now came under the scrutiny of the Naismiths.

Cherry cheeked, wearing a vinyl apron that announced, '*I love to cook with wine*', Mrs Naismith was insistent and a force to be reckoned with.

'Perhaps we should go and check, Mr Hetherington. Are you sure he's dead? Mr Naismith is trained in CPR ye ken,' she said, nodding at her husband. Her broad Scottish accent was soft and hypnotic in the warmth of the Aga, capable of removing the urgency from any situation. Mr Naismith was sitting at the kitchen table, reading the *Salderk Bugle,* unmoved by the conversation.

'Mrs Naismith, he is indeed quite dead.' I too had recently acquired some limited resuscitative skills, after a rainy afternoon spent with my daughter, who was yet again worrying about the increasing number of bodies I seemed to be finding of late. *'Perhaps if you knew CPR they wouldn't be dead,'* she had said. *'You'd be a hero instead of the grim reaper.'* I reassured her, as I now reassured Mrs Naismith, the man was: 'Very dead.'

'Definitely?' Mrs Naismith was disappointed.

'Definitely.'

'Ye see George has saved ten lives now on the island. It'd be ne bother to pop down to the beach and check.'

George grunted.

'Mrs Naismith I really think….'

'No offence Mr Hetherington, but you're nae trained,' Mr Naismith interjected from behind his paper.

'George is,' his wife picked up the cue, 'and he's always saying we can't waste time with nae ambulance on the island. Have to get a helicopter, see?'

'I do see, Mrs Naismith, but I really am sure. My daughter's a nurse and….'

'Ooooo, is she? Saints they are, saints!'

'Yes quite, but I really think we should find Constable … Simmons, was it you said?'

'Yes. Well, if you insist! I'd much rather go and check on that poor man on the beach. Poor soul. Nae much use is Walter Simmons.'

I ignored the slight aimed at the only law enforcer present on the island. Mrs Naismith pulled on an anorak over her apron and turned to me. 'Come on then, we better go to the pub.'

'The pub?'

'Yes, The Fisherman's Rest. That's where he'll be.

That's where he always is. Back soon George.'

There was a second grunt from behind the paper as George acknowledged his wife. I followed Mrs Naismith obediently, Prince tagging along behind, as bewildered as I was with the events of the last hour.

It was a brisk twenty-minute walk to the pub. The interrogation I had just endured had shaken my confidence a little and I hoped I wasn't wrong. The idea of leaving someone in distress to die slowly on a windy, storm-worn beach was not something I wanted on my conscience. I shook off this notion. The pocket watch had clearly said one fifteen. If my assumptions were correct, he had been in the water a long time. I looked at my own watch, eight a.m. What was the local police officer doing in the pub at seven thirty in the morning? Even with the new licensing laws I wasn't sure there were many who would frequent a pub at that time of day, let alone officers of the law.

Featuring in the Good Beer Guide, the pub's proximity to the bed and breakfast had been another reason for me choosing to stay with the Naismiths. From the road leading up to the pub I could see the large oak door was firmly closed and the shutters on the windows echoed this sentiment. The sign, hanging below the upstairs window, showed a white bearded version of Captain Haddock complete with pipe, taking me back to the Tintin comics of my youth. A few steps ahead of me, Mrs Naismith knocked firmly on the door.

'Who is it?'

'Betty Naismith, Walter. Got someone wants to see ye, here. Police business.'

'Police Business?'

'Yes, now open the door, ye …,' but before Mrs

Naismith could get any further there was a clunking of bolts, the sound of a key in the lock and the door creaked open.

Squinting in the sunlight was a short man in his forties, with round steel-rimmed glasses. He was dressed in a woollen sweater, similar to the one I had seen on the dead man, oilskin trousers and, balanced precariously on a haystack of blonde hair, a Breton to top off the ensemble.

'Constable Simmons?' I asked.

'Yesssss?'

'I'm Mr Hetherington, and I'm staying with the Naismiths ....'

'Paying guest he is Walter, so mind yer manners ...,' Mrs Naismith interrupted.

'... Yes,' I continued trying to get to the point. 'I'm afraid I've found a body on the beach.'

'On the beach?'

'Yes, the beach.' I was bemused as to why the location was what Simmons focused on and not the body. Again I was left wondering if dead bodies were a regular occurrence on Salderk. 'I think you should come and have a look,' I continued.

Constable Simmons leant on the door and it swung forward slightly. Frowning, he replied, 'A body ye say?'

'Yes.'

'Hmmm. Probably one of thae poor sailors from last night's storm.'

I looked at Mrs Naismith, who looked down at Prince, who looked up at Constable Simmons. There was a long silence.

'I think you'd better come and have a look,' I repeated.

'Hmmm. I'm Special though,' Simmons replied.

'Right.' There wasn't much I could say to that.

'Yes, I told ye he wasn't much good,' Mrs Naismith started again. 'Special, he is.'

'Right,' I said

My feet crunched against the lose stones on the road as I turned and started back towards the bed and breakfast, contemplating what to do next. I heard a heavy sigh from the doorway behind me.

'I suppose I should come and have a look,' Constable Simmons relented. 'Give me a second I'll get ma coat.'

I stopped and waited for him to join me, Prince sat patiently beside me, the salt water in his caramel coloured fur glistening in the early morning sunlight. Constable Simmons emerged from The Fisherman's Rest and locked the door behind him. It was definitely an odd place to find a constable, but then again, this one was *special*.

'I'm off back home, Walter,' Mrs Naismith said, already level with me. 'George'll be wanting to know where is cup a tea is.' Throwing her hands into the air and muttering something in Gaelic, she trotted off back down the path at a pace. I watched her walking away, truly amazed at the lack of concern for the situation.

'And where are you going, Mr Hetherignton?' Constable Simmons asked, his hands deep in his pockets a frown still set on his face.

'Well, I better come with you to the beach,' I replied.

'It's quicker this way,' he said pointing across the uneven moorland dotted with clumps of heather and cotton grass.

I walked quickly to keep up with him as he started to walk. 'I appreciate you coming to help, Constable Simmons.' Prince bounded ahead, back to his old self again.

'Nae problem,' he replied, head down against the wind.

An awkward silence stretched out before us. I coughed.

'So you live in the pub?'

'I own it,' he laughed.

'Really? I suppose it makes sense, a policeman owning a pub, you're not going to get any trouble,' I smiled.

'I'm nae a proper policeman,' He stopped and turned to face me. 'I'm a Special.'

'You said, I stopped beside him.

'A Special Constable. That's like a policeman with restricted powers. Bit like a volunteer. They didnae pay me; nae enough crime here!'

'Ah ….' Now it made sense. Constable Simmons started walking across the moor again.

'If anything happens, see, I'm meant to phone the mainland, but it takes them a few days to get here.'

'I can imagine.' I was only too aware of how long that journey could be and then I remembered Mrs Naismith's comment about the ambulance. 'Haven't they got a helicopter?'

'Course! But they nae gonna send that for a little old burglary, or a fight in the local. Most of the time, we sort it amongst ourselves. I leave them to it; I don't get involved in much. Bad for business,' he nodded back in the direction of the pub.

'Right. But this is a dead body!'

'True enough, but I don't think it's all that likely to be a crime Mr Hetherington. A ship ran aground on the rocks about ten miles off the coast last night. Hell of a storm, did ye hear it?'

I nodded, there had been no choice but to hear it.

'Seems there was a crew of thirteen on board. So far only two are accounted for. Ye know what they say?'

'No.' I leaned in hoping to hear an interesting

fisherman's adage.

'Thirteen: unlucky for some,' he laughed.

I recoiled. Laughing over a dead body just wasn't normal. I was reminded of the dog walker's cheery wave; perhaps it was normal on Salderk?

'Mind, I didn't see it this morning when I was out,' Simmons said.

'This morning?'

'Aye, fishing,' he said tugging at the oilskins. 'Only just got back. It's a specialty of mine in the pub: fresh fish.'

'I see.'

'You'll have to come in and try it, Mr Hetherington. You can't beat fresh mackerel.'

'Indeed you can't,' I replied.

'What brings ye to Salderk then?'

'My friend's wedding,' I was starting to get out of breath trying to keep pace with Simmons.

'Oh, Lord Blackwood, you're with that lot are ye? Not staying at the castle then?'

'No.' I didn't feel the need to explain myself, it was really none of Special Constable Simmons' business.

'I've seen them around the island. Him and Mrs Darensky, that is. Mrs Darensky is often here. Friends with the Dame she is.' He made an impression of what he thought was a hoity-toity face. I did not reply. Discretion is often the better part of valour and he was talking about my friend's fiancée.

I could see ahead of us the land began to slope away towards the coast and I could hear the sea once more crashing on the shore. This must have been the cliff the dog walker had been on, but I hadn't seen a way down. As we approached the edge, a steep sandy pathway showed itself and I once again cursed the footwear I had chosen.

'I cannae see it Mr Hetherington. You sure it was here?'

'Yes, yes. It was definitely here.'

Looking down to the beach I couldn't see the body either and I began to doubt myself, worried it had been washed out to sea again. Then I realised a small tree, growing out of the side of the cliff, was obscuring the view of the body.

'It's behind the tree,' I said triumphantly.

'There's nae tree on the beach Mr Hetherington.' A look of compassion mixed with pity swept across Constable Simmons' face.

'No, this tree.' I pointed at the frail skeleton clinging to the cliff edge.

A few feet further down, along the path and the body was as clear as day.

'There,' I almost shouted.

'All right, all right, I can see it,' the constable huffed.

The sea had almost completely receded from the beach and it would only be a few more hours before it began its return. Prince ran the last few yards of the path, much steadier on his feet than his human company. Trotting straight up to the body he barked at us from below.

'Plucky little thing, isn't he?' Simmons said.

'He's a good companion. He's saved my life before now,' I replied

Simmons raised an eyebrow but didn't ask the inevitable question; instead he hurried on down the path. His hobnail boots gave him much more grip than my brogues. Finding no traction on the soft sand, Walter got further away from me and as I tried to catch up I slipped, falling squarely on my backside. I whizzed past Simmons, lucky not to collect him on the way, and landed in a heap on the beach. I stood up with as much dignity as I could muster and dusted myself off. Thankfully, the only injury was to my pride.

'In a hurry Mr Hetherington?' Simmons smirked. 'I don't think our man's going anywhere,' he chuckled to himself.

I was terse in my reply as I stalked off to join Prince. 'No. I severely doubt he is.'

I won't say what the early morning wildlife had done to the man's face in the time that I had been gone; suffice to say I was glad I hadn't eaten a substantial breakfast. As Simmons and I stood there looking at the sight, I wondered who would break the silence first. I didn't have to wait long.

'Well, he's dead all right,' Simmons said, hands on hips. 'Seagulls seen to that. How long ago did ye find him, Mr Hetherington?'

I looked at my watch. 'About two hours ago.' I gritted my teeth against my frustration at the speed with which anything happened on this island.

'I'll get the lifeboat boys down here. They can help move him and then we'll set about trying to work out who he is.'

'Don't you think we should leave him where he is and get the mainland police?' I said.

'Why?'

'Well, it could be murder?'

'Nae, it'll be no hassle, the boys are used to heavy lifting.'

'NO!' I shouted in frustration, the surprise at my tone very evident on Simmons' face.

Clearly hurt he replied. 'All right no need to get in a tizz. Look, Mr Hetherington, the man's drowned. It's undignified enough he's been out here so long, best we move him.'

'He's been here since one fifteen.'

'How dae ye ken that?'

'His pocket watch has stopped at that time.'

'Well then, that solves it, that's when the storm was at its highest.'

'I know, but what if he wasn't on the boat? What if he's nothing to do with the boat? What if he's been murdered?'

'What? Murder? On Salderk? Oh no, no, no, Mr Hetherington, things like that daenae happen on this island,' and with that Special Constable Simmons began the ascent back up the cliff to fetch the lifeboat crew.

3.
The Brood Chamber

This is the part of the hive where the young are reared.

Rufus let out a hearty laugh. 'You think murder is following you around Blake? Like some kind of spectre,' he raised his arms, hunched his shoulders and waggled his fingers, imitating a ghostly apparition, mocking my serious tone. 'I'd better watch out hadn't I? I might not survive to marry Matilda!' And he laughed again.

I had no choice but to laugh with him. He was right; without the solitude of my shed and the occupation of hat-making, my imagination was running away from me. After all it was a reasonable explanation that the unknown man was a victim of the storm, why did it have to be murder? All the signs pointed to drowning: sopping wet body, blue lips.

The find had made the front page of the local paper, the *Salderk Bugle*. I hoped it hadn't made it into any of the national press; my daughter would definitely have been on the phone. After losing her mother over ten years ago she found it very difficult not to worry about losing her father, and her phone calls had become a little too frequent. A lack of mobile reception on the island had its benefits. I should be grateful to have a daughter that cares for me in this way; there are many who would envy me I'm sure. My guilty thought was assuaged by the knowledge that on my arrival on the island I had rung her from the bed and breakfast to assure her of my continued survival.

We were sitting in the grounds of Dame Albrecht De

Vries' castle. The walls stretched up to the sky above and were covered in Virginia creeper, which was going to give a fantastic display of flaming red and orange leaves in a month or so. We were sitting at a white wrought iron table that matched the chairs. A further three more sets made up a twee arrangement on the patio in front of the castle. Exactly the way you'd expect to see in the brochure of an establishment marketing itself as a wedding venue. The sun was past the yardarm and we had opened a bottle of Prosecco as we waited for the ladies to join us. Prince slept under the table as Rufus and I talked. Today it was food tasting; final decisions on the canapés and wedding buffet were to be made.

'I'm sure you're right Rufus,' I said taking a sip of my drink. 'All in an old man's head!'

'If you're an old man, does that mean I have to be too?' Rufus frowned in mock annoyance.

I smiled in reply. Neither of us was getting any younger but to admit it was folly.

The sun was shining in defiance of last night's storm. I had left Constable Simmons and the five lifeboat men on the beach. That was one emergency service that did seem to be appropriately staffed. I was still not entirely comfortable with the decision to delay informing the mainland police, but I knew there was little else I could do. I had reported the man's indecent position and that was all I could do. I looked up at the crenellations surrounding the east tower to the right of where we were sitting. It was a magnificent castle.

'It's a beautiful place, Rufus, there's no denying it. I can see why Matilda likes it.'

'Oh, it's not just the setting, the island holds great sentimental value to her.'

'Really?'

'Yes, she's spent a lot of her younger days here.'

'Really?' I had assumed Matilda had spent the majority of her life in Russia. It had never occurred to me she had been brought up on a remote island.

'The Dame's been awfully good to her. Helped her bring up Liliya, made Liliya a kind of ward and looked after her when Matilda had to go back to Russia to care for her parents. That's when she met her first husband. Matilda tells me he didn't like the idea of a daughter that wasn't his and so Liliya stayed here. Out of sight, out of mind.'

Liliya was Matilda Darensky's daughter. I had not been aware of her existence until quite recently and neither had Rufus. It all came out of the woodwork when Rufus discovered he himself had two sons. Matilda had been sixteen when she had Liliya, that much I did know.

'So how does she know the Dame?'

'Oh, some sort of family connection, not really sure of the details, it's not like I can question her too much given my past,' he said winking. 'Still, as far as I can tell, Liliya's grown up to be a perfect lady. I'd be happy if either of my sons found a girl like her to settle down with.'

Female voices caught our attention and we looked up to see Matilda, and who I assumed to be, Liliya and the Dame, rounding the east wing of the castle. A fourth woman accompanied them with a very hassled look about her, chewing the end of a pen and hugging an arm-full of papers.

'Ah, here they are,' Rufus said, concluding our previous conversation and as they reached our table we stood up.

'Blake, Matilda you know and this is Dame Albrecht De Vries, Liliya and our wedding planner, Aurora

Maldonado.'

I smiled 'Nice to meet you all and Matilda, a pleasure as always.'

Liliya placed herself neatly in chair, knees together, back straight, the Dame sat down beside her and Matilda remained standing. Aurora, shuffled her papers and pen in mouth reached forward to shake my hand,

'Nice to meet you Mr Hetherington, I understand you're the best man?'

'I am and I think the first of my duties should be to find Matilda a chair!' I said briefly shaking her hand and moving towards the other chairs.

'Oh no, no, let me do that,' Aurora replied. Despite her exotic name her accent was as English as the day was long. She put the mountain of papers on the table, where they spread in an avalanche across it and hurried off to get a chair for her employer.

'So nice to meet you Mr Hetherington,' the Dame offered a limp-wristed hand, bedecked with pearls, from across the table. I took it and returned the sentiment. 'You too madam, it is an honour. Do call me Blake.'

'Then you must call me Rosalyn.'

There was a pause and I nodded, smiling at Liliya, not sure I should offer a handshake to her also. The youth of today seem to miss out such formality the majority of the time and she was busying herself pouring a glass Prosecco.

'I understand you're a milliner, Blake?' Rosalyn said, squinting slightly in the sun.

'I am.' I was uncomfortable looking down at the Dame from the other side of the table but I was still unwilling to sit, while Matilda had no chair.

'Any relation to John Hetherington?'

'John?'

'Yes, the inventor of the top hat!' The Dame was smug in her knowledge, however, I had known to whom she was referring; I'd played this game a few too many times. John Hetherington was often thought to be the inventor of the top hat and caused a terrible row when he appeared in public wearing one. He was not the inventor though, it was George Dunnage, but my manners would never allow me to correct the Dame.

'I'm afraid not. I'd like to think my millinery has caused ladies to swoon but I am pleased to say it has never frightened horses,' I replied.

Aurora placed a chair down, scrapping it on the patio and saving me from any further millinery quizzes.

'We must get started,' said Rosalyn. 'Aurora, tell the staff they can bring the food out, there's a dear.'

'Of course madam.' Aurora pushed the chair in for Matilda, who sat down with the same grace and poise as her daughter and then went to talk to the staff.

Now that all the ladies were sitting, Rufus and I sat and I thought the conversation may turn to the food but I was wrong. I had not escaped the Dame's questioning yet.

'Blake, I hear your holiday has got off to a rather shaky start. I am so sorry. Bodies on the beach really aren't befitting of Salderk. It was a terrible storm last night so it's no surprise there were some casualties. I understand Simmons is dealing with it?' The Dame finished.

'He is, and I'm fine, thank you. I feel sorry for the poor chap on the beach,' I replied.

'Quite. I understand it's not the first body you've found either, how thrilling, but I do hope you're not going to upset our quiet little island with your cosmopolitan ways, Mr Hetherington.' there was not a hint of irony in her voice. This was clearly a statement and not a question.

I took up my glass of Prosecco before Liliya could pour me more. 'I'm here to celebrate the wedding of my very dear friend Madam and, trust me, I do not intend to find any more bodies; I've found quite enough for one lifetime.'

Rufus laughed breaking the awkward standoff. 'And I'm very glad to have you here, Blake.' He slapped me on the back just as I was taking a sip from my glass. I only just managed to retain the liquid and my composure.

'Glad to be here,' I said coughing back a mouthful of wine.

'What have you dragged us out here to try then, Matilda dear?'

'Rufus! You know it's important. This is our wedding, we can't just serve cheese, crackers and pork scratchings!' Matilda Darensky's accent was subtle but still apparent. A luxurious Russian twang, relaxed the listener.

'Eurgh! I hate the hair on those things,' Liliya screwed up her nose.

'But I thought we'd made a decision already?' Rufus replied.

'We have for the day dear but we need to decide on the evening buffet. I thought an afternoon tea would be appropriate.

'In the evening?'

'Yes, dear.'

'Not a hog roast then?'

'Eugh!' Liliya again.

'No. We'll have scones and finger food. I thought you English liked an afternoon tea?'

'We do indeed,' I said trying to mediate. This was fast becoming a domestic.

'We need to make a decision about the honey,' Matilda continued, ignoring me.

'Honey?' Rufus replied.

'Yes the honey in the wedding cake and the tea bread.'

'We'll use Rosalyn's surely?'

'I rather hoped you'd want to stick with the organic theme. Layland's honey is so much nicer.'

The Dame smiled, a far from benevolent smile, and Liliya shuffled in her seat. With impeccable timing, the food arrived at the table along with Aurora who, oblivious to the conversation so far, announced, 'Here we are ladies and gentlemen.'

Two young men dressed in smart white shirts, bow ties and black trousers placed silver platters of sandwiches and scones on the table and retreated back across the patio.

Aurora pointed at each of the sandwiches in turn. 'Sandwiches are smoked salmon and dill, lamb and mint, crayfish in a chipotle sauce, and for the vegetarians, roasted Mediterranean vegetables. The scones are blueberry, raspberry or strawberry. The tea bread will follow, they're just sorting out the honey.'

'Sorting out the honey?' Matilda required a qualification of this statement.

'Yes, the chef's a little agitated, but not to worry Mrs Darensky, it's all under control.'

'How can he be agitated? It's tea bread with honey!'

'I should think it is the honey that has upset him,' the Dame replied.

Matilda looked at the matriarch with evident surprise.

'I've told my staff that honey from *that* farm is not to enter my kitchen. It's competition dear, pure and simple. Geoff Layland can have his little venture if he likes, but it is not to venture into my kitchen. He knows this, he's probably very pleased with himself right now.'

'I'm sorry Rosalyn but I really want this all to be

organic! Layland's honey is organic. You understand don't you?' Matilda's eyes widened in a look I had seen several times on my then, three-year-old daughter. A look that said I have you well and truly round my little finger.

The Dame's face relaxed and she smiled. 'Of course I do dear; it's your wedding day. Although I have no idea what all the fuss is about. His bees take pollen from the same heather as my bees!' She looked up at the wedding planner who had been holding her breath since the conversation began. 'You better let Nathaniel know he can use the honey.'

'Yes Madam, of course.' Aurora hurried off towards the kitchen her posture displaying her relief.

The incident with the honey resolved, for now at least, we all settled down to sample the afternoon tea. Prince shuffled at my feet but he didn't beg. I'd managed to train him to wait for an offer. Yet again I was filled with nostalgia, as the taste of salmon sandwiches and fruited scones brought back memories of reading Famous Five stories, in front of the fire.

'I'm not sure about the bread dear, what do you think?' Matilda was talking to her daughter.

'Spelt might be better for the lamb ones mummy. Spelt is very à la mode at the moment.'

'Mmm. Make a note of that will you Aurora. I think maybe a different bread for each filling. Spelt for the lamb, white farmhouse for the crayfish, granary for the vegetarians and I think … yes … I think there should be some of my heritage in there, so get them to make Russian black bread for the salmon.'

The wedding planner hurriedly scribbled her notes on the paper, holding a half eaten Mediterranean vegetable sandwich as she did.

'Do we have to be so exotic dear?' Rufus complained wiping his mouth on a napkin.

'I must say, Matilda, it's all very nice, with or without the different bread,' I said, trying to give my friend some solidarity.

'It can't be just *nice*, Blake, it has to be perfect!' she admonished. I chose to be quiet once more. Prince rested his head on my foot in sympathy.

'Constable Simmons!' The Dame announced. I turned in my seat to see Special Constable Walter Simmons walking through the rose garden to the west side of the castle, towards our little group. 'And what can we do for you?'

'Madam. I'm sorry to interrupt.' Simmons doffed his Breton and looked straight at me. 'Looks like you were right, Mr Hetherington.'

'Oh?' I replied.

'Yes. Our man wasn't on last night's wrecked ship after all.'

'But I thought you said they hadn't all been accounted for yet!?' The Dame demanded.

'No Madam, but the surviving two crew members don't recognise him, although I'm sure the seagulls didn't help matters.' Walter coughed. 'He was probably a stowaway, they said, because none of the crew would have anything as fancy as that pocket watch.'

'A pocket watch?' The Dame replied, incredulous.

'This one.' the constable held up the silver cased watch by its chain and the sunlight glinted off it. 'One of the two survivors is Polish. He says the pocket watch is Russian. I thought Mrs Darensky may ken.'

'And why, Constable Simmons, would I have any idea who that pocket watch belonged to?' Distain oozed from

Matilda's person.

'I'm sorry Mrs Darensky, I didn't mean offence, I just thought you might ken whose the coat of arms was. It might give us an idea as to who the man was.'

Matilda stood up slowly and reached across the table. Taking the watch in one hand, she spent a few moments studying it.

'I have no idea. It looks like a cheap reproduction to me. A pretender I'm sure. Now if you don't mind we are trying to decide what sandwiches to eat at our wedding,' she smiled thinly and sat back down.

As she did, the tea bread, spread with honey, appeared.

'Now Rufus, try some of this I'm sure you will see why I prefer this honey.' Matilda turned her attention to the tea bread and her husband to be.

Walter Simmons, not at all put out by the reaction of the Dame or Mrs Darensky, reached out and took a piece of the tea bread. The whole table watched in amazement as the piece of tea bread disappeared in one bite and Walter proceeded to lick his fingers of honey.

'I must say Madam,' he said to the Dame. 'Your bees do produce the most delicious honey!'

Rufus and I held our breath in anticipation.

'That's not my honey, constable, now if you're quite finished questioning my guests …?'

'Canae blame a man for needing sustenance. Helps the old grey cells,' Walter replied with a fake Belgian accent on the words *grey cells*. 'I'm sure we'll get to the bottom of this, don't you worry madam,' he finished and turned on his heel. Walking as tall as his stature would allow, he left our gathering the same way as he had arrived.

'I hope you're not going to pay any attention to him, Mr Hetherington,' the Dame said, once Simmons was out of earshot. 'Russian stowaway, my eye. I've never heard anything so ridiculous.'

I was saved from replying by a mouthful of tea bread.

Rufus stepped in. 'Just another storm victim. Doesn't matter if he was on the crew or not, it was a tragic accident. Right Blake?'

'Right,' I said taking another sip of my Prosecco to wash down the bread and trying to convince myself more than anyone else at the table, that this was indeed the case. If Delilah had been here, she would have had none of it. She would have already invented a back-story and a murky past for our poor dead Russian fisherman. There was one thing Walter Simmons was right about, though. This honey was glorious!

4.

The Cuckoo Bee

The Cuckoo Bee, like the bird, lays its eggs in a honeybee hive and leaves the host bees to raise their young.

'I heard that the body ye found on the beach is an impostor, Hetherington.' George Naismith spoke to me for the first time that morning; a disembodied voice from behind the *Salderk Bugle*.

I'd been reading the front page as he held it aloft. The story entitled, *Body On The Beach,* took centre front, with a windswept picture of the shore and few of the lifeboat men gathered around something that was thankfully indistinguishable. I doubted you'd get away with such a photo on the mainland, but I was learning fast, that here on Salderk, things were a little different. He pulled the paper down, concertinaing it into his lap, and squinted at me over his reading glasses.

'I really wouldn't know,' I replied, a spoon of syrupy porridge half way to my mouth.

'Oh, but ye would Mr Hetherington,' Mrs Naismith chimed in. 'It was ye that found him and I hear you're a bit of a detective in ye spare time.'

I placed the spoonful of porridge back into the bowl, folded my napkin and sat up straight. I'd been enjoying the silence of the morning, peacefully eating my breakfast at the far end of the table nearest the inglenook, surrounded by tights drying on the airer and pots and pans waiting to be washed; normal everyday family life, with only the occasional huff from Prince to express his annoyance at not yet venturing out for a walk. My peace had not lasted long.

'Mystery Milliner, George reckons,' she persisted.

George leant forward scrunching his paper further and waited for my reply.

'I hardly think so Mrs Naismith. That's an error on my website. I didn't realise you could get the Internet round here?' I added remembering I'd had to telephone to book the bed and breakfast. They'd had no website. I booked purely on the recommendation of the local tourist office.

'We're not that backward Mr Hetherington. George's got a Raspberry Pi and a satellite link-up. Didnae understand it myself ….'

'Not for you to ken, love, didnae ye worry,' George interrupted. 'So ye don't make hats then?' He directed the question at me.

'Well, yes I make hats ….'

'So it's the mysteries you daenae dae then?'

'Well ….'

'Well either you dae or you didnae Mr Hetherington, there's no in between I should imagine.'

'Shall we just say I prefer not to. Mysteries seem to find me.'

George tutted and shook his head, pulling the paper back to level with his face. I picked up my spoon to continue my breakfast.

'George was rather hoping ye'd help us solve this one. Not good for business, unknown bodies on oor best beach and ….'

'But it seems ye the very cause of it, Mr Hetherington,' George finished his wife's sentence.

'Hang on a minute …,' I said, still not getting the spoon quite to my mouth.

'No, No, that's what ye said.' George appeared from behind the paper. 'Mystery follows ye. That's nae good for business Mr Hetherington. Nae good at all.'

'Now George, he's oor guest, I'm sure it isn't really Mr Hetherington's fault. Pure coincidence, isn't it?' Mrs Naismith finished, smiling at me.

'Definitely!' I was emphatic in my reply.

'Still, might make us feel better if we thought ye were doing something aboot it,' George said, burying himself back in the paper.

'I'm pretty sure Special Constable Simmons is onto it.' I finally managed to place the spoonful of porridge in my mouth. It was cold.

'Simmons!' Georg huffed, 'he's special alreet, fat lot of good he is,' George muttered into his paper.

Swallowing the cold and now slimy porridge, I played back the conversation in my head. 'Raspberry pie?' I half muttered to myself.

'It's a computer Mr Hetherington. Fits in ye pocket. Only mobile that works on this island,' George chuckled into his paper.

I finished the rest of my breakfast, thinking it best not to invite any further comment on my profession. It was almost unbearably cold but I persevered, my mother's words *'waste not want not'* ringing in my ears. I couldn't believe Delilah still hadn't removed that sub-heading from my website. Actually I could believe it. She was a menace when it came to *helping*. I needed to learn how to sort that website myself. Perhaps George and his raspberry pie might oblige if I solved their problem. Though I couldn't see how it was bad for business; in my experience people flocked to scenes of crime, especially if it involved murder. A habit we'd acquired from the Victorians. Perhaps we were a little subtler with it now; the occasional drive past a scene to rubberneck or a trip to a shop we hadn't visited in years. But the nation as a whole was still as ghoulish and as obsessed with the deadliest of sins, as it ever was.

I pushed my bowl away and wiped my face. What was I thinking? The body on the beach was Walter Simmons' problem, Special or not, it was not mine!

'Come on Prince, we better take you out for a walk,' I said getting up from the table. 'Thank you for breakfast Mrs Naismith.' I turned to leave the kitchen.

'Mind ye daenae find anymair bodies there, Mr Hetherington,' Mr Naismith muttered from behind his paper.

'I can assure you it is not my intention,' I replied and left the kitchen as quickly as possible. I had certainly not endeared myself to the proprietors thus far and I thought it best to retreat from the situation gracefully.

I could spend the morning exploring the cliffs. I was to meet Rufus for lunch in The Fisherman's Rest. He wanted to speak to me in private, although I was sure that little remained private on such a small island. He hadn't let on what it was about but I suspected it was a surprise for Matilda and as the best man I would be chief engineer. Later we were having dinner at the castle at the Dame's request. With a little bit of luck I wouldn't need to be back at the bed and breakfast until well into the evening, and avoid any further discomfort on either part.

Back in my room I packed a small rucksack I'd had the foresight to put in my suitcase at the last minute. Waterproofs, a spare jumper, some thick socks and of course, Bonio for Prince. First stop would be the shops at the heart of the island for a map and a decent pair of wellies.

'Come on then, chap,' I said to Prince. 'Let's go see what else this island has to offer other than shipwrecks and cantankerous locals.'

***

The middle of the island wasn't far. The bed and breakfast was half way between the coast and the row of shops that classed as the high street. There were five shops on offer. A convenience store that encompassed a grocer, butcher and baker. A hardware store that included a post office. As well as a clothing store, a tourist shop selling, in the main, items of little practicality and a cake shop encompassing a café. Each had its niche and I suspected there wasn't much room for any competition.

I tried the tourist shop first for a map. I was sold, not an ordnance survey as you might imagine but instead a hand drawn map, created by the owner who proudly offered me the item for fifty pence. *'Island's so small there's nae point selling anything else. We have a tea towel with a map on it ye might find useful.'* I declined the offer and, cutting my losses, went next door in search of wellie boots.

As expected the clothing store was as unconventional as the rest of the island, selling an eclectic mix of sun hats, woolly gloves and everything in between. Sweatshirts and T-shirts with *'I'd love to bee on Salderk'* emblazoned on them, hung in the doorway, swaying gently in the breeze. Checked shirts, umbrellas and pac-a-macs followed, accompanied by mass-produced sun hats. The kind that meant I'd been unable to sell a decent handmade boater for several years. Then right at the back, heavy knit sweaters, oilskins, deck shoes, heavy-duty boots and finally a solitary pair of wellington boots. I imagined I'd find black, yellow or green full length wellies for sale, on an island that potentially has the majority of its population relying on the sea for their living, but no. These were pink; one solitary pair in a size nine. Who wears size nine, pink boots? I went over to the desk.

'Hi there can I help ye?' The shop assistant asked.

'Er, yes, I was looking for some wellington boots.'

'What size are ye?'

'Nine.'

'Ye in luck, we have one pair left.' She walked out from behind the counter and started to head towards the back.

'Erm, I saw them. Do you have any in a different colour?'

'Oh nae, I'm sorry, the delivery's not for another two weeks.'

'Two weeks?' I replied. My stay here would almost be over by then, making a pair of new wellies fairly redundant.

'Aye, the supply ship couldn't get through the other day because of the storm, so we have to wait for the next one. That's two weeks.'

'I see.'

'What about the heavy-duty boots we have? I have them in black and a size nine.'

'How much are they?'

'£80.'

My eyebrows must have met my hairline because the reply was apologetic.

'We're a working island sir; the men need decent boots. These are good quality ye ken. They last a year of heavy work. Few else do.'

'How much are the wellington boots?'

'Thirty, but I'll let you have them for twenty on account of them not really being your colour,' she winked at me.

'That's too kind,' I replied. I had a decision to make. Overcome my pride and wear pink wellies for the next three weeks, or fork out for some very expensive heavy-duty boots that would no doubt take at least four weeks to wear in, resulting in blisters and sore feet; £80 was a lot of money for a pair of boots I'd probably not wear once I was home. Saying that, I was unlikely to wear the pink wellies anywhere in Tuesbury either, but they were a damn sight cheaper. Really though, who wears size nine pink boots?

'Could you do them for fifteen,' I tried. I wasn't a barterer at heart but if I was going to wear pink boots, they were going to have to be a bargain.

'Oo I'm nae sure. I'd have to check with the manager.'

'Surely there isn't anyone else with size nine feet wanting pink boots?' I tried.

'You'd be surprised sir. Our ladies have surprisingly big feet. The joke is Salderk women will never fall over. Steady as mountain goats they are,' she beamed at me and I suspected she was taking the mickey. I had no reply.

'Let me give my manager a call and see what I can de for ye.' She disappeared off into the back of the shop.

I was considering the purchase of a thick Fair Isle style sweater when another customer entered the shop. She walked up to the counter and called.

'Maria, are ye there?'

'She's on the phone,' I replied for Maria.

'Oh I see. And who might you be?' The girl smiled at

me. Pale, freckled skin, auburn hair and green eyes gave her a very Scottish look.

'Blake Hetherington,' I said smiling back and extending a hand. 'I'm staying at the Naismiths' bed and breakfast.'

'Penny Murray,' she said. 'So you'll be here fur the wedding then?' She smiled back, taking my hand. 'Is that your dog ootside?'

'The spaniel? Yes. He's probably getting fed up, I should have taken him for his walk about an hour ago.'

'Handsome wee chap he is. Mine's an Old English Sheep dog.'

I frowned. 'Were you up on the cliff yesterday?'

'Aye I were. Was that you on the beach?'

'Yes, I was trying to get your attention.'

'Oo, I'm sorry. So it were ye that found the body. I could nae see from where I was, just thought you were being friendly. They still daenae ken who it is,' she said. Her eyes twinkled with curiosity, a look I had seen on Delilah's face several times now and knew what was coming next. I was saved by the re-emergence of the shop assistant, Maria.

'She says aye, just this once but mind don't go telling everyone … oh hi Penny. Here for your dry cleaning?'

'Aye.'

'You have a dry cleaners?' I was surprised.

'Aye, course we do, we are a civilised people, sir, despite our large feet and lack of wellingtons.' I could see Maria was teasing me again and she went off to get the wellies.

Placing them down on the counter, she rang them into the till. 'Just these for you today then sir?'

'Yes thank you,' I said handing her the cash, blushing as I did. It was going to take me a while to get used to the colour of my new footwear.

'They're a fine pair of boots, Mr Hetherington,' Penny smiled. 'She'll be very happy with those.'

'They're for me,' I said sitting on a chair beside the till, changing my brogues for my new purchase.

Both girls assessed my outfit: brown moleskin trousers, dark purple Guernsey sweater and a navy blue Barbour jacket. 'I see, very fetching,' Penny replied and the girls laughed as I pulled on the pink boots.

'He had little choice bless him. Last pair we have,' Maria said. They were both still watching as I finished putting the boots on and packed my brogues into my rucksack.

'At least your rucksack's manly enough,' Penny said smiling at the Pokémon pin badges my niece and nephews insisted on me having on the bag. In my rush to pack I'd forgotten to remove them.

I was yet again without a suitable witty riposte, no doubt as I was walking the cliff tops later I'd think of something. Instead I replied, 'Well, thank you ladies, I better take Prince for his walk before he gets too fed up. Nice to meet you Miss Murray, and thank you for your help,' I nodded to Maria.

'Nae bother,' she said. 'Enjoy your walk.'

I could hear them laughing together as I left the shop. I was pretty sure Salderk women did not have the huge feet Maria had claimed they were famous for, but I wasn't about to investigate further. I suspected, given the layer of dust on the toes, that these boots had been one of those accidental orders that befalls the shop owner on occasion. Still, they would serve their purpose and it was better than ruining a perfectly good pair of brogues for the sake of a few interesting looks.

Outside the shop Prince sniffed the new rubber of my boots and gave me a quizzical look. I was pretty sure dogs only saw in black and white but who knows, perhaps pink has a particular smell. Either way he looked far from impressed.

'Don't worry boy we're off for a walk now,' I said in reply.

It occurred to me that given enough mud I might be able to disguise the colour of my boots sufficiently to avoid any further embarrassment. Unclipping his lead from the bicycle rack we headed back towards the coast. I looked at my watch. I had two hours until I was meeting Rufus; plenty of time to explore the island.

5.
Balling

Balling is where the workers bees surround a queen bee that is no longer considered acceptable, in an attempt to kill her.

After over an hour of exploring the island with Prince, I'd worked up a healthy appetite. I ordered a mackerel sandwich, took my half a pint of *Salderk Buzzing Brown* ale from the bar and I settled myself on a small table towards the back of The Fisherman's Rest. Prince was thankfully tired from our morning's trek and settled happily under the table.

The Fisherman's Rest had a tired, world-weary look about it. Peeling wallpaper, chipped paint on the dado rail, the church pew seats against the walls had sagging threadbare cushions, and old wooden tables and chairs occupied the middle of the pub. The carpet, that had seen better days, was black where it met the hearth of the raised open fire. Dilapidated it may be but the pub had an air of nostalgia that many landlords would have sold their right arm for.

I was sitting at a table that had once housed a Singer sewing machine. The wrought iron was battered but the table was what the pubs in London might refer to as boutique. The chair had an old cushion on it covered in animal hair, suggesting the pub owned a cat or, more likely, the cat honoured the pub with its presence. With one leg shorter than the other three, the chair had a wobble that meant the sitter should sit still.

Simmons was not behind the bar. Instead a young man in his late teens had served me. Surly but efficient enough, the job obviously held little pleasure for him.

When Rufus entered he didn't look in a much better mood than the bar staff. He ordered a pint and he sat down opposite me.

'Not eating?' I asked

'No, I feel like I've been eating constantly since I got here with all this wedding food.'

I nodded.

Rufus was uncomfortable I could tell. He hadn't removed his jacket and yet it was plenty warm enough in here for him to do so. He sat sideways on his chair facing the door rather than me. The fingers of his left hand drummed on the table impatiently. My sandwich and the pint arrived at the same time but the beer did nothing to break Rufus' mood. I waited.

Halfway through my sandwich Rufus burst out: 'Damn it Blake, why now?'

'Why, what?' I said, unsure as to what had got my friend so agitated. Had Matilda revealed more secrets? Had Liliya run away with an unsuitable man?

'It follows you, I swear. You were like this when we were kids, I was always getting you out of some scrape or another, you never could just leave well alone.' He banged his fist on the table and Prince jumped. The young man behind the bar flinched. Lacking any other customers, he'd been asleep, head resting on his hands at the far end of the bar.

I sat open mouthed at this outburst, mackerel sandwich in hand. I could apologise, although I had no idea what for, question Rufus and incur further wrath, or stay silent. I chose silence. I put my sandwich down and waited. Nothing.

'Perhaps I could get you a whisky, old chap?' I said, trying an olive branch instead.

Rufus grunted and I took this as a yes. The youth was already at the whisky bottle pouring the shot before I'd even reached the bar. I thanked him and returned.

'So, what am I meant to have done?' I said, putting the glass down in front of Rufus. He continued to avoid looking at me.

'Murder, Blake,' he replied, quieter and in a more even tone than his first outburst.

'What? Surely you don't think I've killed someone?'

'No, no, don't be so ridiculous.' He turned in his seat, his posture softened. Facing me he held the whisky glass halfway to his mouth and finally looked me in the eye. 'That man you found on the beach; he was murdered.'

'But I thought ....'

'I know! Turns out Simmons got the local dentist to take a look his teeth, see if they could identify him, and the first thing the dentist noticed was a brown stain on the white jumper your victim was wearing.'

'My victim?'

'Yes, well you found him.'

'It's hardly my fault though Rufus … anyway a brown stain could have come from anywhere!'

'Not this one. It was caused by blood from a chest wound. Looks like he was stabbed.'

The youth behind the bar was sitting upright on a stool listening intently to the conversation; his demeanour, now, altogether more attentive. Rufus and I became aware, at the same time, of his eavesdropping and turned to look at him.

'Can I ge' ye gentlemen another drink?' he smiled, caught out.

'No thank you, we're fine,' Rufus replied. 'Haven't you got some glasses to wash?'

I was always surprised with the ease at which my friend gave out instructions; years of having staff no doubt. Myself, I had a solitary profession. Instructing was not something I was used to. The barman hopped off the stool, nonchalantly walked to the dishwasher, loaded the two empty glasses that amounted to the morning's trade, smiled and walked back to his seat.

'I'm still not really sure why you think I've got anything to do with this, Rufus,' I said, lowering my voice so only he could hear it.

'Well, you do seem to stumble across murders with alarming alacrity. I thought we'd be safe on such a remote island.'

'Nice alliteration,' I replied.

He smiled, the whisky thawing his temper.

'It just brings a lot of things up again. Things I'd rather leave where they were.'

'Death always does.' I picked up my sandwich again and started to eat.

'Really though Blake, couldn't you have just walked on by, just this once?'

I gave him an incredulous look as I savoured the mackerel; Walter was right again, it really was good. That man knew his food even if he'd failed to detect a murder when it washed up on his beach.

'I know, I know. Blake Hetherington, man of honour, never able to walk by if injustice is being done. Just like school.'

'Just like school,' I repeated between mouthfuls. He was right. He had pulled me out of some fairly hairy scrapes. I hated bullies and they were often bigger than me. I picked fights I was never going to win, knowing Rufus would sort it out.

'But what are we going to do about it?'

'School? Well I think we're a bit past that now.' Perhaps the sea air had mellowed me but right now I couldn't care a less who was murdered and who wasn't, I was enjoying my mackerel sandwich. 'This is good stuff Rufus, you should get Matilda to put mackerel in the sandwiches instead of salmon.'

'Blake!'

'What?'

'I'm getting married in three weeks and there's a bloody murder investigation going on right in the middle of it. What are we going to do about it?'

'Well, Special Constable Simmons will have to get the big boys over to play won't he,' I replied. I was getting a little fed up of being accused of inviting this murder to occur. The walk along the cliff tops had cleared my head enormously. Rufus and half the island might think I was somehow to blame for this murder, but I did not. Without Delilah here I was free to take a back seat in this particular case. Hopefully they'd have it wrapped up within a week. Well before she and Rob arrived. This murder was nothing to do with Rufus or Matilda, so there was no reason why it should affect the proceedings.

'Fat lot of good they are. They won't be here for another twenty-four hours, the death's not suspicious enough apparently.'

'Well there you go then, maybe the wound is from a bit of flotsam or perhaps his body hit the rocks.'

'That's not what the dentist thinks.'

'He's a dentist, Rufus. Stab wounds are unlikely to be his specialty. What about the local doctor?'

'Ex-army dentist! He fills in for the doctor when he's on holiday, which is where the doctor is.'

'Oh,' I replied, finishing my sandwich and wiping my mouth with my napkin.

I was fully aware the barman was still listening and it was difficult to find a tone that could be heard by Rufus, but not heard by him.

'The problem is, Walter Simmons has puffed out his chest and is behaving like a proper little cock pheasant.'

'He seemed OK yesterday.'

'Yesterday he wasn't in full swing. He's decided he wants to wrap up the case before the mainland police get here. Says he's got something to prove.'

'He doesn't seem to have a great reputation on the island,' I concluded.

'No. Worse than useless by all accounts and now he's got it into his head that the victim's a Russian stowaway; some kind of illegal immigrant with a stolen, Russian oligarch's watch in his pocket. Incredible!'

'It does sound a little incredible, but there aren't that many explanations for his presence on the beach.'

'Now he's gone and dragged Matilda into it,' Rufus sighed. 'He wants her to interview all of the Dame's Polish workers on her honey farm. Apparently there are a few there, that aren't entirely legitimate and they don't speak English. Walter's been turning a blind eye up to now. He wants her help or he'll make trouble for the Dame.'

'I pity the man that tries to do that.'

Rufus gave a small smile and pinched the bridge of his nose.

'I'm sorry for my outburst Blake, but I really can't have Matilda in the middle of all of this when we're about to get married. She's under an incredible amount of stress trying to organise everything.'

'Well then as the best man, it's my job to help!' I smiled and reached over giving Rufus a reassuring pat on the arm. 'Another pint?' I said, moving round in my chair to face the bar.

'Jolly good idea,' Rufus replied.

The barman was back to his surly self and I had to walk right up to the bar this time to order the drinks. I returned with two full pints of the *Salderk Best*. I noticed Rufus had ordered this on entering and thought it might be better than what I had been drinking, which was a little too sweet for my tastes.

'So what can I do?' I said, as I sat back down lowering my voice once more.

'Speak to Walter will you? Make him see sense.'

'I doubt I can do that, I haven't exactly made a great impression on him.'

'I doubt the pink wellies are going to help,' Rufus smiled.

'You noticed.'

'Er, yes, no amount of mud's going to cover those, Blake.'

'They were the last pair in the shop.'

'If they were the last pair in the world I wouldn't be wearing them,' he chuckled. It was good to see him relaxing a bit and if my unfortunate purchase facilitated that then it was worth it.

'I'll see what I can do. I can't promise anything but perhaps I can persuade him not to drag Matilda into it and to wait until the police from the mainland get here.'

'That would set my mind at rest, thank you Blake; and again I'm sorry.'

I waved the apology away as the door opened and in walked Walter Simmons.

'Speak of the devil,' Rufus said, just a little too loud.

'And he shall appear,' the Special Constable replied, smiling. As we were seated this was probably one of the rare occurrences on which Walter Simmons, given his shorter stature, was able to look down on us.

'I see you had the mackerel, Mr Hetherington.' Walter stood hands on hips.

'I did, it was splendid, thank you,' I replied.

'So how can I help you gentlemen?'

'I hear it was murder.' I set him a look that suggested I knew I was right.

'You hear right, Mr Hetherington, in fact I need ye to give me a proper statement. Ye ken. Where you found the body, when etc. etc.'

I doubted Walter Simmons had ever completed a statement before but I was happy to oblige. 'Do you need me to come to your office?'

'This ….' Walter said indicating the room with open arms, 'is my office, Mr Hetherington.'

'Well what do you need me to do?'

'I have some forms here, if we could go through them

and fill them in,' he said walking towards the bar. 'Apologies for interrupting lunch Lord Blackwood,' he said, over his shoulder as he went. I got up from the table and followed him. 'Robbie, ge yersen a break will ya,' Walter said to the barman, voice muffled, his head under the bar digging around for the forms. 'If ye could just fill these out then Mr Hetherington.'

'Certainly.' I replied and looked at the form in front of me. Standard stuff; name date of birth, address, what happened when. Over the last two years, I'd filled in a few of these. 'I hear you have the mainland police coming across tomorrow.'

'Aye, but I reckon I can have this sorted in no time.'

'Really?' I looked up from the form, baiting him to go on with my unbelieving tone.

'I'm going to speak to the men at the honey farm later. They'll ken what's going on. Mrs Darensky has agreed to help me, in case any of them forget how to speak English.'

'Is that really appropriate?' I said, looking him in the eye, my pen hovering above the statement paper.

'Aye, why would nae it be?'

'Well, she's Russian.'

'That's a bit racist Mr Hetherington. I'm surprised what with her being a friend of yours,' Walter was purposely obtuse in his reply.

'The Polish don't always get on with the Russians,' I replied patiently.

'Och I don't care aboot that. I'll get what I need I'm

sure.'

'But it's not exactly protocol either is it? Involving a member of the public in an official murder investigation?' I tried a different tack.

'Protocol Mr Hetherington? I daenae think any of this is protocol.'

'True, but isn't it best to err on the side of caution? What if she's involved, you'd have no idea what she was saying to them.' I had my back to Rufus and I heard him splutter into his beer, but to his credit he didn't say a word.

'You ken she is then?'

'Oh no, but it is a thought,' I said, and started to fill in the form. Walter was silent in contemplation and pulled himself a pint as he waited for me to write my statement.

'Happen you're right, Mr Hetherington,' he said taking a sip of his pint. 'Perhaps I should go on my own, see what I can turn up. Like you say, it's an official investigation.'

I looked up, smiled and nodded. 'This could take me a while, I don't suppose there's any chance of another drink for myself and Lord Blackwood while he waits?' I said eyeing up the whisky. First bartering for boots and now whisky, I was getting used to this place.

'Aye sure. Nice wellies, by the way,' Walter smiled and turned to pour the whisky. His posture told me he was smirking.

I swivelled around in my seat and winked at Rufus. With a thumbs up he indicated he had forgiven me for accusing his fiancée of murder, by removing her from the honey farm situation. Dinner this evening would be an altogether easier affair with Rufus back in good spirits. In my opinion Walter had to be crazy if he thought Matilda had anything to do with the murder. There was no chance any woman was capable of having the time for murder in the middle of planning a wedding, but for Walter, the seed of doubt had been sown; I only hoped he wouldn't take it any further.

6.
Piping

Piping is a series of noises the queen makes before she emerges from the cell as she is born.

Castle Albrecht is an eclectic mix of old and new with the banqueting hall marking the epicentre of the old part of the castle. Dating back to the thirteenth century, the castle had had several refurbishments but it still retains many of the original features. Old pipes frequently mean visitors are regaled with bizarre noises from the central heating. Scuttling in the wainscoting reminds you that in such a large building, even in the absence of human companions, you are never really alone.

An impressive space, the banqueting hall encompasses a huge arched fireplace that dominates the far end of the room. On the south side, six-foot high lead-light windows are framed with heavy, sage green velvet curtains trimmed with gold tassels. Two gigantic wrought iron chandeliers hang from the ceiling, filled with mock candlelight and that evening the prospect of sitting underneath one of them was making me nervous.

'The stone floor is six hundred years old,' the Dame's voice rang out across the table. 'So for goodness sake don't scrape your chairs. Let the footmen help you with them.' She looked pointedly at a tailed, bow tied, auburn haired footman who had already taken his cue to attend to the Dame's chair and was standing behind her patiently waiting. I hadn't been in the presence of servants since the old days of Blackwood Manor. Rufus had long since dispensed with the need for any domestic help. He simply never replaced them once they retired. The Dame referred to them as staff, servants being such an old fashioned phrase, but they were servants no less.

A second footman and a maid stepped forward to assist us with our seats. Rufus and Matilda sat opposite me and to the left of the Dame, who sat at the head of the table. I was seated beside Liliya, to my right. Edward, Rufus' youngest son had not yet arrived. He had been unwilling to leave his new business, for three weeks of wedding preparations, during the height of the tourist season. His second hand bookshop, a welcome addition to Tuesbury, was proving very popular with the American tourists that visited the village. Donald, his oldest son, even with excellent legal representation, was unable to change the judge's opinion that he should not be able to leave the country for the next year. After the events of the spring, he was lucky to get away with a suspended sentence.

It was a small gathering here this evening, but Rufus was in good spirits after our afternoon's endeavours in The Fisherman's Rest. Several more whiskies had also helped relax him further. Matilda was now punishing him with sideways looks and frosty replies in return for turning up ever so slightly inebriated to the Dame's dinner.

The footmen busied themselves filling our glasses with red or white wine, which I noted Rufus, under the glare of his fiancée, refused. The starters were served and, after a rather boozy lunch and pre dinner drinks of Kir royals, I tucked into my ham hock, quails egg and asparagus starter with a little too much gusto, dripping hollandaise sauce on my shirt. I looked up to see if I'd been noticed. The Dame was still talking, about the hall and its history, Matilda's look of disdain was aimed at Rufus who had also been too hasty with the hollandaise and Liliya, thankfully, had not noticed my indiscretion.

'Of course, my late husband's great, great grandfather was from Friesland. So much history, the Netherlands, my husband would spend hours telling me about it on long winter nights, of course not all of it completely true. He always put his spin on things. It's such a shame we were never blessed with children, they would have loved his stories.'

'I remember them, babushka.' It was the first time Liliya had spoken since I had arrived this evening. She had sat on the sofa in the drawing-room smiling politely but not joining the conversation until now.

'Of course, dear, of course.'

'I love the one about Peter the Great. Déduška would tell me how his great, great, great, great, great grandfather met him when he visited the Netherlands in sixteen ninety-eight.'

'He was a story teller, wasn't he?' The Dame smiled

placing her knife and fork across the plate to indicate she was finished.

'He also said he was a relative of the Captain Cruys. A Norwegian who served under Peter the Great.'

'Really dear, I shouldn't believe that.'

Liliya finished her starter and dabbed her mouth with the crisp linen napkin provided. 'It beats my past,' she concluded and avoided the hard stare Matilda gave her from across the table.

'Liliya, don't be so ungrateful,' her mother scolded. 'Rosalyn and Montgomery gave you a fine life. You're a lucky child. There were many in Russia who never had the opportunities you did, myself included.'

This was a rare glimpse into Matilda's past. She never usually volunteered, even the slightest titbit of information.

'Where does the name Darensky come from, Matilda?' I asked, curious and sensing an opportunity. She looked at me from across the table for a few seconds and then gave her one word reply.

'Poland.'

This was not something she wanted to discuss further but the Kir royal drove me on with unusual impertinence. 'I only ask as I'm very interested in genealogy,' I continued leaving a pause for a reply.

'Our family's complicated, Mr Hetherington,' Liliya replied, giving me a broad smile; not at all uncomfortable unlike her mother. 'Déduška told me my father was Russian nobility. You won't get any information out of my mother. I've tried. She's too proud,' she laughed.

'Now Liliya ….' Rufus had stayed quiet during the whole conversation, I suspect as interested as I was, but now he stepped in. 'Of course you're very proud of your heritage aren't you dear.'

'I told you Liliya, you should not believe everything Monty told you. He was a storyteller, through and through. Now that's enough!' The Dame's voice cut across the table breaking the atmosphere. 'There are many Russian dynasties Liliya as you know. I have found people make up stories to be kind, but they are often anything but that. The truth is much kinder.'

I now regretted pushing the conversation further but Matilda and her history intrigued me. Rufus never worried about a person's past and hence he knew little of Matilda's. I, on the other hand, was fascinated by a person's origins.

'This sorbet is delightful,' Rufus changed the subject. 'Do send my compliments to the chef.'

The footman nodded. 'Pomegranate is the chef's specialty sir,' he replied.

'Déduška used to let me have it for breakfast,' Liliya beamed at Rufus.

'I can see why!' He replied.

The main course, confit of duck in a cherry sauce, was served and an array of vegetables circulated the table dished up by the footmen and the maid. The constant questions from your left shoulder as to which vegetables you might like made conversation difficult and I wondered why with so few of us we couldn't have been a little more informal. I noted the women were completely at ease with the situation, it was only Rufus and I that were bewildered by the whirl of vegetables.

'So what about our mysterious body on the beach?' Liliya said through a mouthful of duck. The question was aimed at me. 'How exciting to be the one who found him, Mr Hetherington. Exhilarating!'

'Liliya …,' Matilda growled at her daughter. I was unmoved. I suspected the Kir royals had affected the young lady as much as they had myself.

'That's hardly dinner conversation, dear.' Dame Albrecht De Vries gave a look that had it been a deadly weapon would have been extremely effective.

'So?' Liliya continued un-hindered and nudged my elbow in encouragement.

'Constables Simmons has it under control,' Rufus replied attempting to cut the conversation dead.

'He wants mummy to interview the honey farm staff!' Liliya grinned at me and placed a tiny new potato in her mouth.

'Not any more,' Rufus was stern this time. A fatherly, admonishing tone I had never heard him use before.

'Really dear? Oh thank goodness for that,' the Dame replied.

'Yes, Blake had a word with him and pointed out how inappropriate it was,' Rufus concluded.

'Mr Hetherington?' The Dame replied.

'Yes.'

The Dame turned to look at me, askance. 'Walter Simmons did as you asked?'

'Well, I simply pointed out that ….'

'Walter Simmons has agreed not to involve Matilda in the investigation, so that's the end of it,' Rufus said. Thankfully before I could dig myself a hole.

'Well I must say, that is a revelation.' The Dame turned her attention back to her duck. 'Walter Simmons is a pompous fool and never one to do anything that doesn't suit himself.'

Rufus looked at me from across the table and remained silent. I wasn't sure if I'd impressed the Dame or annoyed her.

'Don't be mean babushka, Walter does his best,' Liliya pouted.

'Oh you've always had a soft spot for him, I've no idea why, not a brain cell in his body. An intelligent girl like you could do a lot better.'

Liliya ignored the implication that she may have feelings for Simmons and ploughed on with the previous line of interrogation.

'So, Mr Hetherington, was it awfully gruesome?'

What was it about young women and murder? As soon as Delilah arrived I was going to have trouble with these two.

'I really think your mother and the Dame are right. This isn't dinner conversation.'

'Well then, you'll have to take me out for a drink and tell me all about it,' she nudged me again waving a fork laden with potato at me.

I couldn't decide if she was flirting or just being mischievous. She was more than thirty years my junior and the soon-to-be stepdaughter of my oldest friend. Surely it couldn't be the former. I finished my dinner and put my knife and fork together, neatly on my plate.

'How are the Naismiths treating you, Mr Hetherington?' The Dame rescued me from further embarrassment, although having refused to stay in the castle, I wasn't entirely sure I wasn't walking into another trap. I proceeded with caution.

'The lodgings are very comfortable thank you, Rosalyn,' I replied.

'They are adequate I suppose,' she finished her dinner and placed her knife and fork down. 'Although I've heard it's a little draughty there. That storm must have rattled the foundations. Not like Castle Albrecht, solid as a rock this place. We had a storm here in 1992. Brought an old oak tree down on the east wing; hardly a scratch on the place. The oak tree was fire wood of course.'

'Such a shame,' Matilda joined the conversation once more. 'The tree had Rosalyn and Monty's names carved in it.' She pulled a face at me across the table that implied pity but not too much.

'It was a sign of course. Two months later Monty died.' The Dame was very matter-of-fact about her late husband.

'I don't know why you never married again, Rosalyn,' Matilda said. 'An eligible woman like you.'

'Never found the right man, my dear. All too soft in my opinion; hard to find a man with a backbone these days what with all this women's lib. You don't know how lucky you are, dear,' she finished smiling at Rufus as the plates were cleared.

Rufus beamed at his fiancée. 'I think it's me that's the lucky one here.'

Liliya sighed breaking the romance. 'What's for dessert babushka?'

'You'll have to wait and see,' the Dame replied.

'I do hope it's sticky toffee pudding. The chef's sticky toffee is amazing, Mr Hetherington,' she nudged me again.

I pulled my elbows closer in and held my hands in my lap, waiting for dessert. When it arrived it was indeed sticky toffee pudding; one of my favourites and more than compensation for the fact that I was beginning to sober up. As I sat there considering the evening's conversation, I wondered what was more likely to happen; the Dame poisoning my pudding on account of my refusal to stay in the castle, or the chandelier falling from the ceiling creating a spectacular end to the dinner. Neither were satisfactory outcomes.

I thought of Prince snuggled up by the fire back at the bed breakfast, safe and sound and completely unaware his master's jeopardy. The Naismiths had been more than happy to look after him for the evening. Despite their eccentricities, they really were very accommodating.

It felt like weeks ago, not two days that I'd arrived on this island. Rufus was right; murder did seem to follow me. I could try solving it as I had before and as the Naismiths had suggested, or, as I was here for the wedding of my friend, I could do as Rufus wished and not invite more of it. The latter was infinitely preferable. It was just under three weeks until Rufus would be safely married. If I could avoid being dragged into a murder investigation, crushed or poisoned I'd consider it a result.

7.
Scout Bees

These are bees that search for new pollen, nectar, propolis and water for the hive, or even a new home for a swarm.

After desert, a cheese course, port and then drinks in the drawing-room, it was getting on for midnight. The Dame tried to insist that I stay in the castle, ' … *for a night of luxury.*' When I politely declined she decided to tell me about the Beast of Salderk that roamed the island in the dead of night and that a walk back to the Naismiths' residence was out of the question. I had to use my trump card. Prince would be worried if I did not return and she conceded with the acknowledgement that perhaps it would be rude if I did not return to the Naismiths' hospitality.

***

I awoke to the sun streaming in the window and the noise of the Naismith household in full swing, in the kitchen downstairs. I looked at my watch. Nine-thirty a.m. Much later than my usual time of six-thirty; the Kir royals had definitely gone to my head.

Prince was awake and watching me from the end of the bed. As he saw my eyes open, his head lifted and he looked hopeful that I might, at last, be awake. My head spun and I cursed the ever-efficient footmen who filled your glass when you weren't looking. I could smell bacon from the kitchen downstairs. Bacon always smelt better if you'd been drinking the night before. However, as I stood, buoyed by the idea of a bacon sandwich, my stomach was decidedly queasy. A walk along the beach was just the ticket. The fresh air would sort me out. I could investigate the bakery and the teashop afterwards.

Pulling on my dressing gown I walked across the landing to the shared bathroom, safe in the knowledge there was no one else upstairs. The room I was in was part of the Naismiths' extension. On opening the door to my bedroom, the circle of the old water tower felt as if it surrounded my doorway. A wave of nausea rose from my stomach and for a moment I was reminded of my age. A youthful body would have been more forgiving of a couple of pints of beer at lunchtime and the odd glass of champagne, oh yes and the port. I gave an inward groan. Gathering my composure I walked to the bathroom, washed, shaved and cleaned my teeth. Feeling better, I opened the door and found Mr Naismith leaning against the wall opposite the bathroom reading the paper.

'Wife wants to know, will ye be wanting breakfast, Mr Hetherington?' he said, not looking up from the paper.

'Good morning Mr Naismith. Thank you for looking after Prince last night. I'm going to pass on breakfast this morning I think.' I took a step forward to walk round him and into my room. He lowered the paper and leant forward towards me, peering over his glasses.

'Late night last night?'

'Er, yes I'm sorry,' I blushed involuntarily and, conscious of the proximity of my bedroom to the Naismiths' accommodation, I added, 'I do hope I didn't disturb you when I came in.'

'Nae not at all, Mr Hetherington. I cannae sleep at the best of times and it was a full moon last night.'

'I see.' I went to walk on.

'Are ye sure ye won't have breakfast. Tasty bit of bacon down there ye ken. Thick cut too.'

'Really I'm fine,' I said, holding my stomach at the thought.

'Aye well, all the more for me I suppose,' he chuckled folding the paper and heading back downstairs to the kitchen.

Back in the safety of my room I saw that Prince was missing from the end of the bed. No doubt he'd found his way to the kitchen for breakfast. The Naismiths had been happy for me to leave his food bowl there and he'd quickly become accustomed its new location.

I dressed quickly. I could hear Mrs Naismith talking in the kitchen: *There you are then you wee chap, but don't tell Mr Hetherington.'* I needed no further evidence to know that Prince had conned some bacon out of Mrs Naismith. I packed my rucksack once more, this time removing the Pokémon pin badges. I lifted Prince's lead off the chair where it hung over last night's shirt. I noted the hollandaise sauce stain and remembered Mrs Naismith had said she'd be happy to do any washing for me. I gathered it up and headed downstairs.

In the kitchen, I found Prince wolfing down a sausage or two and a guilty looking Mrs Naismith. Mr Naismith had resumed his position at the head of the table, behind the paper.

'Could I impose upon you to wash my shirt Mrs Naismith?' I asked, ignoring the guilt on her face. 'Had a bit of an incident with some hollandaise sauce last night.'

'Aye, nae bother Mr Hetherington. Is there anything else?'

'No thank you, just the shirt, that would be very kind, thank you.'

'It's nae bother, I could do your tie too if that was a casualty?'

'Thankfully it wasn't,' I replied.

'Leave him alone Betty,' Mr Naismith said. Then looking over the paper at me. 'She'd have your troosers too man, watch her, she loves to wash. Never known a woman like it.'

'Now George, hearty meals and clean shirts, that's all a man needs, that's all I'm trying to do.'

'Aye and you'd have me eating in ma pants if you could woman!'

I stifled a smile at the thought.

'I'm off out for a walk, get some fresh air. It's such a lovely day out there,' I said, nodding at the window.

'Aye it is.'

'Well I'll see you later.'

'Will ye be wanting dinner?'

'Oh no, I won't put you out, I'll probably go to the pub.'

'It's nae bother Mr Hetherington.'

'Betty, leave the man alone!' Mr Naismith repeated from behind his paper.

'That's very kind of you Mrs Naismith, but really I'm not sure what I'm doing this evening.'

'Right ye are then. Enjoy your walk.'

'Thank you.'

I went to leave the kitchen, Prince at my heel still licking his lips from the contraband breakfast.

'Oh and Mr Hetherington …,' Mr Naismith said.

'Yes?' I said turning back.

'Nice boots,' he laughed the paper disguising the full extent of his glee at my pink wellington boots that were waiting for me by the door.

***

I breathed in the fresh salt air of the beach. I may not have made it out the door of the bed and breakfast with my dignity intact, but at least I hadn't been quizzed any further about the murder. For that I was relieved. Fresh sand on the beach and a new lot of flotsam meant all trace of the body had disappeared. Prince rushed around the beach barking at the seagulls. It was good to see him settling in. I began to think perhaps it was just a tragic accident after all, a coincidence. Even if an ex-military man had carried out the initial examination, the man's injuries could still have been caused by debris in the storm. I was no pathologist myself, but I could see how it could happen. Or was I just trying to convince myself?

Rufus was convinced. I could see he was under a lot of pressure. The wedding preparations were getting to him and I hadn't helped. I was meant to be there to support him and so far all I'd managed to do was create problems. Granted I'd dissuaded Walter Simmons from involving Matilda in the investigation, but in the same breath I'd implied she was involved in some way. A notion, if his reputation was to be believed, I doubted Walter Simmons would let go of. The mainland police would be here later today and I hoped they would find that our Special Constable had got far too over-excited at the prospect of a murder investigation, concluding that the death was accidental.

I called out for Prince to come back. It was gone lunchtime and, head clear, I now needed some food. I headed back up the steps that had been built into the cliff face. I was starting to get my bearings and I knew this side of the beach led to the row of shops at the centre of the island; unlike the slippery path that Simmons had led me down. That path went in the direction of the pub.

As I walked up the steps I wondered if the café sold almond croissants. For several years I had enjoyed Albert Pane's almond croissants from the bakery on the High Street in Tuesbury. The bakery had now passed to his brother-in-law and the croissants were not the same. I was yet to find an almond croissant that lived up to Pane's.

At the top of the cliff, I paused to look down on the beach, serene in the mid-morning August sun. Not an inkling of the events of two days ago. Had I imagined the whole thing? Turning to my right I could just see the ferry docking at the little landing station in what the locals called, Donkey Bay. The enthusiastic ferryman had told me on my way across, that donkeys were used to transport deliveries up the long sloping path to the top of the cliffs. Now the only donkeys left were on the Jameson's small holding and they were not used for hard labour these days. Instead the Jameson's tractor, with a quaint canopied trailer attached, transported visitors to Salderk to and from the ferry.

From my vantage point I was able to watch the tractor snake its way down to meet the ferry and the small crowd of passengers alighting from the boat. The ferry rocked lazily against the dock, the fenders rubbing against the stony edge of the quay. I could have stood there for hours watching the comings and goings if it weren't for the protestations of my stomach. My queasiness blown away by the salt air, I was now well and truly in need of sustenance.

'Come on the Prince, let's go and get some breakfast.'

***

I tied Prince up outside, not sure if dogs were allowed in the bakery. With a sufficient supply of Bonio he didn't object. Entering the café I could see there were only a few other people in there. A couple in their sixties and a young mother with a baby. Approaching the counter I was greeted by a familiar face. I had not expected to meet Penny Murray again so soon.

'Well, hello Mr Hetherington, boots doing you well I see and what can I get for you?'

'Good morning Miss Murray, lovely day out there; the boots are very comfortable thank you,' I smiled, showing there were no hard feelings. 'What coffee do you do?'

'You're in luck, the coffee machine's working for a change so you can choose from the list,' she replied, handing me the menu across the counter. 'And can I tempt ye to a cake?'

'I'm rather partial to an almond croissant if you have any?' I scanned the counter. Cakes, choux pastry, quiches, the list went on. For such a small island there was plenty to choose from.

'No, nae almond I'm afraid and we just ran out of plain. Our specialty's the Salderk Honey Cake though. Ye should try that. I believe Mrs Darensky likes that one? Having it for her wedding cake she is.'

I had not had the pleasure of tasting the wedding cake, leaving that privilege to Rufus and Liliya. Trialing the buffet had been quite enough excitement for me.

'Then I better have a slice of that,' I said. 'And an espresso I think; double, thank you.'

'Aye nae problem, take a seat, I'll bring it over.'

I settled myself on a seat in the window so I could keep an eye on Prince. He'd sat down next to the heather border outside and was taking a nap in the sunshine. The white and rose pink heather was alive with bees. Thankfully Prince had seen fit to leave them in peace. I heard the coffee machine spring into action and watched as another couple in walking gear, entered the café and became hypnotised by the cake counter.

'Here ye are then,' Penny said as she placed the cake and espresso down in front of me. 'Recovered from finding that body then?' she smiled. I looked up, confused by the question. Lost in the beauty of the day I'd almost forgotten the whole thing. 'Bad news travels fast round here. Police from the mainland came in on the last ferry, no doubt you saw it if you were up on the cliff, with yer wee pooch there,' she said looking in the direction of Prince.

'I did,' I said. 'You can see a lot from those cliffs can't you?'

'Aye that you can. Douglas, my dog that is, loves it up there.'

'Well, Prince is definitely settling in.'

'Aye, looks like he is. He can come in ye know, if he's well behaved enough. As long as he doesn't come behind the counter.'

'Thank you, I'll bear that in mind,' I said, hungry now. My stomach needed food rather than to retrieve a perfectly happy Prince from outside. I lifted my fork to start the slab of cake. Golden yellow in colour it was light and fluffy and covered in thick buttercream, drizzled with honey.

'Simmons's been in asking questions,' she carried on,

pulling out the chair opposite me and sitting down. My stomach was beginning to rumble.

I smiled, hoping to dissuade further conversation so I could eat my cake.

'He said the same as you.'

'Me?' I was surprised.

'Aye. That you can see a lot from those cliffs. But I told him, I daenae see anything that morning. Just ye on the beach waving at me, like a loon.'

'A loon?' I couldn't help but pick her up on this last point

'Aye, I weren't to know you were trying to get my help now was I? Plenty of tourists wave from the beach. It's a pastime of theirs I reckon. How about you and Prince come with us next time?'

'Come where?'

'For a walk! Douglas'd like the company, we go about seven most mornings, before work. De ye fancy it?'

It occurred to me that Penny Murray seemed very keen to tell me she hadn't seen anything even though we'd already discussed this in the shop yesterday. Then again, small talk was a peculiar thing. People often repeat themselves just for something to say. I couldn't resist the opportunity. I was once again curious about the events that lead to the body on the beach. If she did know something then surely going for a walk with her and her dog was the way to find out.

'OK,' I said.

'Great, I'll see you tomorrow morning then?' she smiled.

'Where should I meet you?'

'Just come up to the cliff where you saw me, we'll be there.' I nodded and Penny went back to her duties behind the counter.

I dug into my honey cake. Food at last and it was worth the wait. The sweet honey was balanced by a not-too-sweet icing made of crème fraiche, not butter cream as previously thought. Prince opened an eye as someone stopped to scratch his ears on the way past. Despite their sometimes obtuse ways this was a close knit and friendly community. It would be nice for Prince to have the company on his walks, he was used to having Delilah's dog, Bertie around. It would be company for him before they arrived.

Delilah would be here in three days. The Saturday ferry was bringing Rob, Bertie and her across. I knew she'd be furious to have missed out on the excitement of a potential murder. Rob on the other hand, would not. I could only imagine what he would say. The poor man was coming for a holiday. I was like a pendulum in my interest and reticence with this case. I could only hope the mainland police would have it all wrapped up before Delilah and Rob arrived, saving us all from any unnecessary shenanigans other than those that normally preceded a wedding.

8.
Travel Stains

Travel stains are the dark marks found on the surface of honeycomb caused by bees walking over it.

The next few days passed in a whirl of wedding favours, place names and visits to suppliers. A trip to the local microbrewery was not at all a trial and Matilda had not been pleased when Rufus and I returned in a boisterous mood from the beer tasting.

Each morning I met Penny on the cliffs, with Douglas. He and Prince were becoming firm friends. Now Saturday was here I wondered how Bertie would react to the new alliance when he arrived today with Delilah and Rob.

On one of our walks Penny informed me that the mainland police had left the island within two days. I was pleased to hear that they had concluded the wounds to the victim were caused by debris in the water from the shipwreck and therefore the body became another accidental death of an unknown person. The case was to stay open until they could establish an identity for the victim but that part of the investigation could be better conducted on the mainland.

According to Penny the ferry had put on an extra service dedicated to the transport of the body and its police escorts. Up until that point the body had been kept in the local doctor's surgery, where there was a small mortuary that was only meant to hold two people until their funerals could be arranged. Not really an appropriate place for unidentified, suspected murder victims.

I picked up many useful bits of information on my walks with Penny. She told me tales of Walter Simmons' policing efforts that included lock-ins in The Fisherman's Rest, the history of the Dame and her honey farm; far more information than I'd ever gleaned from Rufus. The heather was the key to the wonderful local honey, and the island's best-kept secret was the Singing Caves on the northeast side of the island.

At her insistence, we'd visited the caves on Thursday, Penny's day off. She had said the tide would be at its lowest mid-morning. Standing in the cold damp cave listening to wind as it whistled through the caverns, it was indeed as if the caves were singing.

Several times I'd said to her she must have better things to be doing on her days off, than showing me around the island. *'Oh nae,'* she'd replied. *'I love the island, it's great to have someone who's interested. I used to go exploring all the time with ma grandda', te find fossils on the beach.'*

I wasn't sure how I felt about the implied comparison to a grandparent but I took it as I believe it was meant; kindness not insult.

I'd told her about Delilah, Rob and Bertie, and Penny was now curious about the impending visitors to her island, so she had joined me for lunch in The Fisherman's Rest where I was waiting for my friends to arrive. So here we were. I was enjoying a mackerel salad and half a pint of Salderk Best and Penny was tucking into a ham and pickle sandwich.

The pub was busy but the increase in business hadn't snapped Walter out of his sulk. His shot at solving a big case had been snatched from him. The arrival of the mainland police had made him redundant before his investigation had even begun. He had said nothing more of the John Doe on the beach when I'd ordered my lunch. I felt sorry for him; he'd not even mentioned my wellies today.

Prince and Douglas were sat on the rug in front of the fire. The fire wasn't lit but it was about the only space big enough for Douglas to sit without being in the way. Prince had almost disappeared into Douglas' long shaggy coat and the two looked content after their walk. The smell of old ash as the wind pushed down the chimney was comforting.

This lunchtime was particularly busy and the pub was full of walkers, I suspect many were tourists who'd arrived on the mornings ferry from the mainland. The beach discovery had made it to the mainland papers and I wondered if perhaps unknown bodies on remote beaches weren't so bad for business after all? A couple of locals sat on the other side of the pub setting the world's to rights and a group of fishermen sat by the bar complete with oilskins and black heavy-duty boots; five in total, two older men, two younger men and a woman. All five nursed pints of Salderk Bitter. Their conversation moved easily from Gaelic to English and back again. The English referred to the football. The Gaelic, I imagine, to hide subjects they did not want the tourist to overhear. It was fascinating to watch. The Naismiths spoke Gaelic but they were always very polite and so spoke English if I was in the room. To watch the flow of a bilingual conversation like this was a treat and one I hadn't seen since my time studying millinery in Paris, many years ago now.

I was also the first time I'd seen the small, fuzzy TV that was hanging behind the bar, actually on. The picture was grainy but the gist of the game could be gathered. I was grateful the sound was off. Football had never really been an interest of mine. Penny glanced at the screen occasionally but offered no comment.

'So Delilah's an archaeologist?' Penny asked in between mouthfuls of mackerel. She was keen to meet Delilah and as she had previously confessed to being an amateur collector of fossils, I assumed this was why Penny was so interested in my archaeologist friend.

'Yes. Although I blame her studies wholly for her fascination with death!' I replied.

'Death?'

'Yes, she has a propensity for finding trouble. We had a little spate of murders in Tuesbury earlier in the year. Delilah was in her element.'

Penny laughed. 'You seem to take it in your stride yerself, Mr Hetherington. I'm sure the two of ye together make a grand team.'

'Hmmm,' was my reply. 'I just hope she doesn't try digging any of that business on the beach up again. She's bound to want an in depth description of events.'

'Well, I can't help you with that,' Penny smiled wiping her mouth with her hand and taking a sip of the half pint of *Buzzing Brown*. 'Perhaps I can distract her with the identification of some of my fossils though?'

I was saved from further questioning by the entrance of Liliya Darensky. In the week that I'd been here I'd yet to see her in the pub. There was silence at the bar as she entered. Wearing faded jeans and a baggy t-shirt, her looks were not out of place, it was more her demeanour that was juxtaposed to the environment. Confidently superior she held herself with an air often found in the landed gentry. The Dame had probably instilled this subconscious arrogance in her from an early age.

'Liliya.' I stood up from the table. 'Nice to see you, can I get you a drink,' I said trying to be as welcoming as possible, unlike the locals.

Penny now turned in her chair, she'd had her back to the door and hadn't realised who it was that had caught the fishermens' attention. 'All right Liliya, how ye doing?'

'I'm good thank you Penny,' Liliya replied. 'I shan't have a drink thank you, Mr Hetherington I'm not stopping, I just needed a quick word with Penny.' The pub resumed its hubbub and Liliya took the two steps to the table sitting down at a chair between Penny and myself.

'Sorry to interrupt your lunch.' Liliya turned towards Penny, her back now towards me.

'Nae bother, what's up?' Penny spoke as if Liliya was an old friend. Her body language was in no way formal or tense, in fact she continued to eat her lunch.

'It's about the wedding cake.'

'Aye?'

'We want you to make it. I know there's only two weeks to go, but mummy's really not happy with the one from the shop.'

'Why's that? She really should tell them, they'll change it in a jiffy.'

'They won't that's the problem. The want to make it from the Dame's honey but mummy wants to use Geoff's honey.'

'So she wants it organic? Nae bother, just tell them.'

'She has but the Dame's threatened to up their rent if they ever used Geoff's honey and she's not budging.'

'Is she? I thought she was family? Benevolent ye ken?'
I'd never heard anyone dare to speak of the Dame like this before, never mind in front of one of her relatives.

Liliya gave Penny a pleading look. 'I know, but you know what she's like. She's a businesswoman. If people see one person can have cake made from Geoff's honey, they'll all want one. She doesn't take kindly to what she sees as disloyalty.'

'Well she nae gonna like me if I make the cake then, is she?' Penny laughed ironically. 'I like me job in that shop.'

'She won't know about it, it'll be our little secret,' Liliya winked at Penny.

Penny sighed and put her knife and fork down on the plate. 'OK, just this once mind. I'm not in the habit of going against the Albrecht De Vries. It's not gud for ye health, but as it's ye.'

'Penny you're a darling,' Liliya reached forward and hugged Penny hard. Penny laughed patting her on the back to indicate she'd like to be released.

'All right, all right. When do you want it for?'

'The night before will be fine. Will you have enough time?'

'Aye course I will. My kitchen at hoom's tiny but Mrs Jameson, up at the farm'll let me use her kitchen, no doubt, so I'll have to let her in on it. She'll be pleased to get one over on the Dame.'

Liliya turned to me now. '… And I can rely on your discretion, Mr Hetherington?' she said.

'I am the soul of discretion,' I replied with a little mock bow.

'Oh good, then it's sorted.' She turned her back on me again and got up from the chair.

'I suppose I better go and see Geoff,' Penny said.

'You needn't look so down about it, you're supposed to be his girlfriend,' Liliya teased. I tried to hide my surprise. I had no idea Penny had a beau. Goodness knows what he thought about her gallivanting around the countryside with me.

'Aye, he's just … you know … a bit clinging sometimes,' she said lowering her voice. 'I've been trying to avoid him for wee while.'

'You're not breaking up are you?' Liliya too lowered her voice and leaned down to put a hand on Penny's shoulder.

'Oh no, nothing like that, just needed a wee bit of breathing space, ye ken?'

This went some way to explaining her insistence on showing me around the island. I suspected I was part of an elaborate ploy to avoid poor Geoff Layland. I'm not a naïve man and I am sure there were better ways Penny could have spent her time but I was clearly a safe option.

'Well he is a little intense sometimes, I can see that,' Liliya said.

'Aye.'

'I better get back,' Liliya concluded. 'Penny I can't thank you enough. We'll speak soon, I'll bring round the designs mummy has in mind.'

'The designs?' Penny looked worried now.

'Oh it's nothing you can't handle, don't worry.' She turned to me again. 'Penny's the island's cake maker extraordinaire,' she said and with a pat on Penny's shoulder she left the pub.

'Too proud that one,' came a voice from the bar as soon as the door was safely closed behind Miss Darensky. In English, the comment was clearly aimed at our group.

'Rog, leave her alone,' the female at the bar retorted,

again in English. 'She's the haves, we're the have nots, that's the way it is.'

'The problem is, Ruby, she likes to let us know that,' one of the younger men replied.

'She doesn't mean any harm and be careful what you're saying, her friends are sat just there,' Ruby hushed the men.

'Daenae mind us,' Penny shouted from the table where we sat. 'Ye entitled to ye own opinion,' she smiled. It had the desired effect. The men at the bar blushed and turned back to the football.

'Karma,' the older man muttered into his pint.

'Giv it a rest Rog,' Ruby tried again.

'I'm telling ye lass. Wherever ye go, ye leaves a mark. Even the sea's marked by men,' he replied.

'Aye,' the men said in unison raising their glasses. 'To the sea.'

Ruby stayed silent this time and Walter came out from behind the bar to collect our empty plates.

'Can I get ye anything else?' He said, sullen and gloomy.

'I'm fine thank you Constable Simmons,' I replied.

'Call me Walter, Mr Hetherington, you're the only one that calls me constable round here.'

'Only one daft enough to,' Penny laughed.

'You may laugh, but just you wait, there's more te that death than an accident, I'm telling ye. Mr Hetherington agrees with me don't ye?' He looked at me with earnest eyes, begging me to back him up, but I couldn't.

'I am given to understand the mainland police thought it was an accident and I have to say I'm inclined to agree,' I said with an apologetic shrug.

'That's not what you said on the beach though is it! Murder, that's what you said.' Walter raised his voice and it got the attention of the fisherman again.

One of the younger fishermen spoke up. 'It weren't murder Walter, plenty o' men die at sea and don't we know it lads?'

'Aye, to the sea.' They all raised their glasses in unison again.

'It's murder I tell ye, and you'll all be laughing on the other sides of your faces, when I prove it,' Walter shouted, waving the empty plates in his hands so hard I worried the knives would fly off and hit someone.

'What's murder?' Came a familiar voice from the doorway, accompanied by the patter of tiny doggy feet running to greet me.

Delilah, Rob and Bertie had all arrived, right on cue.

9.

Windbreaks

These can be constructed or occur naturally, and protect the hive from the winter winds.

Delilah and Rob made a handsome couple with her chestnut brown hair and dark brown eyes sparkling beside Rob's brooding, green eyes and dark hair. I imagine they would have been the envy of most, at any graduation dance. That's if they have them anymore? Now, standing in the pub doorway, all eyes were on the new arrivals. Once it was established that they were our friends and members of the Dame's wedding party, conversations in the pub soon resumed. Hugs, introductions, luggage stowed behind the bar and food and drinks orders, only delayed the inevitable.

'Now, stop stalling! What murder Blake?' Delilah finally asked. She lasted much longer than I'd expected. We'd even managed to get a round of drinks in and Bertie had introduced himself to Douglas who had been more that happy to act as a beanbag for two dogs. All three were now settled on the rug. I stalled a little longer trying to decide how to answer. Savouring my mouthful of beer and swallowing, I looked at Delilah. There was no getting around this one.

'Blake found a body on the beach,' Penny said in a very matter-of-fact manner.

Delilah looked at me for confirmation. Rob needed none. Instead he bowed his head, covered his eyes with a hand and groaned.

'Don't be so dramatic,' was Delilah's answer to the groan. I could see his predicament. The man was on holiday.

Rob removed his hand and looked at me. 'Why?'

'Well I didn't exactly engineer it,' I replied. 'Anyway, it was Prince that found him.'

'Him?' said Delilah.

'Yes him and it wasn't a murder it was a tragic accident.'

'So why was he saying it was a murder?' Delilah said, jabbing a thumb over her shoulder in the direction of Walter, who was now stood at the bar watching us.

'He, is Walter Simmons, the island's Special Constable and he thinks it was murder.'

'So isn't it?' Delilah pushed.

'No. It was an accident. The man was drowned. He just happened to have a chest wound.'

Rob groaned again.

'Don't worry Rob, the police on the mainland are dealing with it and they say the wound was caused by debris from the shipwreck.'

'Shipwreck?' Now Delilah was really interested. I really wasn't helping myself out of this hole. Her recent archaeological field trip to Haiti had taken her to the site of the shipwreck of one of Columbus' flotilla.

'Yes. The first night I was here the island caught the tail end of hurricane Bertha. The ship was a casualty of the storm.'

'How exciting,' Delilah's eyes glistened.

'It was quite frightening really. Douglas howled all night!' Penny chipped in. 'Mind ye, we're used to extreme weather out here, sat in the middle of the North Atlantic.'

Rob drained his half pint of bitter and banged the glass on the table. 'I need another drink! Anyone else?'

We all shook our heads.

'Nae thanks,' Penny replied. 'Can't drink too much at lunchtime, I'm working a shift in the café this aft.'

Rob walked to the bar and ordered a pint this time. Robbie was serving him. The young man seemed to be a regular barman in work in the pub, although I had wondered how Walter could afford staff given the irregularity of his trade. Robbie poured the pint and as he did, Rob beckoned Walter over to where he was standing. A hushed conversation took place between the two of them. Rob produced his warrant card and for a moment, the look on Walter's face meant I thought Rob was going to arrest him. I wasn't sure what for. Inciting a one-woman riot in the form of Delilah? I was pretty sure encouraging Delilah in her morbid interests wasn't yet an arrestable offence neither was it a particularly difficult task.

'So you've already been having adventures without me,' Delilah continued, unwilling to sit in silence and wait for Rob's return.

'I'd hardly call them that. Penny's been showing me around the island. You'd like the Singing Caves.'

'Aye, I'll take ye there if ye want? That's where you'll find the best fossils,' said Penny, leaning forward, enthusiastic once more.

'Fossils?' Delilah replied.

'Aye. Blake said you were an archaeologist?'

'I am but European history is more my thing.'

'Oh,' Penny sat back deflated.

'But I used to collect them, it might be fun to go looking for them again,' Delilah smiled at Penny.

'Aye, and there's plenty there,' Penny beamed back, shuffling to one side as Rob joined the table once more.

'Nothing to worry about,' Rob said setting his pint down on the table.

'What do you mean?' Delilah said.

'Accidental death, pure and simple,' Rob replied.

'How do you know?' Delilah replied. I watched the conversation with interest. Rob relaxed and confident, Delilah bristling at having her fun cut short.

'He's a Special, Delilah. He just got a bit over-excited, that's all. I had a word with him and he agrees. Accidental death.'

Delilah sat back in her chair arms folded, frowning. 'But what about the wound?'

'Like Blake said, the mainland police say it's from the debris in the water. No mystery there.'

'But ….'

'Delilah, please, can you leave it alone? We're on holiday. It's Blake's friends' wedding for God's sake, we don't want any mystery, murder or subterfuge in the next fortnight, thank you. I want to relax,' Rob finished the conversation taking a sip of his pint and before anymore could be said he changed the subject completely. 'So, Blake, tell us about the bed and breakfast. Is it comfy?'

'Splendid. It's an old water tower, as you know, so plenty of history in the old building. A bit rattly in a high wind but perfectly pleasant.'

'Good, I could do with a few good night's sleep away from the town.'

'Well ye'll get that here,' Penny said. 'Nothing like good sea air! I'll warn ye though. Mr and Mrs Naismith are a little, eccentric,' she laughed.

'Not as eccentric as Delilah I'm sure,' Rob said goading his girlfriend. It had the desired effect.

'Oi, who you calling eccentric?'

'You! I've never known anyone so interested in the gruesome aspects of life. Well, apart from our pathologist.'

'Outrageous!' Delilah replied.

Before any real argument began, Penny interrupted. 'I better be getting on. Shift starts in half-hour. Nice te meet ye both and Bertie of course. Ye'll be coming for a walk with us tomorrow?' She asked.

'We'd love to.' Delilah's manners snapped her out of her sulk.

'Good I'll see ye then.'

When Penny and Douglas left, Bertie and Prince looked dejected. After some more chitchat about the island, where I'd met Penny and the plans for the wedding so far, we decided to head to the bed and breakfast to get the new arrivals settled in.

We were now sat around the table in the Naismiths' kitchen enjoying a cup of coffee and a slice of Mrs Naismith's homemade cherry bakewell. George Naismith was out but Mrs Naismith was busying herself with the washing.

'Nice to have a full house,' she grinned. 'Homely!'

'This is really lovely bakewell,' Rob said.

'I can give ye the recipe if ye like lass,' Mrs Naismith said to Delilah.

Rob almost choked on the crumbs from his bakewell, at this suggestion. He knew only too well, cooking was not Delilah's forte.

'That would be very kind, thank you Mrs Naismith,' Delilah replied, her eyes daring Rob to say anymore on the subject.

'So ye be here for the whole two weeks?' Mrs Naismith continued.

'Yes, we're here for the wedding,' Delilah confirmed.

'And a holiday!' Rob added.

'Ye deserve it. Grand job ye policeman do, not like our Walter.'

'It's a difficult job being a Special Mrs Naismith. You're lucky to have such a dedicated man on your island,' Rob rallied with his colleague.

'Aye, but it'd be better if he actually did something. N'er does anything unless it suits him, ye ken?' she replied. Rob decided to stay silent and ate the last of his bakewell.

'Nae, ye the guys that do the work,' she smiled at him, patting his arm. 'I best go check on the chickens,' she said getting up.

'You have chickens?' Delilah said.

'Aye.'

'But Bertie, he'll go mad!' Bertie's head looked out from under the table at the mention of his name.

'Nae, bother, their fenced in and they're well used to dogs. Come and see if you like. Bring the wee dog, introduce him, I'm sure they'll be fine.'

'I'm really not so sure.'

'Och, come on, they'll be fine. Best he gets to know them, then he won't bother with them.'

'OK. I'll bring his lead,' Delilah said, getting up from the table.

Prince hadn't paid the chickens any heed what so ever but Bertie on the other hand was a different breed of dog entirely. I could see Delilah's concern and I kicked myself mentally for not thinking about it.

The two women left. Delilah was hesitant and Bertie had picked up on her mood. Mrs Naismith, on the other hand, was the epitome of unconcerned and I hoped the meeting would go well. If it all went wrong, at least I knew there was room at the castle for them and there'd be chicken for dinner.

'Nice place this. Cosy,' said Rob as he heard the front door closing. 'Mrs Naismith doesn't seem that bad either.'

'No, they've been the perfect hosts,' I replied. 'They were a little put out that I found a body on the beach on my first day but what can you do?'

'I can't say it surprises me, Blake. Things like that do seem to follow you around. I can't quite decide if knowing you helps my career or hinders it?'

'Thanks!' I huffed.

'Just saying,' Rob replied.

'I have to say this place has been a godsend.'

'I bet. Weddings are dangerous,' Rob chuckled. 'Both my brothers are married, I should know.'

I'd had no idea Rob had two brothers and yet again I realised how little I really did know about him. Up until now our conversations had been primarily about Delilah or murder. This holiday would be a good opportunity for me to get to know him a bit better.

'Matilda's ferocious in her planning and her daughter's not a lot better; determined women the Darenskys. Oh, and don't get me started on the Dame,' I concluded.

'Women!' Rob said. 'Mention the word wedding and you've had it.' He got up and started to wash his cup in the sink. The front door opened again and Delilah and Mrs Naismith entered. In the time they'd been gone we'd heard no excessive clucking from outside or screams of terror; the meeting had gone well.

'Who's a good boy Bertie,' Delilah was crouched down, scratching Bertie's ears as he nudged her pockets, expecting a treat.

'He's a fine wee dog, that one,' Mrs Naismith agreed. 'Not at all interested see, I told ye.'

'You did, thank you Betty. I still won't be letting him out on his own though,' Delilah replied.

'Oh no, I wouldnae dae that anyway. Not with the Beast of Salderk wondering around. Eat a little scrap of a thing like your wee pooch he would.'

'The Beast of Salderk?' Delilah stood up.

'Aye. Takes the odd chicken sometimes,' Mrs Naismith replied.

Delilah looked along the hallway to Rob and myself, in the kitchen.

'She's having you on,' Rob said turning from the sink.

'Nae I'm not young man, and ye don't need to be deaing the dishes here,' Mrs Naismith replied. I couldn't be sure if she was cross at the domestic chores being undertaken or Rob's impudence.

Rob knew the tone well and stopped his task instantly drying his hands on a towel.

'Has nae one told you about The Beast yet?' The question was addressed to all three of us.

'The Dame mentioned it,' I said. 'But I wasn't sure if she was just trying to get me to stay at the castle, rather than walk back here.'

'Probably a bit of both,' Mrs Naismith replied. 'The

Dame doesn't like the idea of anyone outdoing her hospitality, ye ken?'

I nodded.

'Still, ye best be careful. Rumour is The Beast's a wild cat. Been on the island for centuries.'

'It can't be the same cat then,' Delilah said.

'Aye, no, probably more than one, but nae one's ever really seen it. Well, I say that, what I mean is nae one's got evidence they've seen it. It's normally when they're on the way back from The Fisherman's Rest.'

'How exciting!' Delilah said.

'I wouldnae say that hen, trouble that thing is. I'm nae even sure it's of this world. George's sat up all night before now to try and catch it at the chickens. The Beast took two that night. George didnae see a thing and he swears he was awake the whole time.'

'In my experience, rumours and tradition always hold some truth,' Delilah said.

'Aye I 'spect they dae,' Mrs Naismith said taking the towel from Rob's hands and hanging it up.

Rob sat back down at the table. 'There you go, Delilah,' he said. 'There's a mystery for you, solve that one!' He chuckled.

10.
Chilled Brood

This is a brood of immature bees that have died from exposure to the cold.

The next day we were honoured with bright sunshine. The accompanying blustery gale served to remind me of the remoteness of the island. At times it almost blew us from the top of the cliff, as we walked the dogs. I was glad of my cap to keep out the worst of the wind although it was a great effort to keep it on my head. Talking was also difficult but Penny and Delilah managed quite well. Rob and I were content to take in the fresh air and the view.

Delilah was quizzing Penny about the Beast of Salderk. The subject had well and truly piqued her curiosity and Rob and I were pleased it had steered her away from the subject of murder.

'Where's it been seen?' Delilah asked Penny, shouting above the gusts of wind.

'Oh, here and there; n'er the same place, by the same person. It's like a mirage.' Penny moved her hand across her face to demonstrate the ethereal nature of The Beast.

'Have you seen it?'

'Oo no, I haven't. Me pa has, but he doesn't like to talk about it.'

'No?'

'No. He says it's a load of old rot. Truth is, it scared the living daylights out of him.'

'How big was it?'

'Size of Douglas, he reckoned. Big beasty but quick.'

'Aw Douglas isn't that big, you'll give him a complex,' Delilah smiled at the dogs as they played together along the cliff top.

'Aye, true but I wouldnae want to meet him on a dark night,' Penny replied.

'So, where has it been seen?' Delilah persisted.

'Where hasn't it? Across the moor, obviously, in the castle grounds where the deer are, up on the Jameson's farm too many times and even in the school playground one night.'

'The school playground?'

'Aye, but that were old Roger said he'd seen it there. He's a fisherman, likes his drink. Fisherman are always seeing things.'

'True enough,' Delilah replied. 'Any profession that makes a habit of mistaking manatees for beautiful fish-tailed women, shouldn't really be trusted,' she chuckled to herself. 'Where on the moor then?'

'All over!' Penny swept an arm out in front of her. 'The last one was by the old well, near the bothy. One of the local lads fell asleep against the well on his way home from the pub. Must ta been freezing. Story is he woke up when he felt the hot breath of The Beast on his face.'

'Eurgh.' Delilah shuddered involuntarily.

'Creepy eh?' Penny replied.

'Yup. Can you show me where?'

'Of course. I'll take you up there now if you like, I've got enough time before I start my shift at lunchtime.'

'If you're sure? Do you always work shifts?' Delilah changed the subject slightly as they moved to walk in the direction Penny had pointed in.

'Aye, not enough work for me to do all day.'

'I see. So what else do you do for fun?'

'This and that, I'm seeing a local guy, Geoff, he owns the honey farm up the road from the castle. Sometimes I help there.'

'I bet that's interesting.'

'Aye, you need thick skin.'

'He insults you? I wouldn't have my man insulting me,' Delilah frowned.

'Nae not like that, for the bees. They're fine most of the time but you do get the odd sting.'

Delilah and Penny laughed and a singsong of notes was carried out to sea.

'We're going over the moor lads,' Penny called over her shoulder. I wasn't sure if it was directed at Rob and I or the dogs, either way we followed, as they headed west across the moor.

After fifteen minutes of walking, Penny pointed at a ramshackle old bothy that stood beside a well. A few sheep were scattered around it so we called the dogs back. Leads on, it was safe to continue. There weren't many sheep on the island. Penny said the Jamesons owned most of them, but the ones that did live here, roamed pretty much free and they didn't take kindly to dogs.

'I've got a bad feeling about this,' Rob said as Penny and Delilah pushed on ahead towards the bothy. The grey stone of the building was stark against the blue sky. No roof and half a chimney added to the overall dilapidation. It did indeed have a bad feeling about it.

'What's the worst that can happen?' I replied. 'At least she's not going on about that body on the beach anymore.'

'True,' Rob shook his head. 'I can't believe you Blake.'

'It's not my fault.'

'No I don't suppose it is,' he shrugged.

The girls had reached the bothy and the sheep scattered. The dogs pulled on their leads, impotent in their efforts to reach their fluffy quarry. They disappeared around the back of the bothy and Rob and I were left with the moor.

'No, not a good feeling at all,' Rob said.

'Cheer up,' I replied. 'Come on, we better not leave them on their own for too long, there's a beast loose on these moors,' I laughed.

'Don't tempt me,' was Rob's reply.

We picked up the pace and rounded the bothy to see Delilah and Penny, sat against the back wall of the building, shielded from the wind. The dogs sat with them, preferring shelter to exploring the moor.

'Do you want one?' Delilah said brandishing a packet

of mints. 'Found them in my pocket.'

'As tempting as that sounds,' I replied. 'I think I'll pass.'

'Suit yourself,' she said offering Penny one, who took it and rested her head back against the bothy wall. Delilah did the same. 'Can you feel the history?' she said.

'Aye, oozes out of this place. I love it. Great place to come to think,' Penny replied.

'Imagine all the shepherds that have stayed the night here with their flock. Someone lost has stayed here, maybe or a lovers tryst?' Delilah enthused.

'Hard to get lost on this island,' Penny said, her eyes closed, head still resting against stonewall. 'Still some daft beggars have managed it.'

'I bet,' Delilah closed her eyes now too.

'I shouldn't think it's anything as romantic as a tryst,' Rob said. 'In my experience it looks like an ideal hang out for youths or passing drunkards to use as a convenient latrine.' He stuck his head through a small window in the brickwork of the bothy and sniffed. 'Smells like it too,' he concluded.

'Thanks Rob.' Delilah opened one eye scowling at her boyfriend.

'He's probably right,' Penny agreed. 'Something does smell a bit funky round here. I'm not sure it's the bothy though.'

Something indeed didn't smell quite right. We all stood there for a few seconds, noses in the air, trying to work out where the smell was coming from.

'It's just the sheep,' Delilah said eyes closed again, head back against the wall.

'No, it smells familiar,' Rob sniffed the air again. 'I can't place it though. It's probably just the bothy.'

'Could be the farm,' Penny said. 'Day like today, with this wind, you'd smell the slurry from here.'

Bertie was getting fidgety. Now the sheep had gone, Delilah had given him a free rein to explore on his extending lead. He'd been happily exploring the smells around the wall of the bothy but now he had moved out a little further, away from us. Extended to its full five-metres, the lead locked and Delilah opened her eyes. Bertie was sniffing around the bottom of the well.

'What've you found now Bertie?' Delilah squinted at her dog and the ground where he was sniffing but she didn't move. 'Leave the sheep pooh alone, you horrible thing,' she said tugging gently on the lead. Bertie would not be dissuaded. He turned and barked at Delilah. Douglas and Prince raised their heads to look at him, from where they sat by the wall.

'What's that Lassie?' Rob said. 'Is little Jimmy stuck down the well?' He laughed at his own joke and we couldn't help but join him.

'Come on Bertie, let's go then,' Delilah said getting up and brushing herself down. Penny followed. Douglas and Prince got back on their feet ready to start walking again. 'Got time for a drink in the pub, Penny?' Delilah asked.

Penny looked at her watch. 'Aye. Just a soft drink

mind,' she said smiling.

'I don't know what you mean, Penny?' I replied smiling at her.

'Nae, I've got to work again later,' she replied, embarrassed by her inference.

I looked down at my burgeoning waistline. It was true that since I'd been spending more time with Rob and Delilah my beer intake had increased. I breathed in and made a mental note to have a coffee in the pub when we got there. I was meeting Rufus this afternoon for final suit fittings; I couldn't allow my belly to expand any further.

'Come on Bertie,' Delilah said again tugging on the lead, but Bertie wouldn't move. A gust of wind whipped around the bothy, ruffling the hair of both man and beast.

'There's that smell again,' Rob said. 'It really is familiar. Hang on a minute ....' His face changed. He became serious and his cheeks flushed. He walked over to where Bertie was standing. Putting both hands against the wall of the well he tested its strength before he leant over and looked down into it.

'Blake, could you come over here a minute?' Rob said.

'What is it?' Delilah said walking across to join him.

I got there a few feet in front of her. Penny was just behind.

'I don't suppose you have that pocket torch do you?' Rob said to me, knowing I always kept a torch in my pocket, coming from a village with a high frequency of power cuts.

Patting my Barbour I located and retrieved the torch. 'You're in luck.'

'No luck required,' Rob smiled at me. 'You were definitely a boy scout Blake.'

'Yup, always prepared,' I said. We both leaned into the well and shone the torch into it.

Delilah and Penny had moved around the well and were now leaning on the other side also looking down. The torch fell on something at the bottom of the well.

'Oh my God,' Penny blanched and put her hand over her mouth, turning away from the well.

Delilah peered a little longer before understanding the full extent of Penny's distress and turned quickly to comfort her.

It was a sickening sight. A pale grey face stared up at us. A young man in his twenties from the look of it, wet through from several days in the well. With the torch beam full in his face and not a squint from his glassy eyes, he was very dead. The body was up to its midriff in the water that sat in the bottom of the shaft and a red stain of blood ran the side of his face.

'I had to look didn't I?' Rob said as he pulled the torch back and rested his head in his hands, elbows on the side of the well.

'Well, you can't blame me for this one Rob,' I said, just loud enough for him to hear but not to cause further distress to Penny. 'This one's all yours!'

11.
Propolis

A resin that is used to stiffen the honeycomb and fill in any cracks there may be in the hive.

It didn't take us long to reach the pub. We walked in silence. Penny was in shock. She told us she knew the boy in the well but was unable to say anything more. Delilah comforted her as we walked. Rob was frustrated at the lack of mobile signal, more used to being able to contact colleagues at any time of day or night anywhere.

Arriving at the pub, Rob walked straight to the bar and asked to see Walter Simmons. Sensing the urgency in Rob's voice Robbie did not procrastinate and disappeared out the back to find the landlord.

There were very few people in the pub. The fishermen were in their usual spot and a couple I'd seen around the island over the last week sat in front of the fireplace. Delilah, Penny and I sat down on one of the old pews near the bar and waited for Rob. Walter appeared and there was another hushed conversation until:

'Murder!' Walter's voice cut through the pub and all eyes turned to Rob.

'Yes,' Rob replied. The dam holding back Penny's tears finally burst. 'I think we need the mainland police again STAT! Perhaps there's a room out the back where we could discuss this?'

'Aye, there is.' Walter puffed out his chest. 'I telt ye, I telt ye I did, and ye all laughed.' He was pointing at the fishermen sat at the bar. 'Murder!' He muttered and beckoned Rob and the rest of us to follow him round the bar. He didn't object to Douglas, Bertie and Prince as they followed us, curious as to what all the fuss was about.

'Is there any chance of a drink for Penny?' Delilah asked eying the optics.

Walter looked at Penny, her eyes red, her faced streaked with tears. 'I think we need whisky for this one,' he said, and stopped to pour a double on the way to a back room.

We all entered a large games room with faded curtains, a dartboard at the far end and a pool table in the middle. There were chairs around the outside, not terribly sociable but it suited our purposes.

'I think we should call it in first,' Rob said to Walter. 'Then we can start working out what it is we're dealing with.' His air of authority silenced any further peacocking from Walter as he led them both into an office adjoining the games room. Door closed, I assumed this must hold some kind of landline or satellite phone that allowed communication with the mainland.

I did my best to offer sympathy to Penny but crying women have never really been by forte, especially since there was a distinct lack of tea and biscuits to distract her with. I was glad Delilah was there and soon Penny was inhaling great gulps of air in between gulps of whisky.

The door to the office opened again and Rob and Walter appeared. Rob pulled a chair away from the wall and sat in front of Penny. Walter stood in the doorway to the office watching the sergeant. Rob leant forward and touched Penny's hand.

'I know this is difficult Penny, but I need you to tell me what you know about the man we just found?' Rob asked, gently.

Finally she spoke. 'Poor Robin, I hadn't seen him for a day or two, but I just assumed ….'

'So you knew him?' Rob asked.

'Aye, I've seen him around. His names Robin Everall, he's working for Geoff.' Penny blew her nose.

'And what did you assume Penny?'

'That he'd gone home! Summer holidays or something, you lose track of time on this island. He's a student, working at Geoff's farm. Doing some work for him. Or rather he was.'

'And where did you normally see him?' Rob asked.

'He was doing some research on the cliffs. There are some wild flowers there, vetch I think he said; it's poisonous for the bees. He was studying entomology.'

'I see. Can you tell me anything else?'

'He liked the bees.' Penny gave a weak smile and drained the last of her whisky, putting the empty glass on the baize edge of the pool table.

Rob stayed quiet, as did the rest of us, allowing Penny

time to tell us what she knew.

'He'd never o' bothered anyone. He didn't even get in huff with Douglas when he stuck his nose into whatever he was counting up on the cliffs,' she sniffed and Delilah handed her a tissue from a fresh packet she had in her pocket. 'Said he was counting the bees and studying when they came and went and what plants they took the pollen from. Came to Salderk because we're famous for our heather honey,' she said.

'Best in the world,' Walter interrupted. Rob gave him a look that he'd probably subjected many a constable to in the past.

'This is great Penny, you're doing really well,' Rob encouraged. 'Is there anything else you can tell us?'

'I don't think so. Geoff said he kept himself to himself. I'd never seen him in the pub. Always had his head in a book Geoff said. He'd even helped him with a bad case of varroa mite in the beehives. Said he'd found a new organic solution to it.' Penny started to cry again. 'I have no idea why anyone would want to kill him.' Huge sobs shook her body this time.

'I think we should get you home now Penny, the mainland police will want to ask more questions when they get here. For now you need some rest.'

'But I have to work,' Penny gasped between sobs.

'Oh, I think they can give you the day off today don't you? Walter? Do you think you could let them know at the café?'

'Aye nae problem.' Walter ducked back into the office.

'Be discreet Walter, don't mention the boy, just say Penny is sick.' Rob was firm in his statement.

'Aye, ye can count on me, Sergeant.' I could not see Walter's face but I could tell he was grinning from ear to ear, pleased to be in the epicentre of the drama.

'Delilah, could you take Penny home for me.'

'Absolutely,' Delilah said, already gently ushering her charge out of the games room, Bertie and Douglas following obediently. Prince remained at my feet, waiting for the next move. That was Rob's decision; he was well and truly in charge of this one.

'Well Blake, we better go and talk to this Geoff. Fancy a visit to a honey farm this afternoon?'

'Should we not wait for the mainland police?' I asked.

'Since when did you wait for any man, Blake?' Rob smiled.

'Shouldn't you take Walter?'

Rob screwed up his face. 'Na, I'd much rather take you. You see things I don't.'

I felt my cheeks redden. I've never been very good at taking compliments and I was pretty sure Rob was more than capable without my help, as he had been on previous occasions.

'Rufus needs me for a suit fitting at two o' clock,' I said.

Rob looked at his watch. 'Plenty of time, come on, Blake, you know I value your opinion.' He stuck his head in the office where Walter had just hung up the phone. 'Walter, can you stay here and wait for the mainland guys?'

'Aye, course,' Walter beamed. 'And where can I find ye when they get here?'

'I'm off up to the castle with Blake, I won't be long. I'll be back down here by two o' clock.'

'Right ye are.'

'And Walter ….'

'Aye?'

'Discretion,' Rob said tapping the side of his nose with his index finger.

'Aye!' Walter puffed out his chest again and gave a little salute. I was impressed at the effect the sergeant had on the Special Constable and I wondered how long it would be before Walter couldn't hold the news in any longer.

The three of us walked back out into the bar and the fisherman fell on Walter, hungry for answers. Walter was suitably obtuse in his replies.

'No murder here lads, that what ye said and that's what ye's got,' he smirked.

Rob and I left the pub; Rob satisfied that Walter would hold off the gossips for at least a few more hours.

'Castle?' I asked, once we were outside.

'No. Why would I go there? Layland's Honey Farm!' Rob smiled. I had suspected the castle story was a diversion to prevent Walter from insisting on joining us and I had been right. We had an hour and half before I had to present myself for my suit fitting.

The visit to Geoff Layland's Honey Farm was far from successful. On arrival at the farm there were no staff to be found. Just as we were about to give up, a receptionist appeared who apologised for the wait. She had just come back from her lunch. It then took her a further fifteen minutes to find Geoff Layland in the apiary and we'd been there almost three quarters of an hour before Mr Layland was ready to talk to us.

When he did, what he told us wasn't much more than what Penny had been able to tell us. In fact he was more concerned for Penny than he was our dead student; although that was understandable. We left with the promise that he would dig out any information he had on Robin Everall, but that at the moment his computer wasn't working and all his records were on it. A guy from the other side of the island was due to fix it tomorrow. Rob had left as frustrated as I had been on my first day on Salderk. The ambivalence of the island's community when it came to doing anything that might involve expedience was infuriating. I, on the other hand was getting used to the slower pace of life; I was even beginning to enjoy it.

'Have they no sense of urgency?' Rob said as we headed back towards the castle. 'I know I'm trying to play it down, keep it on the low, but it's still a murder!'

'They're all the same, Rob. I think it must be the sea air,' I laughed.

'Well they better buck up when the mainland guys

arrive! They won't take this kind of laid back attitude.'

'I'm surprised you are?'

'Strictly speaking I have no jurisdiction.'

 I nodded. 'When did you say they were arriving?'

'This afternoon sometime. They are coming by ferry.'

'No helicopter then?'

'No that's expensive. Police don't like expensive,' Rob smiled.

'And what's happening to the poor boy in the well?'

'When we were in the office ringing the mainland, Walter gave me the number of the local carpenter, Calum Brown his name is, he can be trusted apparently, but we shall see. I've asked him to seal up the top of the well until a proper unit can get here. It's not ideal, I don't want anything disturbed, but we have no choice.'

I looked at my watch. Ten to two. 'I better hurry, I don't want to be late,' I said.

'OK, thanks Blake.'

'I'm not sure I did anything.'

'It's always good to have reliable back-up in these situations. A right hand man if you like. Anyway I better go and take a look at the well before I head back to the pub. Check it's all been sealed up.'

'Did Rufus say, he has arranged for us to have a tour of Layland's Honey Farm tomorrow, as a surprise for Matilda? There will be sparkling wine and honey tasting. Perhaps we can find out a bit more as undercover agents if you like,' I smiled, only half serious.

'I think I've well and truly blown my cover. You're right though Blake, perhaps the direct approach isn't the best way with these people.'

We parted company, no further forward than we had been a couple of hours ago and as I headed towards Castle Albrecht, I pondered the significance of the body in the well. Had the man on the beach actually been a murder after all and were the two deaths in anyway connected? Our only clue as to the identity of the man on the beach was the pocket watch and identifying him was our only way of finding out if there was some kind of connection between the two victims. If indeed the first was a victim.

I reined my thoughts. We hadn't actually established that Robin Everall was murdered. His death could also have been accidental. An intriguing set of circumstances that had certainly sparked the synapses. However, I should not forget that my primary reason for being on the island was Rufus' wedding. I was the best man, not the best detective. Prince padded alongside me quietly, not stopping to sniff tufts of grass, stones and the corners of buildings on the way, sensing I was in a rush.

I arrived ten minutes late.

'You're late, Blake!' Rufus laughed from the chaise longue were he was waiting for my arrival. 'I've never known you to be late!'

I was flustered, pink cheeked, moisture in the corners of my eyes from the wind and my hair was a state as I removed my flat cap.

'What on earth have you been up to?' Rufus took in the sight.

'Just a walk on the moors with the others.'

'The others?'

'Yes, Penny, Delilah, Rob, the usual.'

'There's nothing usual about you lot,' Rufus replied, as a tall thin gentleman took my coat and ushered me behind a screen. Prince sat down at Rufus' feet. 'Now come on spill!' Rufus finished.

I was given a short respite as the tall thin man was now handing me parts of a suit to try on, including a top hat. I knew the top hat would fit fine - after all I had made it. Distracted further by my creation I stroked the hat, reunited with an old friend. The hours of work had been worth it to see the smile on my friend's face when I'd handed them over on my arrival on the island. Dove grey silk or *hatter's plush* as it's referred to in the trade; they were a simple affair, circled with a plain silk ivory ribbon for Rufus and lilac ribbon for Edward and myself, to match the bridesmaid's dress. The bit I loved most was on the inside of Rufus' hat. I'd embroidered his and Matilda's names and the date of the wedding on the inside band. My own top hat was the first formal hat I had made myself in many years. Of course I'd completed many commissions for weddings but few for myself. Eleanor would have loved to see me in top hat and tails.

I put the hat down on the chair that was also behind the screen. 'Spill what Rufus?' I tried for nonchalant and ended up with harassed.

'Look, Blake I know there's something going on.'

I peered at Rufus from over the dressing screen as I wrestled with a lilac bow tie that matched the colour of the hatband.

Rufus changed his tone. 'Sorry, old chap, it's probably a surprise isn't it? Well as long as it doesn't involve leaving me naked on the moor on my stag do, that's fine.' Rufus picked up a tumbler of whisky that was sitting on the small table next to the chaise longue.

I raised my eyebrows. The idea that I would do this to anyone was not something that had occurred to me. Why it had occurred to Rufus I had no idea. Aside from the practicalities of undressing a fully-grown man in his sixties who was stronger than me and had been the boxing team captain at school, there was the distinct possibility of hyperthermia!

'I can assure you Rufus, I have no intention of disrobing you.'

Moving out from behind the screen I pulled on the front of the jacket as the man assisting me pulled on the back. The result was ripping sound from the shoulder.

'Ah!' Rufus said. 'Well that's torn it.'

I looked at the shoulder and suit fitter tutted and fussed, as he pinned the shoulder back into place. Thankfully it was the tacking that had ripped and not the fabric of the suit.

'Sorry about that,' I said, as he the tailor flitted around

me, smoothing fabric, measuring and pinning.

'No matter, no matter, easily fixed,' he replied.

'So what's up then?' Rufus asked again.

'Nothing!' I replied forcing a smile.

Rufus got up, whisky in hand and walked over to where I stood. 'I'll get it out of you,' he said looking me square in the eye.

'You won't like it,' I said picking some fluff off the sleeve of my jacket.

Rufus took a silent sip of his whisky.

This time it was my turn to look him squarely in the eye. 'We found a body on the moor.'

12.
Play Flights

These are short experimental flights taken by young bees to orientate themselves to their hive's location.

Rufus had been furious.

'I thought we'd dispensed with all this nonsense!' he'd bellowed.

The suit fitter and I had disappeared back behind the screen while Rufus paced the length of the drawing-room.

'I'm getting married in less than a fortnight!'

He'd only stopped pacing to pour himself more whisky. I pointed out that, technically it wasn't me that had found the body this time but he was having none of it.

I'd retreated to the bed and breakfast and spent the afternoon in their kitchen reading a book. George was behind his paper and Mrs Naismith was busying herself washing shirts. One of which was mine. She had practically taken it off my back as soon as I'd walked in, after announcing I looked a state from my morning on the moors. News of the body in the well had not yet reached the Naismiths and after some brief questioning about the wedding suits and the colour of the bridesmaid dress, by Mrs Naismith, I was left to read my latest Colin Dexter. I had decided to avoid the pub and therefore Walter, completely.

Delilah and Rob had returned at about nine and to her credit, Delilah made no mention of our discovery. After hot chocolate and slabs of homemade flapjack, we all retired to get a good night's sleep before the next day's events. Rufus had asked us all to be at the castle by ten a.m. ready to walk to Layland's Honey Farm. I hoped the tour would provide a welcome respite from the subject of murder, although by that point I had no doubt the whole island would know about it.

A clandestine conversation with Rob, on the landing between our rooms, had revealed the police had arrived at the pub in the early evening. The extraordinarily long summer evenings meant the police had been able to examine the scene as soon as they arrived and make arrangements to preserve it. The two constables sent to evaluate the situation had agreed with Rob that the well should be cordoned off and a Scene Of Crime Unit should be called. They arrived by helicopter this time, an indication they were now taking the whole thing more seriously. I doubted the presence of a helicopter on the island had gone unnoticed. I hadn't seen or heard its arrival but I was sure others on the island would have.

The constables drafted in had been about to finish their shifts on the mainland and had not been at all impressed by the diversion. They had had to *pull a double'*, as Rob referred to it. Thankfully Walter had provided them with beer and mackerel sandwiches, softening the blow a little.

They had returned in the helicopter to the mainland, sated and a little less annoyed by the Island of Salderk; it was now up to the detectives to investigate the death on the moor.

Now, as Rob and I talked on the Naismiths' landing, the Scene Of Crime Unit was still up on the moor. As Rob pointed out, he was here on holiday and so he would leave this case to the homicide team. Although his comments, in regard to the unravelling of this particular murder, lead me to understand that he had no intention of leaving the case entirely alone. *'We'll have to see what the honey farm holds for us tomorrow,'* he finished with a wink and disappeared into his and Delilah's room, before we'd attracted the attention of our hosts. I had a feeling, that contrary to his earlier sighs and protestations, Rob was actually enjoying himself.

Now, as we assembled at the gates to Layland's Honey Farm, the whole business of the beach and the moor felt very far away; almost a parallel universe. Rufus was still livid, but thankfully the buzz in the air, if you'll excuse the pun, was all about the wedding. His manners and no mention of bodies or murder, allowed him to put it to one side, for the morning at least.

'I really want people to understand why it's so important we have organic food,' Matilda was saying.

Delilah nodded. 'I agree Mrs Darensky.'

'Matilda, please darling. Besides I'll be Lady Blackwood soon.' She waved her left hand as she spoke and the diamond in her ring on her finger sparkled in the sun.

'Ladies and gentleman, if I could have your attention please ....' The tour guide clapped his hands. In his twenties, tall, thin, scruffy around the edges in that way that's fashionable at the moment and with a very English accent, this was definitely another student; perhaps a Leisure and Tourism undergraduate this time? I wondered if all Geoff Layland's staff were students on work placement? It would make sense. There couldn't be a lot of people on the island to sell the honey to, especially if the Dame was to be obeyed. I imagined it made for some tricky business dealings.

'I bet he knew Everall,' Rob said, just loud enough for me to hear but no one else.

I nodded, curtly. I was conscious that, not only was Rufus looking in my direction but that I'd been brought up not to talk over tour guides, even if they were a third of your age and looked like they'd been dragged through a hedge backwards.

'Follow me, this way please, and we'll begin the tour.'

We entered the Layland's Honey Farm through the large farmyard gate and began the tour in the small herb garden, in front of the main building, or should I say hut. Bees busied themselves amongst the thyme and the scent of fresh herbs wafted up to meet us.

'The tour will start in the Visitors Centre in front of us, where you'll find plenty of information about the *Apis mellifera* or honeybee, and their work at Layland's Honey Farm. There will be a short video of a year in the life of a honeybee and then we'll move on to the apiary itself. Then the bottling room and finally the gift shop. I hope you'll enjoy the tour and if you have any questions along the way, please do ask.'

Inside the hut, we filed into a room on the right that contained nine chairs in three rows and a white screen hanging on the back wall. I found myself looking forward to being educated in the ways of the hive. Delilah, Rob and Liliya sat in the middle row of chairs, Liliya placing herself next to Rob so he became a rose between two thorns. I sat behind them. I've never liked the front row. Matilda and Rufus were the last to enter and they occupied the front. The tour guide dimmed the lights and sat down on a solitary chair behind me flicking a switch to set the video going. As the lights went off, Liliya giggled and touched Rob's arm in a way that was definitely flirting, the type seen on the back row of a cinema. Delilah seemed not to notice and Rob did his best to ignore it. I was reminded of Liliya's flirtations at dinner the other night and I was beginning to build a picture of a bit of a man-eater, or at the very least a compulsive flirt. I was glad I was behind them, although I felt bad that I was not with Rufus at the front.

Predictably, Rimsky-Korsakov's, *Flight of the Bumblebee* introduced the film and honeybees filled the screen. An authoritative voice explained the difference between drones, workers and queens and just as it was beginning to tell us about the brood chamber a whisper came from over my shoulder.

'I need to talk to you about Robin, Mr Hetherington,' the tour guide said.

I did not turn in my seat, not wanting to draw attention to myself.

'It might be better for you to speak to Sergeant Claringdon,' I whispered pointing in Rob's direction.

'I think he was in trouble,' the tour guide continued. I could hear the chair creaking as he leaned forward, I assume, lifting both back chair legs off the floor; his chin was almost resting on my shoulder.

'Sergeant Claringdon will be more than happy to speak to you I'm sure,' I tried again.

'Penny says you'll help. Delilah told her you always get to the bottom of mysteries.'

'Did she?' I said a little louder eliciting a stern look from the front row and another giggle from Liliya.

The video showed us Summer and the bees gathering honey from the heather.

'He knew something, but he wouldn't tell me what,' the tour guide continued in, what was to my old ears a barely audible whisper.

Sensing he was not about to give up, I asked, 'What do you think he knew then?'

'Something about the man on the beach.'

I turned slightly in the chair. 'Did he know who he was?'

'No. I don't think so but he said you could see for miles from those cliffs and that he'd seen something that would put an end to his money troubles.'

'Really, what do you think it was?'

'Well murder of course. He must have seen whoever killed that guy on the beach.'

'But that was an accident.' I must have raised my voice a little because Rob turned his head a little as if attempting to hear. His body language suggested he was no longer watching the video.

Autumn arrived on screen and the room felt cold.

'I doubt if he was talking about a rare breed of bee!' The tour guide was being sarcastic.

'Have you reported it?'

'No.'

'Well, I suggest you should.'

'I am now.'

'I'm not a policeman,' I insisted, once more.

'But you know one ….' He nodded in Rob's direction. 'I don't want any trouble and I don't want to end up dead. I don't get paid to do this job, I'm sure as hell not getting killed over it.' He raised his voice this time and everyone turned to see what he was so indignant about.

I smiled. 'Well I suggest you don't swing on your chair like that then,' I said, breaking the atmosphere.

I turned back around to face winter and the bees were being treated for diseases. The tour guide was silent.

I turned in my chair again. 'If you know anything Mr …?'

'Wilt, Tom Wilt,' the tour guide smiled through a

whisper.

'Well, Mr Wilt, I suggest you speak to the sergeant.' Now I nodded in Rob's direction. I turned back in my chair and managed to catch the last few minutes of the video. Spring arrived once more, the hive regained consciousness and the cycle of life began again. If only it were that simple.

Mr Wilt got up and turned the lights on again and as everyone squinted to adjust their eyes he held the door open for us to continue on our tour.

Rob held back from the others and I was thankful Delilah was being distracted by Liliya and Matilda, with discussions of heather in the bouquets.

'What was all that about,' Rob asked.

'He thinks Robin Everall knew something and that's what got him killed.'

'Knew what?'

'That's just it, he wasn't sure but he seemed to think it was something to do with our Russian on the beach.'

'Russian?'

'Well he had a Russian pocket watch beside him when I found him.'

'I see, I think I need to read through that report again,' Rob said frowning.

'No reports today, Sergeant Claringdon.' Rufus' voice was loud and clear from the doorway to the garden and the apiary outside, where he stood waiting for us. 'You're on holiday!' His smile was threatening in a way that suggested neither Rob nor I were going to do anything that may upset today's proceedings. Murder was not on the agenda.

'I'm not sure what you're talking about, Lord Blackwood?' Rob smiled as he walked into the garden to join the others.

'I mean it, Blake,' Rufus said in a quieter voice now I was nearer, almost desperate. 'I don't want Matilda upset. Leave it to the police.'

'I have every intention of doing so,' I replied smiling.

We walked together into the garden and onto the orchard and the apiary. This case was starting to get interesting. It seemed to me that Mr Wilt might well be right. If he was then there was indeed a connection between the two deaths. They both appeared accidental, but accidental they were very possibly not. I hoped the police would see this and for my friend's sake get to the bottom of it quickly and efficiently without disrupting the wedding. I didn't want Rufus' big day spoiled in any way. When I said I would leave it to the police I wasn't lying. After all, Rob was the police.

13.
Requeen

This is the introduction of a new queen to a hive that is queenless.

The next day passed without comment. Penny was absent for a second morning from our dog-walking group. Not a great surprise considering what we had discovered on the last walk. Afternoon tea at Castle Albrecht meant talk turned, once again, to the forthcoming wedding. Delilah chose to discuss colour schemes and floristry arrangements, rather than murder, with the bride-to-be. Needless to say, Matilda was delighted that someone was finally taking an interest in her wedding plans. A pleasant afternoon was spent on the terrace and as dusk arrived the Dame retired to her drawing-room whilst the rest of us adjourned to the pub for steak and chips.

The next day, Rufus' youngest son Edward and his girlfriend, Miss Derby, one of Tuesbury's local school teachers, arrived on the three o' clock ferry. Delilah, Rob, Rufus, Bertie, Prince and I formed a welcoming committee. Matilda, Liliya and the Dame were once again ensconced in wedding trivia. Miss Derby had bought more bags than I thought possible to fit on the Salderk ferry and the expression on Edward's face when Rob, Rufus and I all offered to help, was one of pure relief.

Assembled once more, on the terrace to the rear of the castle overlooking the grounds, we were treated to the sight of a small herd of deer grazing in the distance. Dinner was to be served at six. A gentle breeze rustled the trees that surrounded the estate. The chirp of house martins toing and froing from their nest, the occasional shrill shriek from a greenfinch sat in the cherry trees to the left of us, and the odd squirrel venturing across the lawn made for a very diverting afternoon.

'You do see now why, Layland's honey is so important to me?' Matilda was saying to Rufus, who simply nodded, aware of the Dame's feelings. 'But you do darling don't you?' Matilda persisted.

'Yes dear, of course. It's your wedding day, you should have whatever you want.'

'Having whatever you want isn't always a good thing,' the Dame cut across the conversation looking pointedly at Liliya who was giggling at something Edward had said.

'Oh, Shush,' Matilda waved a hand playfully in the Dame's direction, but playful or not, the Dame did not appreciate the sentiment.

'Really dear, why is it so important? My honey is really very high quality and much cheaper. In fact free to you!' The Dame was indignant as she sat up straight in her chair and took a sip of her pre-dinner sherry.

'It's the bees that are important, Rosalyn. We need to look after them, treat them with respect. Layland's farm does that. If we have no bees we have no future, isn't that right Blake?' Matilda looked to me.

'Well ....' I was uncomfortable at being pulled into such a conversation. Admittedly insects such as bees were the very foundation of our ecosystem but I wasn't sure about using it as an argument against the Dame. I knew nothing about her honey farm or the honey it produced.

'Don't drag poor Mr Hetherington into this.' The Dame rescued me and I smiled appreciatively. 'What on earth makes you think I don't have respect for my bees?'

'You don't have respect for your workers.'

'Matilda,' Rufus warned his fiancée against continuing by placing a hand on hers.

'You haven't a clue about business dear. Don't pass comment on something you don't understand,' the Dame replied.

I'd never seen this side of their relationship before, more mother and daughter than equals. It showed them both in a whole new light.

'I understand when a worker is being taken advantage of, just because of where they are from,' Matilda was now shouting.

'Mother, really. Don't get yourself upset. Babushka treats the workers on the farm very well.'

'Does she? I've known hardship young lady. I've been paid far less than I am worth and I know what that feels like.'

'I really think this is not the time to be discussing this,' Rufus interrupted. 'The Dame's business, is well, the

Dame's business darling.' Rufus squeezed Matilda's hand this time.

'And that's exactly why this sort of thing happens. We all sit around saying nothing about it, drinking champagne.' Matilda crossed her arms out of Rufus' reach.

'And you've drunk your fair share of champagne dear, don't you forget it,' the Dame replied. 'All this fuss over a little bit of honey, really! Layland's honey is no different from mine. The bees go to the same heather for the same pollen. The only difference is the label on the jar!'

We were saved from further argument by the arrival of a footman and the suggestion that we all might like to come in for dinner.

Up until this point, Delilah, Rob and I had been observers of the conversation. Liliya had been entertaining herself with Edward, and Miss Derby had been quietly seething at the attention Liliya was paying to her boyfriend.

'What was all that about?' Rob said as we walked into dinner.

'I'm not at all sure,' I replied.

'Perhaps we should find out. We've seen one honey farm, what's to stop us going to the other.'

'Politics?' I grinned.

Rob rolled his eyes. A shriek from Liliya behind us suggested Edward had said something she found hilarious.

'I'm not sure it's that funny,' I heard Miss Derby say.

'Lighten up Rose,' Liliya replied with a snort.

'I think there's going to be trouble in paradise,' Delilah

said under her breath. Rob and I frowned in reply. 'Man-eater doesn't quite cover it,' Delilah answered.

'And I thought it was just me she found irresistible,' Rob said winking at Delilah.

'Watch it you,' Delilah thumped Rob playfully on the arm. 'There's no such thing as off limits with that one, you might find yourself in a compromising situation,' she nodded back in Liliya's direction as we filed into the dining room for dinner.

'Sounds promising,' Rob replied ducking into the doorway to the dining room to avoid a second thump in the arm from Delilah; this time not so playful.

I did my best to avoid sitting under a chandelier and placed myself to the left of Rob, Delilah the other side of him, Matilda the other side of me. Rufus sat at the end of the table, next to Matilda and opposite the Dame who sat in her usual position at the head of the table. On the other side of the table were: Liliya, Edward and Miss Derby, or Rose as I was now to call her.

The starters arrived and the wine was poured giving enough of a gap in the conversation for the topic of honey to be well and truly dropped. The peace did not last long.

'So, Blake, come on, tell us all about the body you found on the moor,' Liliya said between mouthfuls of bruschetta.

'Liliya, haven't we been over this before? It's hardly dinner conversation, dear. I'm sure we can find something better to talk about. How about your mother's wedding.

Tell us about your bridesmaid dress, your mother's being coy about it and I'm dying to know,' the Dame cut it from the far end of the table.

'Oh, you don't mind do you Blake, you love a good mystery and I know Delilah does!'

Delilah blushed.

'I'm not sure there's anything to tell that hasn't already been reported in the *Salderk Bugle*,' I replied in an attempt to shut down this particular topic.

'Oh, but Rob must know more. He's a policeman!' Liliya batted her eyelids across the table at the sergeant.

'A policeman on holiday, Miss Darensky,' he replied.

'Rubbish, you guys never take a holiday.'

'Contrary to popular belief we do like a holiday every now and then.'

'I think you chose the wrong man to holiday with then,' Liliya grinned.

'Liliya!' Matilda chastised her daughter.

'What? I've read his website, it says *'Hetherington's Mystery Millinery,'* Liliya finished.

I glared at Delilah. Another Salderkian who clearly had a raspberry pudding, or whatever it was. As soon as we were home again, she was removing that byline. Far too many people were paying attention to it.

'That's just a gimmick,' Delilah said waving a hand. 'Something to pull the customers in with you know. Isn't that right Blake?'

I chose to concentrate hard on a basil leaf, balanced on

my bruschetta, rather than reply. There was nothing, absolutely nothing, gimmicky about my business!

'Have you heard from Penny recently?' I asked Delilah, changing the subject. 'I do hope she's OK it was a terrible shock for her.'

The Dame sighed. 'She'll be absolutely fine. Complete drama-queen that girl anything for a bit of attention. You know she dressed up as a bee and paraded around outside my honey farm with a placard protesting about my beekeeping methods. The cheek of it!'

'It's still a shock for the poor girl,' Rufus spoke up from the other end of the table.

'Yes, yes, I suppose it is,' the Dame relented, indicating to the footman it was time to remove the starter plates.

'Eddy, darling, I heard you had a lot of murders in Tuesbury in the spring?' Liliya fluttered her eyelashes at Edward and put a hand delicately on his forearm provoking a thunderous look from Rose.

'Er, yes,' Edward coughed on some crumbs as he finished his last mouthful of starter.

'You make it sound like a spring/summer collection, Liliya,' Rose huffed. 'It was very traumatic and 'Eddy' doesn't want to talk about it.'

'OK. Wow! I was just making conversation.' Liliya looked down for her plate to discover it had been taken. She flicked her hair back from her eyes and set them on Edward once more. 'You have a brother don't you?'

'Yes, I do.'

'Two of you, what a treat; is he coming?'

'No he's not!' Rose interrupted.

'What a shame,' Liliya turned to look at Rob across the table who had been watching the exchange, and cocking her head, she said, 'I wonder why that is?'

'Liliya!' Matilda, again, attempted to control her daughter. 'You know perfectly well why it is, don't embarrass Rufus, it's not fair.'

Rufus said nothing, instead choosing to give all his attention to the sorbet palate-cleanser now sat in front of him.

'I'm worried about Penny too,' Delilah broke the awkward silence. 'She hasn't been out with us walking with the dogs for a couple of days now; I hope she's not hiding away. Perhaps I should go and see her?'

'She's fine!' Liliya replied a little too forcefully.

Delilah looked up, intrigued by Liliya's tone. 'Have you seen her then?' she smiled.

'Yes and she doesn't want lots of people visiting her with pitying looks.'

'I was only going to see if she wanted to come out with Douglas and get some fresh air.'

'Well, there's no need, she's fine.' Liliya's hands gripped the table as she leant towards Delilah.

'OK.' Delilah widened her eyes holding a hand up to Liliya's verbal attack.

'And what are the police doing about this awful mess?' The Dame's voice rang out across the table and the sorbet cups were cleared.

'Like I said,' Rob replied. 'I'm on holiday. I'm sure the mainland police would be more than happy to answer any of your questions. I believe Walter Simmons has given them accommodation at The Fisherman's Rest, while they investigate.'

Serving dishes clattered as the plates for the mains were placed in front of us with words of warning as to the heat that emanated from them. I did appreciate a hot plate to eat my food from and the Dame had it covered.

'Honey mustard chicken,' the Dame announced and the footmen began serving. 'Not organic I'm afraid, Matilda dear, but local. They're from the Jameson's farm. Lovely people the Jamesons.' The Dame looked at Rob, who was admiring his plate of food. 'The honey's mine of course,' she smiled at him.

'Of course,' Rob replied.

'As you're on holiday sergeant, perhaps you'd like a tour of the farm?'

Rob couldn't believe his luck. 'I'd love to see what goes on there,' he replied eagerly.

'Not half as much as Matilda thinks, I can assure you. Mr Hetherington, perhaps you'd like to join the sergeant?'

I looked up from my plate, hypnotised by the peas as the footman served them. I mustered a reply, not sure what I was agreeing to, 'I'd love to.'

'May I come?' Delilah asked.

'Of course, the more the merrier,' the Dame enthused,

happy the topic was back to her estate and businesses. 'Would Friday be good for you all? I won't be able to join you, I have some business to attend to, but Bob, my farm manager, gives a fine tour, you won't be disappointed.'

'You have another suit fitting at ten, don't forget, Blake,' Rufus answered for me, annoyance in his voice. I couldn't decide if this was because of the rip in the suit or the return of honey as the topic of conversation. It could even have been both!

'Then the afternoon it is, shall we say two o' clock?' The Dame took charge once more.

Rob, Delilah and I nodded.

'Excellent. Do start eating people. Chicken is always best piping hot.' The Dame picked up her knife and fork and attacked her dinner with gusto. A moment of quiet fell upon the table as we all ate once more. I considered the last half-hour's conversations. Matilda and Rufus lost in their world of wedding planning, the Dame fighting to maintain her authority, a flirtatious Liliya, a fuming Rose, honey farm politics and Rob trying somehow to give the illusion that he was on holiday and not involved in investigating any deaths. Family dinners of this size may well be a challenge but they were certainly interesting.

14.
Starline Hybrid

This is an Italian hybrid of bee bred for its increased honey production.

I awoke the next day in a positive mood. Last night the Naismiths had not questioned me further on the subject of my mystery millinery. Mrs Naismith seemed more than happy to wash my shirts and feed me more cake than I had seen in my lifetime. George remained behind his paper, which meant I'd been able to catch up with the front page news over breakfast. A rogue ferret had killed five of the Jamesons' chickens, the headline read, *'The Real Beast Of Salderk'*, and a new lifeboat had arrived, which had created some excitement amongst the local volunteers. However, there was no further mention of murder or bodies. It was refreshing to discover that Salderk journalists preferred to leave such investigations to the professionals. Delilah and Rob had passed up the offer of Mrs Naismith's porridge, choosing to visit the pub for one of Walter Simmons' famous fry-ups, instead. I was to meet them at the Dame's honey farm after my suit fitting.

It was hard to believe only two days had passed since the discovery of poor Robin Everall. Things were beginning to settle. The stormy weather had passed, shipwrecks and hurricane Bertha were distant memories and it was beginning to feel more like a holiday.

My appointment with the tailor revealed the rip was now undetectable. Rufus also seemed to have forgiven me, content that I was not about to find any more corpses on Salderk if I could help it. Preoccupied with dinners, tours of honey farms and long dog walks across the heather strewn island, I too was content that there was little chance of me having time to become involved in this particular mystery. In the absence of any further information, I had decided the two deaths were indeed accidental and that it was simply an overactive imagination that thought otherwise.

I was looking forward once more to celebrating Rufus' union with Matilda and I began to relax. How foolish I was to think that after Tuesday night's dinner conversations, this would be the end of it and we'd be allowed to continue our holiday in peace. I should have known a professional detective such as Rob, would never have left the case to what he considered to be local plodders, even if they were from the mainland. A couple of observations of Robs' activities over the last few days should have given away his intent to solve the mystery himself. Lingering on the cliff top, where the student had last been seen, insisting on visiting the beach one morning at about the same time as the unknown Russian had been discovered and leaving our table in the pub to engage in clandestine conversations with Walter Simmons. I had done my best to ignore it, for Rufus' sake but it was no good. Rob was looking different angle from which to approach the problem. I wasn't so sure. I didn't have to wait long.

'So our student was on the cliff top when the Russian was washed up on the shore.' Rob said, when Delilah was safely out of earshot discussing the pros and cons of hybrid bees with the Dame's honey farm manager. We'd finished our tour of the farm and Delilah had taken to take the subject. As we'd reached the Dames' bottling plant, huge in comparison to Layland's, Delilah had been so impressed she'd asked how to set up her own hive. Bob was now explaining the basics to his enthusiastic pupil.

I gave Rob a sideways glance. 'I'm not getting involved. I promised Rufus.'

'Robin Everall must have seen something. Come on Blake, help me out here. The night of the storm he was in the pub. He'd treated himself to a dinner of lobster, hardly student fare. He wasn't seen again after that. You'd arrived that day, did you see him?'

'No, I went straight to the bed and breakfast. It doesn't sound that odd though. Students today don't seem to have much restraint when it comes to spending,' I replied.

'True, but Walter said he'd never even ordered a packet of crisps in there before that night. He'd come down for half a pint of shandy and then leave. So why did he suddenly decide to dine on lobster?'

'His birthday?'

'Come on, be serious Blake. Walter tells me all his lobster is frozen, people don't eat enough lobster in the pub to keep it fresh. They catch their own or they buy it from the fishermen straight off the boat, it's cheaper. Walter says there was something odd about him. Apparently the mainland guys aren't interested in anything Walter says. It's a mistake to write people off, you never know what they might tell you.'

'Well, Walter is a little, shall we say, eccentric and a man's entitled to a lobster dinner,' I said.

Rob sighed. We sat on a bench amongst borders of lavender. The farm manager was showing Delilah the inside of a display hive and was explaining something in great depth and Delilah was nodding.

'Always after a new hobby,' Rob said, 'Hard to keep up with her sometimes; perhaps a murder investigation is preferable to a beehive. Less chance of me being stung,' he laughed.

I laughed with him. I wondered what Bertie would think of the addition of a beehive to his garden. We'd left the dogs up at the castle, with the Dame, as the honey farm had strict rules. So did the Dame and I feared Prince and Bertie may not forgive us easily for leaving them behind.

'So you think they are linked?' I said.

'Bee keeping and stings? Definitely!' Rob replied.

'No the murders.'

'Ah ha! I thought you weren't getting involved?'

'Well you can't make a statement like *'students don't eat lobster'* and not expect me to get involved.'

Rob grinned, turned in his seat and began talking

excitedly, 'I want to know what that kid was doing up on the cliff at that time in the morning. Tom Wilt and Geoff Layland say he was doing some research. Penny says she doesn't know anything else. Says she just used to see him each morning when she walked Douglas. It's almost like she's scared.'

'You've seen her?'

'Yes, I spoke to her in the café yesterday when Delilah and I went for coffee.'

'She's back at work?'

'Yes, but listen. She was up there at the same time as Robin Everall, but she's insisting she didn't see anything. She said he wasn't there that morning.' Rob bit his nails viciously as he watched Delilah and the beekeeper. 'And another thing, it's a bit of a coincidence that the majority of the Dame's workforce are Polish and our man on the beach was a stowaway. I think he was coming to work here. Matilda Darensky's certainly not happy about the situation on the Dame's farm. I didn't exactly see smiling faces on the way round, did you? In fact the only person here so far who's been even remotely happy is that guy over there and I suspect it's because he thinks he stands a chance with my girlfriend.'

I raised an eyebrow at the reference to Delilah as '*my girlfriend*' as opposed to by her name. The apiarist was getting to the detective.

'I just can't help feeling someone's not being straight.'

'I don't think you've got anything to worry about

there,' I reassured. 'Delilah's just being friendly, you know how enthusiastic she is about new projects.'

'I'm not talking about Delilah, I'm talking about the murders,' Rob was curt in his reply.

'Has it occurred to you that both deaths could be accidental?' I replied.

'Hell of a coincidence. How?'

'Well, the first one was a stowaway, illegal immigrant whatever you want to call him and struck upon some bad luck, or rather a storm and a nasty bit of flotsam that did for him.'

'Flotsam, come on Blake, you don't believe that? I read the report; it was a clean cut between the fifth and sixth ribs, on the left hand side. Pierced his heart. If it was flotsam there'd be something left in there, a splinter or something.'

I stayed quiet. Rob obviously knew far more than me and had access to records I didn't.

'Come on then, how do you explain Robin Everall in the well?'

'He fell in,' I shrugged, 'Died of exposure, simple.'

'He did die of exposure, you're right, but that's because he had a whacking great hole in his head.'

'Hit it on the way down?'

'Now I know you can't believe that, Blake,' Rob scoffed. 'You'd have to lean into the well for a start, what was he looking for in there? I've done two honey farm tours now and as far as I know, bees don't live in wells.'

'He could have had a drink with his lobster and what's bees got to do with it?'

'Are you being purposefully obtuse Blake? Everall was studying bees and no he only had one glass of wine according to Walter.'

I stayed quiet again. Obtuse wasn't natural for me.

'Why are you so keen for these deaths to be accidental?' Rob finally asked.

'I'm not keen for them to be deaths of any kind. My oldest friend gets married in less than two weeks. This is important to him. He needs my support. All the Dame, Matilda and Liliya seem to do is bicker. I need to show him a bit of solidarity and he doesn't need me snooping around the family's honey farm trying to solve a murder.'

'You're not snooping, you're helping me organise my thoughts,' Rob replied. 'I'll do the snooping.'

I sighed, relenting at last to stating what I thought was the obvious. 'If you ask me, which you are, no one's bothered to look into that pocket watch. It's got a family crest on it. Matilda said it was Russian but she didn't know whose family. Surely that will tell you more about the person on the beach, then this might start making some sense. If Everall did see something, he can't tell us now, so doesn't it make more sense to concentrate on working out who the man on the beach was?'

'You see! That's it; I knew there was something missing. There was no mention of the watch in the report. It's probably in his effects. I'll ask Matilda.'

'For God's sake no, don't ask Matilda, Rufus will have my guts for garters,' I almost shouted. I only just had my friends back on side. I didn't need any more trouble.

'Maybe I should go to the mainland then ....'

'Are you going to the mainland?' Delilah strolled across the beautifully manicured grass lawn from the hives. 'There's some bits and pieces I need that I can't get here. I'll come with you. I could get you some sensible boots too, Blake?' Delilah eyed my pink wellies. I hadn't bothered to change them after my walk on the moor.

'I'm growing rather fond of these,' I said waggling my feet at her. 'Besides it would be a waste to get a new pair these are hardly worn.'

'Getting in touch with your feminine side?' Delilah replied, plonking herself down on the bench between Rob and me. The farm manager had disappeared, possibly deciding that Delilah was more interested in the hive than him, or finally needing to do some work.

'Steady, I wouldn't go that far,' I said, 'but there is something quite liberating about wearing pink wellies.'

'So, are we going to the mainland?' Delilah turned to Rob who looked at his watch.

'We've missed the last ferry, we'll have to go tomorrow instead.'

'OK, it'll give me time to make a list.'

'A list? How much do you need woman?'

'There are some books I want that Bob recommended.'

'Bob?' Rob replied.

'Yes the farm manager, he's written a book on natural beekeeping, apparently he's not allowed to sell it in the Dame's shop but you can buy it on the mainland.'

'I know who he is!' Rob huffed.

'I should think he'd get sacked if the Dame caught him even recommending it,' I interjected.

'Then we better not tell anyone,' Delilah grinned at me. 'Come on let's go and get a coffee at the café. All this talk of honey has me fancying a large slab of Penny's honey cake.'

'You don't need to ask me twice!' I said, getting up from the bench. 'I need a decent coffee, not that instant stuff the Naismiths have, although I'll pass on the cake, Mrs Naismith won't stop feeding me flapjack.'

'Me neither,' Rob stood up, breathing in and patting his stomach.

'Lucky you,' Delilah rolled her eyes. 'She never gives me any.'

'If I can get away with it, I'll stuff mine in my pocket next time and you can have it,' Rob winked.

'Gross! Thanks, but no thanks. I've seen the insides of your pockets. Come on, let's go and see Penny. I want to know she's OK. I don't care what Liliya says, she's as sensitive as a brick, I doubt she'd notice whether Penny was OK or not. We'll pick up the dogs on the way, Bertie's missing Douglas.'

We all left the honey farm with an aim. Delilah's was to check on her new found friend, Rob's was to gather evidence on the mainland and mine was to get a decent espresso!

15.

Winter Hardiness

Some strains of bees are able to survive long harsh winters by careful use of stored honey. These bees are referred to as winter hardy.

The silver metal shone as it flew through the air. Rufus caught it deftly on the back of his hand, slapping it down with the other, to prevent a ricochet.

'Heads!' he announced, 'ladies first.' He gave a little bow and Liliya approached the red ball and, placing the croquet mallet perfectly behind it, she rocketed it into play, just centimetres from the first hoop.

Croquet was something I'd enjoyed in my younger days. A chance to sip Pimms, chat and play a sedate game without breaking a sweat. Cricket and rugby were my preferred choices but if you wanted to court a lady, there is nothing better than croquet. Eleanor, my late wife, loved croquet and I have happy memories of playing on the lawn at home and Jane running around, trying to move the balls when I wasn't looking so '*mummy would win*'.

In danger of becoming maudlin in my rose tinted memories I had chosen to sit this one out. Rufus joined me on the little wooden bench at the end of the croquet lawn and we watched the younger members of the party play. Liliya and Matilda against Edward and Rose. Liliya had tried to suggest they *'mix it up a bit'* and she and Edward form a team. Edward declined the invitation, guided by Rose's tight lips and frown. Being a gentleman, he prefixed it with the fact that he'd never played before and would be a handicap. I'm not sure this helped his case with Rose. Still pouting at her rejection it was clear what was motivating the power behind Liliya's first shot. Matilda was in a fine mood after her final wedding dress fitting and cheered her daughter's more than adequate play.

Approaching the starting marker Edward punted the blue ball so it sat neatly beside Liliya's.

'Bravo,' Rufus cheered from the bench. And then to me. 'Where are our intrepid duo today then?'

'Rob wanted to go to the mainland and Delilah never misses an opportunity to shop,' I replied, watching Matilda pitch the yellow ball towards the first hoop. Her less than perfect technique still managed to push the red and the blue balls out of the way, so her yellow now sat neatly in front of the hoop.

'I see. Rob seems to get on well with Walter Simmons.'

'I suppose they're colleagues in a way. Hardly surprising,' I replied.

'From what I hear, no one speaks highly of Salderk's Special Constable, but Walter does speak highly of Rob.'

'Really?' I clapped as Rose Derby's shot landed just behind the other three; I've always been a supporter of the underdog.

'Yes. Matilda said Walter had been round asking for

Rob the other day, said he had some more information.'

The game began in earnest now as Liliya pushed her ball through the first hoop and claimed her extra shot, hit Edward's ball and then roqueted it as far away from Rose's as she could. Giggling she feigned an *'Oops!'* followed by a *'Sorry Eddy Darling, had to be done.'* I could see this game was not going to be harmonious.

Edward trudged across the lawn to retrieve his ball from under a small Hebe and placed it on the boundary line, as instructed, ready for his turn. He took his time eyeing up his shot and he seemed reluctant to take it, especially as Rose was staring at him with a look that suggested their relationship depended on it.

'I hope he's not trying to dig up more information on these deaths,' Rufus continued.

'Who?'

'Rob of course. I know, as professional myself, who also loved my job, it's hard to take a holiday. Especially when something this interesting falls in your lap.'

'So you think these murders are interesting?' I turned in my seat to look at Rufus.

'No, you're taking that all out of context. I don't want anything to do with them. I just don't want Matilda bothered.'

'And is she being?'

'No.'

'Well then ….'

'Would you like me to help you with your shot?'

I turned back in my seat in time to see Liliya smirking as she went to clasp the mallet above Edwards's hands. He abruptly stood up straight almost knocking Liliya off balance. Catching her by the elbow he apologised.

'I'm just fine thank you, I learn better on my own,' he finished, turning his back on Liliya who slouched off to stand with her mother at the other side of the lawn.

'She's been through a lot you know,' Rufus said watching the interaction as intently as I was.

'Liliya?'

'Good God no, that girl's been afforded every opportunity. No I mean Matilda.' This was the first time Rufus had imparted any personal information with me in regard to his future wife and certainly the first time he'd been even remotely critical of Liliya. He already thought I considered Matilda a gold digger. The truth? The more I got to know Matilda, the less I felt able to draw any conclusive opinion of her.

A little whoop from Liliya indicated Matilda had managed to hit Edward's ball in the wrong direction again leaving the visiting team at a severe disadvantage.

As the game played out on the lawn, Rose was taking her revenge on Liliya's ball by knocking it off the pitch, sacrificing a hoop point and thereby ending her turn.

'You're supposed to knock it through the hoop, Rose,' Edward called. 'I thought you said you'd played this before?'

'I have!' Rose gave him a dangerous look.

This time Rufus and I both clapped. 'I think Rose might have the measure of Liliya,' Rufus said, quietly enough for those on the pitch not to hear. He continued in the same tone, 'Matilda's not the hard woman she appears, you know?'

'I'm not sure I ever thought she was,' I replied.

'Come on Blake. I know what you've been thinking.'

'Do you?' I always became indignant when someone claimed to know what I was thinking. Regardless of whether it may or may not be true.

'Matilda had Liliya very young, with no family to support her in Russia. She had to make her own way. She scraped by on very little for a long time. Liliya was five when she came to England. Rescued from Astrakhan, Matilda says, by the late Sir Albrecht De Vries.'

'Rescued?' I gave a short laugh, cutting myself short. I couldn't help myself. It did all sound a little melodramatic.

'Yes! They were living in a slum!'

I regretted laughing. Having never visited a slum myself I could only imagine what this must be like, but either way the word conjures an image of such deprivation as to think oneself very lucky.

Taking in my repentant look, Rufus continued. 'She wasn't always well heeled. The Dame and Sir Albrecht De Vries saw Liliya on the street paying for half a loaf of bread from a street vendor. With no children of their own, Liliya's angelic blonde hair and blue eyes captivated them. They followed her home and offered Matilda a lot of money, so that they may adopt Liliya. Matilda of course refused. They said they'd give her time to think about it and that they would return the next day.'

'They wanted to pay for her child?' I was astounded.

'Shush!' Rufus raised his finger to his lips.

'Sorry,' I replied in more hushed tones, 'But this really is too fantastical. People don't just go around offering to pay to adopt children.'

'The Albrecht De Vries do.'

'Outrageous.'

'I know.'

And then I drew the inevitable conclusion, 'So Matilda sold her child?'

'No, No, Matilda wouldn't do that. They had to come up with an alternative. They offered Matilda employment as a maid and in exchange they would help her to bring up Liliya.'

'Matilda worked here, as a maid?' This was incredible; I couldn't help the involuntary rise in my tone.

'Do I hear my name being used in vain?' Matilda called from the far side of the croquet lawn. The players were rounding the far end and approaching the third hoop. Edward was standing, one hand in pocket, and mallet over his shoulder, watching Liliya as she took her shot. Her bottom stuck out just far enough as to be alluring to the unsuspecting male. From the look on Rose's face I was surprised she hadn't used her own mallet to keep the pert derrière in order.

'Blake was asking how you were getting on with the wedding preparations.'

'I was just saying how nice it must be to have your daughter as the maid-of-honour,' I smiled.

'It's perfect,' Matilda replied hugging her daughter to her side.

'I'm trying to take my shot mother, do you want us to lose?' Came the loving reply.

The focus of the players turned once more to the game.

'I'd rather you didn't mention any of this to anyone,' Rufus was earnest in his request.

'As you wish,' I replied, not entirely sure why Rufus had felt the need to tell me any of it at all. Perhaps he felt Matilda's past was a burden, one he needed to share. The next statement answered that for me.

'I'm not at all ashamed of Matilda's past you understand, and neither is she, it's just … you know?'

I smiled. I did not know. People who professed not to be ashamed of something were generally the antithesis of this. I wondered if the novelty of his new family was wearing off. Rufus had been through a lot of change over the last six months and a wedding might not be the right way to cement it. However, this was not something I was about to point out.

I watched as the players made their way back down the lawn towards the fourth hoop. The sun had gone behind a cloud and for once I was at a loss as to what to say to one of my oldest friends.

Here I was, best man to his groom. Matilda was an undeniably attractive woman; polite, dignified and soon-to-be Lady Blackwood. I wondered who her last husband had been. Had he been the butler? Darensky was a Polish name and so far during my trip to Salderk it was evident the Dame liked to employ staff from the Baltic block. I was venturing into dangerous territory, so I turned my attention instead to Liliya's behaviour.

Desperate for attention, flirting with every man that came near her, I wondered if this was how she'd learnt to survive. At a very young age she'd been taught her looks could get her what she wanted. Now, twenty years on, why would she think any different?

I had always taught Jane to work hard for what she had. Told her that no one was going to hand her anything on a plate. She, like myself had a strong sense of right and wrong. I knew she felt she had earned her place in society through her nursing career. Liliya on the other hand, had been given all she had, with little effort. Her mother had had to work as a maid, while she was treated like royalty.

I remembered the Dame's words; *'having whatever you want isn't always a good thing.'* Did she think the fruit had been spoiled? Did she now regret her decision to *'rescue'* Matilda and her daughter? Could she be referring to the offer of employment she made Matilda, allowing her to stay with her daughter, or was the Dame referring to Liliya as the thing she wanted but should not have received? There was, indeed, far more to this family than met the eye, far more intriguing than any mysterious body on the beach.

'She's a lucky woman, Rufus,' I said, not knowing if I was referring to Matilda or Liliya.

'I'm the lucky one, Blake,' he replied.

16.
Robbing

Robbing is where bees steal honey from other hives.

'Trouble in paradise, Mr Hetherington?' George Naismith asked from behind the paper.

'Hmm?' He'd caught me by surprise. I was eating my porridge and assimilating the information Rufus had given me yesterday, trying desperately not to make judgements. Prince sat by the Naismith's Aga eating his biscuits and some cold ham, Mrs Naismith had snuck into the dish. Mrs Naismith, herself, was out feeding the chickens. Delilah and Rob had already departed for their morning walk with Bertie. They had persuaded Penny she should join them on the cliff top and didn't want to be late. I on the other hand was content to dawdle this morning and savour my porridge. Prince was happy to wait for his walk especially with the opportunity of treats from Mrs Naismith. I had a bit of a thick head this morning and I was blaming it on Walter's over efficient cleaning regime. You could clearly taste the chemicals when he'd cleaned the pipes through.

'Cogitation!' George lowered his paper. 'I know when a man's cogitating and that's what ye're doing.'

I considered my reply.

Naismith tried again. 'No Miss Delibes and her man

this morning? Left ye in a thoughtful mood, has it?'

'I suppose it has,' I replied, having no desire to reveal the true reason for my contemplative mood.

Pushing the paper into his lap and leaning forward he squinted at me over his reading glasses. 'Or is it this mystery that's got you thinking?'

Now used to this kind of interrogation over breakfast, I took another mouthful of porridge before replying. 'What mystery would that be?' I smiled.

'Oh now come on, Mr Hetherington. These bodies that keep following ye around.'

'Following me around?' I laughed.

'Aye, I'm surprised ye aren't daeing something about it.'

'And why would it be anything to do with me?' Swallowing my last mouthful of porridge with purpose, I pushed my empty bowl forward, intrigued as to what George Naismith was going to accuse me of next.

'It's a bit strange, don't ye think?'

'Oh, I don't know. I'm beginning to grow fond of Salderk's eccentricities.'

'Not the island Mr Hetherington, ye!' Naismith flapped his paper open again.

I couldn't resist, 'Me?' I asked.

'Aye ye! I've been doing a bit of Googling and ye seem to have cropped up in connection with a fair few murders,' he squinted at me again.

I stayed quiet, I was pretty sure of his implication. I took a sip of my tea.

'Is it ye?'

The tea almost returned to the mug but I managed to retain my composure.

'What on earth do you mean?' I replied. Prince trotted over and sat under the table, replete after his breakfast. I heard the front door close as Mrs Naismith came back into the house.

'Is ye a murderer?'

You had to admire the man. He always came straight to the point. No qualms about etiquette, or in this case fear for his life.

'George!' A gasp from Mrs Naismith informed me she was back in the kitchen and standing behind me.

'We canae have a murderer staying here Betty! Bad for business!' George pulled his paper back up and began to read the news once more, turning the pages aggressively.

'I'm sorry Mr Hetherington. He spends far too long on the Internet. I've told him before, it's the devil's work.'

'Devil's work woman, what ye on about? Devil's work is what *he's* been up to,' Naismith finished, pointing an accusing finger at me.

'Mr Naismith. Mrs Naismith,' I said addressing each in turn. 'Please believe me when I say, I am not a murderer! Why would I be travelling with a police sergeant if I was?'

'Perhaps you're under surveillance?' George offered.

An involuntary feeling of guilt entered my person. Naismith had touched a nerve. 'And besides, nobody's said there has been any murders.'

'You did. Walter Simmons says you did. When you were stood with him on the beach.'

'The police don't think it is, otherwise they'd be questioning everyone, surely?'

'No yet maybe!' Mr Naismith muttered, 'but things happen a little slower here Mr Hetherington. Mark my words, they were murdered.'

'What makes you think that?' I knew I was getting dragged into a conversation I couldn't win but this man fascinated me.

'I daenae think, I know!' Mr Naismith waited to be questioned further but when no prompt came he continued anyway, lowering his paper once more. 'There's always been trouble brewing between those honey farms. I told Betty, I said Betty, there's going to be trouble at those farms one day.'

'He did.' Betty nodded earnestly from the Aga where she was stirring a stew for dinner. Prince looked up hopefully, in the direction of the slow cooking meat.

'And now look, two people deid!' George finished.

'I see,' I replied draining the rest of my tea.

'Would you like another cup, Mr Hetherington?' Mrs Naismith hovered with the pot, 'Or a wee piece of cake?'

'No, no really I'm fine, thank you Mrs Naismith.'

'Leave him alone woman.' George Naismith had gone from accusing me of murder to defending me from an onslaught of cake. Interesting. I wondered if perhaps he was suffering from a multiple personality disorder. I obviously did not voice this concern.

'So what makes you think the deaths are connected?' I asked

George Naismith leaned into the table once more. 'Well, that Dame employs immigrants on her farm. The body on the beach is Russian, ye ken?'

I nodded. I had no idea how he knew this and didn't really want to endorse the statement, but I wanted him to continue.

'That young lad was a student, right?'

'Right.' This I could confirm.

'Well he's from the Layland's farm, ye ken?'

'I do.'

'So it's tit fe tat!'

'Tit-for-tat? I'm not sure I see the motive?'

'One worker for another. Their trying to dae fe each other's business. Like I said, it's bad for business, murder!'

'Right.' I sat back in my chair. The simplicity was charming. I wondered if Rob had considered it. Perhaps Robin Everall hadn't seen anything from cliff top. Penny said she hadn't seen anything and she had been up there at about the same time. Could he simply have been a victim of circumstance? Was his presence on the cliff top that day merely a coincidence? But there I was again with the notion of murder and not accidental death when there had been no mention of murder by the mainland police. Could it instead have been a dodgy lobster dinner that had caused Robin Everall to lean over the well, vomit and in the process overbalance, sealing his fate. All this was supposition. I was a funambulist walking a fine line of assumptions without a safety net of facts. However, the straightforward nature of George Naismith's proposition was alluring.

I hadn't yet had a chance to ask Rob what information he had gathered on the mainland. We were meeting in the pub for lunch. I looked at my watch. I had enough time to walk Prince and clear my head, gather my thoughts along the cliffs, before meeting them. The more innocuous the deaths appeared to be in my head, the more my subconscious nagged at me and found its way to a murderous conclusion.

George Naismith was watching me from the far end of the table. 'So ye interested now?'

'Do you still think I'm a murderer? If you're right, what have I got to do with the honey farms?'

'Nae, I never thought ye were really. Just testing, ye ken?' He winked at me. 'It's got ye thinking though.'

'I'm sure the police have every angle covered,' I replied.

'Every angle eh? We haven't seen them since they were up on the moor pulling that poor boy out the well. Have ye?'

I couldn't deny it I hadn't. I needed to speak to Rob, see what he had uncovered. I was involved whether I liked it or not and I didn't like being accused of murder. Joking or not. George Naismith might not be the only one to have reached this conclusion.

'I thought things moved slower here?' I smiled.

'Nae that slow.'

'I better take Prince for his walk,' I said getting up from the table.

'Will ye take some flapjack for the way?' Mrs Naismith asked.

'The man daena want flapjack woman! For God's sake, leave him alone.'

Mrs Naismith looked hurt. 'Perhaps a small piece wouldn't go amiss,' I said.

'It'll give ye something else to chew on other than those murders eh?' George returned to his paper and Mrs Naismith handed me a very large piece of flapjack wrapped in a paper towel. I thanked her and, returning to my room, collected my rucksack and Prince's lead, and headed out.

I felt a wave of guilt and excitement as I left the Naismiths. Rufus had specifically asked me to stay out of it all and yet Rob was actively investigating and despite the lack of the word murder officially associated with the case, I felt sure there was more to this than two, completely separate accidental deaths. I'd had very few wedding duties, other than delivering the hats, trying on a suit and attending food tastings. Fairly early on I realised I was here more as moral support for Rufus than anything else and I felt bad that my mind was wandering away from the purpose of my visit. As I walked across the moor to The Fisherman's Rest I ran through my best man's speech again in my head in an effort to refocus. The words blurred and my brain would not allow me to think of anything else. The facts of the case were the only thing I could focus on; two suspicious accidental deaths, but if they were murder, how were they linked? I had to know and Rufus wasn't going to like it.

17.
Clarifying

The process of removing foreign material from the honey or the wax to purify it.

The Fisherman's Rest housed the usual suspects: Robbie serving at the bar, Walter chatting with the fishermen at the other end, and a few walkers. Rob, Delilah and I sat in front of the fireplace with the dogs. The only two faces that were out of place were two men in suits sitting at the back of the pub with laptops. Based on their appearance and recent events I drew my conclusions. They were probably a couple of detectives from the mainland. So they were investigating something.

Delilah said Penny had joined them for their walk but now had to work. They hadn't spoken much about the discovery of Robin Everall and Rob felt it was best to leave it that way. Not an official component of the investigation he didn't want to be accused of harassing witnesses. Delilah, for once, had agreed with him.

I relayed my breakfast conversation with the Naismiths to Rob who listened with amusement.

'I thought you weren't getting involved?' he said once I was finished.

'He accused Blake of murder,' Delilah defended me, 'of course he's going to get involved, aren't you Blake?' Delilah grinned her eyes alive with the idea of a mystery to solve. As she finished she nudged Rob almost spilling his pint as he drank. Rob coughed and wiped his mouth with a clean napkin. We were waiting for lunch to arrive. I'd gone for a crayfish salad this time, still not sure if it was the lobster that had done for Robin Everall.

'Warring honey farms eh?' Rob said. 'It's a theory I suppose.'

'There's another thing,' I said, 'I found this on my walk this morning.' I produced a see-through plastic bag I carried with me for obvious purposes on dog walks. This one was, of course, clean and I had used it instead to pick up a spiral bound notebook I'd found up on the cliff top. Placing the bag on the table I pushed it towards Rob. 'It was stuck in a gorse bush, probably blown there by the wind. I think it's Robin Everall's.'

The notebook was turned to a page showing a square drawn in pencil, it was a wonder it hadn't been washed away. I recognised some of the names of the flora and fauna within it. It was dated at the top of the page with the same day I'd found the man on the beach. Delilah leant over Rob's shoulder as he read. The notes beneath the square diagram stopped halfway through a sentence.

'It certainly looks like a notebook Everall might have and it looks like whoever owned it left in a hurry.'

'Maybe he did see something?' I ventured.

'Maybe. It would make sense. I'll have to hand this over to the mainland police,' Rob said nodding in the direction of two suited men in the corner of the pub. 'They were a bit stroppy when they realised I was staying on the island.'

'They are police, then?' I said confirming my suspicions.

'Yeah. They heard I'd been over to the mainland. Treading on their toes I think. Some people find collaboration threatening. This might build a few bridges. I'll go and talk to them once we've had lunch.'

'How long are they staying?' I asked.

'I should imagine they'll be here until all this is cleared up. They should be. Still, I'm glad I went to the mainland; they let me look at Robin Everall's autopsy report, much more friendly than those guys,' he said nodding in the direction of the suited men.

'Tell, Blake what we found out,' Delilah said, before Rob had a chance to say any more about the unsociable officers.

'They are treating them both as murder,' Rob lowered his voice a little with the word *murder*. 'It's like I said, the man on the beach has a clean wound consistent with a knife and Everall was hit on the back of the head with something like a hammer before he fell or, what is more likely, was pushed into the well.'

'So why aren't the police all over the island?'

'They're keeping it hush hush. They took statements from everyone at both honey farms the day after we found Everall, but the Dame wants it kept quiet. Bad for business.'

'Everything's about business on this island,' I replied. 'Two murders and all they are worried about is business! What if George Naismith's theory is right? What if it doesn't matter who the Russian was; it was simply that he worked on the honey farm?'

'It's possible, but it's a bit random,' Rob replied, 'A hell of a risk just to get ahead in business and why was he in the water? No I think you're right Blake, the key to this case is who that man is. It might well lead us back to the farms but either way we need to find out who our man on the beach is.'

'Did you get another look at the watch?' I asked.

'I did, I've taken a copy of the picture from the evidence file. I'm not supposed to but it can be our secret,' he grinned at me. 'The mainland guys have had an antiques expert look at it.' Rob took a mouthful of beer.

'And …?' I was interested. The watch had just looked wrong in the pocket of a fisherman.

'It has a double headed imperial eagle on it. The enamel work is very high quality. It was made by Pavel Buhre in Russia towards the end of the nineteenth century. It's a very nice piece.'

'Do they know who it belonged to yet?'

'No. It's possible it was a Russian dynasty of some kind. The one thing we do know for sure is that these particular watches were only ever made for the Czarist court, never anyone else. They were presentation pieces given as awards. The serial number can be traced to the court of Tsar Nicholas II. All the dates tie in but it doesn't get us any closer to working out who our man is. He certainly wasn't over a hundred years old and he didn't look like a Russian aristocrat, although, what does one of those look like? There's an inscription in it, in Russian. A rough translation is, '*For honour and duty*'.

'So we have ourselves a hero of some kind?'

'Possibly, although the watch could have been sold or stolen. An item of high worth that old could have passed through many hands; antique dealers for example.'

'And we all know they're not to be trusted,' I said thinking back to the very first time I met Delilah.

'Interpol is involved,' Rob continued, 'but they haven't worked out who he is yet.'

'Do they even know he's Russian?' I asked, 'After all it's only the watch that suggests he is.'

'It's the only lead they have and they've got to start somewhere,' Rob shrugged. 'His jumper had a Russian label in it, so it's more than likely.'

'Perhaps he admired Russian workmanship?' I suggested, playing devil's advocate. Rob raised an eyebrow.

'Walter's been very helpful, hasn't he?' Delilah said.

'He has actually. He might appear a fool but he's not. He knows the people on this island and what they get up to and he's a gossip.'

'So how have you got him to stay quiet?' I asked.

'I suggested if he helped me solve the case he'd be a

local hero. If he told other people they might solve it before him. I also mentioned that island or not there are still licensing laws and his all night lock-ins weren't entirely legal. He doesn't have a twenty-four hour license! Contrary to popular belief not many of them exist.'

'Threats and logical reasoning,' I chuckled, 'I like it.'

'He's been very forthcoming. Hardly any need for me to ask questions of anyone else.'

'He thinks it's all about the honey farms too,' Delilah said.

'Really?' I replied, looking in Walter's direction. He was laughing at a joke with the fishermen. Running a pub, fishing in the mornings and being the island's special constable certainly meant Walter had his finger in many pies.

'Walter says, Penny and Geoff Layland have been together for a year,' Delilah said.

'I thought we knew that,' I replied.

'You didn't tell us!' Delilah huffed.

'Delilah you know I don't gossip and that's gossip. I don't see what bearing it has on the case.'

'I suppose you know Geoff asked Penny to marry him two weeks ago and he's still waiting for his answer!' Delilah replied.

'No I didn't know that. Poor chap, you girls really shouldn't leave men dangling like that.'

We paused the conversation as lunch arrived accompanied by a surly Robbie. My stomach growled its appreciation.

'I still don't see how it's any of our business,' I said once Robbie had returned to the bar.

'The interesting thing is,' Rob cut in before Delilah could reply. 'Liliya and Geoff Layland were engaged until he set up his honey farm in direct competition with the Dame's farm.'

'Now that's interesting,' I replied tucking into my crayfish salad.

'It's gossip Blake,' Delilah smirked.

Rob ignored Delilah's comments. 'As we already know the two honey farms do not co-exist in harmony and it's rumoured the Dame put a stop to Liliya's engagement. The Dame does everything she can to make sure Geoff Layland does not succeed, but he seems to get by somehow. There's no way of telling exactly what's going on, without looking at his accounts, and there's no chance of me getting a warrant, off duty!'

'I see.' I savoured a mouthful of crayfish and mayonnaise. 'Do you think that's why Matilda Darensky's so keen to use the Layland farm honey?'

'Well she does seem to like to bate the Dame, whether she means to or not,' Rob smiled.

'Oh I think she means to,' I replied, immediately regretting it.

'Is there something you're not telling us Blake?' Rob frowned at his lunch. 'Come on spill.'

'Well ….'

At that moment the heavy wooden door to the pub burst open, saving me from a reply, and Rose Derby strode towards the bar.

'Gin and tonic, make it a double,' she ordered. The pub watched in silence, the hum of general conversation shattered. Rose handed over the money without asking how much it was and started to rifle through her handbag for something.

Delilah looked across at the bar. 'Hi Rose,' she said, as cheerily as possible. 'Come and join us.' She pulled the spare seat at the table out in invitation.

Rose looked up from her handbag. 'Delilah, hi.' She seemed to have been completely oblivious to anyone else in the pub until that moment. 'Thank you, I will.' She walked across to our table with her drink and sat herself down with some force, causing the pints of beer Rob and I were drinking to slosh around in their glasses.

The pub returned to its conversation but I could see Walter watching us out the corner of his eye.

'So how are you? No Edward with you?' Delilah was putting on her best innocent face but she was digging and Rob and I knew it. Neither discretion nor subtlety had ever been part of Delilah's personality. We ate our food and observed the women.

Rose finished rooting in her bag and pulled out a compact mirror and a lipstick. She applied the lipstick as she answered with a blunt, 'No!'

'Shame, we would have invited you to lunch if we'd

know you were on your own.' Delilah took another bite of her bacon and brie sandwich.

Rose snapped the compact closed and threw it and the lipstick back into her bag. Picking up her gin and tonic she drained her glass before replying, 'How did you find a good one, Delilah?'

'A good one?'

'Man,' she said. I could tell it was one of those conversations that men really shouldn't be present at but occasionally had to endure.

'He found me,' Delilah smiled at Rob.

'Well good for you,' Rose huffed folding her arms across her handbag. She hadn't removed her coat and the lipstick she had just applied was now around the rim of her glass. 'Anyway, she's welcome to him!'

'Liliya?' Delilah guessed.

'Yes, that little tramp. I saw her coming out of his room.'

'Edward's?' Delilah guessed again.

'Yup. So I thought screw him, I'm going for a drink!'

'I'm sure there's an explanation,' Delilah tried to offer a rational explanation to an angry Rose. 'Their parents are getting married, are you sure it wasn't something to do with that?'

Rose burst into tears. Delilah stopped eating, wiped her fingers on a napkin and put her arm around Rose's shoulders who now began to sob hysterically. The pub was watching once more.

'Perhaps I'll get Rose another drink,' I said, trying to extricate myself from a tricky situation.

'We were having such a nice holiday,' she managed between sobs. 'We found a lovely bed and breakfast on one of the other islands. I don't know why we couldn't have stayed there. There's a regular ferry. There's no reason at all why we had to stay in that awful castle with that awful woman.'

I wasn't sure to whom Rose was referring at this point but I was very aware the whole pub had heard this last comment.

'Shush,' Delilah said stroking Rose's hair. 'I'm sure there's a perfectly good explanation, you'll see. We'll get you sorted out and go and speak to Edward. Blake, I think a coffee might be a good idea,' Delilah shouted after me and I made the order.

So Edward hadn't been diligently tending to his shop after all. He'd been holidaying on a neighbouring island with Rose. And what was Liliya doing in Edward's bedroom? I was sure, from what little I knew of Edward, it was as Delilah suspected but I knew Liliya was trouble. I doubted Liliya had made it look innocent even if it was. Had she set her sights on Edward? The Dame couldn't object to that match, even if they were about to become stepsiblings. I couldn't help but feel sorry for Rose stuck in the middle of it all.

The Darensky seemed to be at the epicentre of most events recently. With the wedding this may seem inevitable but even the watch lead us back to Russia. I couldn't help thinking there was something else that the family was hiding. The question was, would we ever find out what it was? Perhaps I was over complicating things? Maybe this was all simply down to the bees and a whole lot of red herrings!

18.
Africanized Bee

This term is used widely to refer to the African honeybee. This species is well known for its aggressive temperament.

Rose's unfortunate situation had sadly interrupted my lunch and whilst I had the utmost sympathy for her, my stomach did not. Incapable, due to my upbringing, of continuing to eat whilst a lady was in such distress, half a crayfish salad was not going to cut it and for the first time during my visit to Salderk, I found myself hoping there would be cake available at Castle Abrecht.

Delilah had convinced Rose, after three cups of coffee, that she had misunderstood what she had seen and that there must be a simple explanation. Back in control of her emotions for the time being, we made the decision to return to the castle to try to resolve the issue. No one wants a family rift less than two weeks before a wedding.

Rounding the corner, the worst possible scene greeted us. Sitting on the terrace enjoying the afternoon sun, a pot of tea and a large slice of honey cake, Edward and Liliya were laughing, loudly. Liliya had her hand on Edward's shoulder as his arm rested on the back of her chair. In normal circumstances one might observe a scene of sibling bliss, however Rose was not about to believe this for one minute. Edward's guilty face and quick retraction of his arm compounded the issue.

'Go on, laugh all you like!' Rose doubled her pace, leaving no time for deep breaths or counting to ten. 'You'll be laughing on the other side of your face when she drops you for someone with more money.' The words were spat at Edward in a ferocious torrent fuelled by gin and caffeine. There was little any of us could do to stop it.

'Rose,' Edward stood up, 'You've got it all wrong ....'

'It doesn't look that way to me. First I see Liliya leaving your room, then I find you laughing and joking with her, paws all over each other like love struck teenagers.'

Liliya burst out laughing. 'Really Rose, we were just talking.'

'She's near enough my stepsister! Am I not allowed to laugh with my sister?'

'It didn't look like sisterly love from where I was standing!' Rose glared at Liliya who was stifling a second laugh.

'Rose, why don't you sit down and we'll talk about it,' Edward said, 'You really have got it wrong.'

'Come on Rose,' Delilah took hold of Rose's elbow. She soon discovered this was a mistake.

'Get off me,' Rose yelled, jerking her elbow away violently and following it with an elbow jab. Delilah landed squarely on her backside on the slabs of the patio. Taken aback by the sudden movement, she sat there stunned. Rose didn't even acknowledge the injury.

'Rose!' Edward raised his voice for the first time in the

argument and Liliya got up to walk round the table and help Delilah up. I too moved to do the same but Rob got there first.

'I think you better calm down, Miss Derby,' he said, in what I know to be his, *'I'm about to arrest you voice."* He helped Delilah to her feet as he spoke. Delilah dusted herself off and moved back a few steps to avoid further mishap from Rose's flailing elbows.

'Calm down? Calm Down! Would you calm down if it was you?'

'Why don't we see what Edward has to say?' Rob tried.

'I'm not interested in anything that bastard has to say. And as for her, well she's no better than the day I first met her.'

'I beg your pardon?' Liliya replied.

'Oh, I don't expect you to remember. You were a trollop then and you're a trollop now!'

'I have no idea ….'

'What's going on?' Rufus's voice cut across Liliya's. Matilda, Rufus and the wedding planner had arrived in time to hear the last insult flung at Liliya.

'Liliya?' Matilda asked.

'This woman's crazy, mother! I don't know what you see in her Edward,' she said turning to her stepbrother. 'Will you please take her away. If you don't I'm sure Rob will oblige.'

'Hang on …,' Edward was about to try and defend his girlfriend's indefensible behaviour as Rob stepped forward to take hold of Rose's arm.

'I think it's best Edward,' Rufus said.

'Don't worry yourselves, I'm gone. Edward good luck. I told you they were crazy.' Turning on her heel, Rose Derby left the party on the terrace open mouthed and in stunned silence. All except, that is, Liliya.

'Well she's clearly lost it,' she said tapping the side of her head with her index finger and sitting back down beside a stunned Edward.

'She's never done anything like that before,' Edward replied.

'I should hope not! Where on earth did you find her?' Liliya chided.

'Liliya,' Matilda was stern in her tone. 'She seemed to think you had done something you shouldn't have. Have you?'

'Mother, how could you, I'm the picture of innocence.' Liliya was smirking.

'I should go after her,' Edward said walking away from the table in the direction Rose had left.

'In my experience it's best to let them calm down,' Rufus said, placing a hand on Edward's shoulder as he passed him.

'You might be right,' he replied. I didn't blame him. Any sane man would have accepted this excuse rather than go after a woman as furious as Rose was.

'So did do something?' Rufus said to Liliya.

The wedding planner spoke up. 'Why don't we all sit

down and have a cup of tea. Calm the nerves a bit,' she smiled.

'Good idea,' I said eyeing up the cake on the table. Although I had been silent throughout the argument, unwilling to say anything that might make the situation worse, my stomach had not. I walked across to another of the tables on the patio picked up an extra two chairs to take over to join Liliya's table. Rob followed suit and soon we were all sitting around the table. More tea was ordered and, now things appeared a little calmer, Matilda returned to the overriding question.

'So Liliya, what did you do?'

'How …?' A look from Matilda silenced her daughter's attempt at protest. 'OK, OK. She saw me coming out of Edward's room this morning.'

'Really! What were you doing?'

'Mother!' Liliya feigned indignation and Edward blushed involuntarily.

'Liliya I know my own daughter. You love to stir the pot, now what were you doing in there, or do we have to ask Edward,' she looked pointedly at her soon-to-be stepson.

Liliya huffed, 'If you must know, it's a surprise.'

'I don't like surprises,' Rufus said.

Liliya looked across at the wedding planner who was staying very quiet.

'Aurora will tell you. We were planning a slideshow for you. *Our Two Families Unite*,' Liliya said moving her hands in a dramatic semicircular motion. 'Edward brought some photos across with him and we were deciding which ones to use.'

Matilda and Rufus looked at the wedding planner. 'She's right,' she replied, holding her teacup to her lips and blowing on the hot tea. 'They swore me to secrecy. I thought it was rather lovely; a personal touch,' she smiled over the rim of her cup.

Rufus served himself a slice of cake on a side plate and started to eat. At last I could legitimately eat without looking callous. I started on the piece in front of me. I was tempted to say something like, *'that is a lovely idea'* or *'how thoughtful,'* but playing through these additions to the conversation in my head, any way I said them sounded sarcastic, so I stuck to the cake eating.

'It is a lovely idea, darling, but why do your ideas always have to come with such drama?' Matilda replied finally.

'I don't know what you mean?' Liliya smiled.

'I really should go after her,' Edward said again, pushing the piece of cake he'd been handed, back into the middle of the table.

'Would you like me to go?' Delilah said. 'It might be better. She's probably gone back to the pub.'

'Huh, well that explains a lot,' Rufus said.

As we had all come from the pub, Delilah, Rob and I looked at Rufus for further explanation.

Rufus sat forward. 'Well she must have been drunk!'

'I doubt it the amount of coffee she drank,' I replied.

'She looked drunk to me,' Rufus asserted, 'and a schoolteacher as well. You've picked a right one there Edward.'

'She doesn't normally drink coffee.'

'Well I don't want her at the wedding if she's going to behave like that after a glass of champagne.' Rufus scraped some icing off his plate with his fork. 'She's insane!'

'She's really not, Rufus,' Edward said. 'I don't know what's got into her. She said she'd met you before,' Edward looked at Liliya.

'I don't know what she's talking about,' Liliya replied.

'She was reluctant to come to the wedding but I thought it was because she didn't know any of you, not because she did,' Edward said to Rufus.

'Well I don't know her, Edward, other than around the village. I know she teaches at the school, but I've only ever heard good things,' Delilah said, trying to offer Rose some support.

'Exactly!' Edward almost shouted. 'She's never done anything like this before. Are you sure you haven't met before?' Edward looked at Liliya.

'Positive!' Liliya dabbed her mouth with her napkin.

'Romany blood, that's what it is. You can't fight it,' Matilda said finishing a mouthful of cake.

'Pardon, darling?' Rufus said

'She's got Romany blood, you can see,' Matilda replied. 'You'll never tame that one, Edward,' she smiled across the table.

'I never intended to. She really is a very caring, loving person. I don't know what's got into her.'

I thought about Matilda's comment. I hadn't considered Rose's dark hair and dark eyes before, the slight tan to her skin. She was as English as the day was long but I could see where Matilda had drawn her conclusions.

'It comes from a history of itinerant relatives. Never settling in one place. You often find yourself defending yourself for the smallest of things. The result? A passionate people,' Matilda said, almost to herself. 'I can empathise. Liliya you shouldn't have wound her up.'

'But I ….'

'I know you,' Matilda interrupted. 'You would have done nothing to stop her thinking what she did.' Matilda turned to Delilah. 'I think it's a good idea you go and see her, you stand a better chance of explaining. Edward you stay here, if you're lucky she'll forgive you.'

'Forgive him?' Rufus laughed. 'She was the one standing on the terrace screaming like a banshee!'

'And she had good reason. I know what it's like to be an outsider, Rufus. You have to fight for what you have.'

'Huh, not on my terrace you don't,' Rufus replied.

'Your terrace, dear?' Matilda smiled.

'I'll go and see where she is,' Delilah said, before any further argument could ensue between the affianced.

'Do you want me to come with you?' Rob asked.

Delilah stood up from the table, 'No I'll be fine. She'll have calmed down by now.' Delilah turned to Edward. 'I'll try and explain,' she smiled.

I watched Delilah go with admiration. I'm not sure I would have gone after anyone who had knocked me down for no reason but a fit of rage; other than to give them a piece of my mind, that is.

'So this slide show? How would you like it to fit into the wedding?' Aurora the wedding planner, who'd sat quietly, discreetly drinking tea throughout the conversation, deftly brought us all back to the wedding.

'We'll have to talk about that later,' Liliya smiled at her mother, 'It's a surprise!'

19.

Absconding Swarm

This is where an entire colony of bees abandons the hive due to disease or infestation.

'I found her down by the quay,' Delilah said. Delilah, Rob and I had returned to the Naismith's after giving Edward the bad news: his girlfriend had left the island and was not coming back. Delilah was now filling in the gaps. We were sitting round the Naismith's kitchen table, the Aga was still warm and with the mild August evening Rob and Delilah were wearing T-shirts. I had conceded to rolling my shirtsleeves up and undoing my top button, and I was trying not to stare at the travesty of millinery, which Delilah now wore; a black, two-a-penny, cap that touted the phrase *I love Salderk* on it. A heart replaced the word love.

Delilah had bought a bottle of wine from the pub on the way back from talking to Rose and we all had a glass to go with a very fine stew, Mrs Naismith had left in the Aga for us. One of the most obliging bed and breakfast owners I had ever come across. Mrs Naismith was more than happy to cook an evening meal for guests for the princely sum of £5 a head; much cheaper than eating in the pub. I wished Delilah would have the courtesy of removing her hat for such a fine meal. It certainly used to be the custom.

My only reason for not partaking every night was, other than dinners at the castle, which I could not avoid, was the interrogation the Naismiths enjoyed and you normally suffered, while eating. It was a Friday evening and Mr Naismith was in The Fisherman's Rest. Mrs Naismith was up at the Jameson's farm collecting a joint for the Sunday roast. Both, I had discovered, were Friday night traditions that were never missed despite their compulsive hospitality. It made for a rare opportunity for those staying at the bed breakfast to enjoy a wholesome meal in peace.

'She blames herself,' Delilah continued.

'Well that was quite a performance,' I replied between mouthfuls of stew and bread.

'Perhaps three cups of coffee wasn't a very good idea after all,' Rob said.

'She did admit she'd always had a short fuse when it came to men. *'Give me a five-year-old to teach any day,'* that's what she said.' Delilah took a mouthful of wine.

'I don't know,' I said. 'Eleanor was always complaining I had the attention span of a five-year-old. That would imply we're not so different.' I smiled and started to pour us all some more wine. For such a small pub, The Fisherman's Rest really did do a very fine bottle of Sauvignon Blanc.

'So she's gone?' Rob asked.

'Yup, gone back to the bed and breakfast they were staying at last week,' Delilah replied.

'Is Edward going after her?' I asked. Making the natural

assumption that he would.

'I told him she didn't want him to.'

'Since when did a woman ever say what she meant?' I was glad it was Rob who'd proffered that suggestion and not me given the glare he got from Delilah.

'We frequently do, you just don't listen,' she replied. 'You always think you know best.'

'And does Edward?'

'Well, he said he wouldn't go after her if that's what she wanted, so I suppose that's that.'

'He can't really care about her,' Rob concluded.

'What makes you think that? He was very cut up about it.'

'If it was you who'd just stropped off, I'd damn well go and get you back.'

'That's sweet Rob, but I think this is a bit different.' Delilah gave her boyfriend a withering look and then frowned. 'Anyway I don't strop!'

Rob looked at me and I looked at my stew, unwilling to enter this particular debate.

'Edward blames Liliya,' Delilah continued. 'She admitted to remembering Rose but wasn't going to let a, and I quote, *'crazy woman like that,'* get the better of her. Edward thinks if she'd admitted it, Rose might have calmed down. I'm not so sure.'

'What makes him think that?'

'Apparently ever since Rufus announced his marriage to Matilda, Rose has done nothing but talk about what dress she was going to wear for the wedding and how exciting it was Edward finding a new family. That was until Salderk was mentioned.'

Rob and I waited patiently for the rest of the story as Delilah ate a mouthful of stew.

'Apparently, Rose hadn't made the connection between Matilda Darensky and the island. As soon as she did she was refusing to stay on the island at all. It took Edward several weeks to get the truth out of her. Rose and her family used to holiday here. That's how she met Liliya, or at least a ten-year-old version of Liliya. They used to play together on the beach until Liliya got spiteful, as she put it. Rose had been a bit of an ugly duckling until one summer, when they were both fourteen. Rose arrived for the family holiday and one of the local boys paid and interest in her; a crush, nothing serious. It involved bunches of heather and a picnic on the cliff top. Liliya couldn't stand it and made every effort to divert the attention away from Rose and onto her. She managed it. Rose found them eating ice-cream together on the bench on the cliff top, him with his arm around her. Rose has never forgiven her.'

'But that's a silly childhood crush, surely,' Rob laughed at the idea.

'It's amazing how seriously our fourteen-year-old selves take these things,' Delilah replied. 'I've never forgiven Tracy Smith for kissing Brad Travers behind the science block. He was supposed to be taking me to the school disco.'

Now we all laughed.

'Seriously though,' Rob said, 'that's a hell of a grudge.'

'I suppose Liliya brings out the worst in people,' Delilah replied.

The conversation paused as we all concentrated on finishing our stew before it was stone cold. Clanking cutlery as the meat was scraped up, plates of remaining gravy mopped with bread and more wine poured. I sat back in my chair.

'It's interesting though, don't you think?'

'What's that?' said Rob.

'Well, what Matilda said about Rose's origin.'

'Rose's origin?'

'Yes, that she's Romany.'

'Oh she was right about that. Rose's grandmother was Romany. Settled down when she met Rose's grandfather. Matilda would have known that.'

'How?' I asked.

'She knew Rose's family. Rose would come to tea with Liliya here at the castle.'

'Why didn't she say?' Rob said.

'No idea,' Delilah replied.

'Curiouser and curiouser,' I said.

'Hardly!' said Delilah. 'Just a bunch of women playing mind games with each other.'

'Do that often do you?' Rob smirked.

'No, I don't thank you very much.'

'Blake's right though, it's interesting. Aren't some

Romanies from Russia?' Rob asked. I could see where his brain was going. Exactly the same way as mine.

'Some are, but not originally I don't think. A large proportion of them are from Russia or even Slovakia,' I said. There was a wealth of information to be learnt on Radio Four these days and I often enjoy listening whilst doing washing up.

'And Rose said in the pub they were staying on another island last week, didn't she?' Rob directed the question at Delilah.

'Yes. Rose said that she and Edward wanted a holiday. Given what I've just told you it's not surprising she persuaded him to stay on another island.'

'No, but it is interesting ….'

I picked up Rob's train of thought. 'If Rose Derby was staying not too far away and her family has Russian connections ….'

'… then the Darenskys aren't the only ones who could be connected to the body on the beach!' Rob finished.

'What are you two on about?' Delilah said as the front door closed announcing the arrival of one of the Naismiths. 'Rose Derby is a victim in all of this, she's been manipulated by the Darenskys into behaving like a crazy lady.'

'I think she did that all by herself,' Rob said.

'Rose Derby? Manipulated? What planet are ye on woman?' A voice came from the doorway. It was George Naismith. 'Well this is a happy gathering,' he said, looking at the table of empty plates and wine glasses. The dogs, lying beside the Aga, raised their heads as he came in but lost interest when they realised it wasn't Mrs Naismith and therefore there was no chance of a treat. 'Mind if I join ye?' George Naismith asked.

'Not at all, I think Betty's left you some stew in the pot at the back there,' Delilah said. 'No wine though I'm afraid.' She lifted the bottle moving it from side to side to indicate it was empty.

'I daent want wine woman, whisky's all a man needs. Can I interest you gentlemen in a drop?'

'That would be very nice,' I said, and Rob agreed. Delilah declined ignoring the implication that as a woman she wouldn't have been interested anyway.

'So, what ye talking about Rose Derby for?' George Naismith said, once he'd furnished us all with whisky, and himself with a large bowlful of stew and hunk of bread. I observed that the fact he didn't use a knife and simply tore a lump off the loaf, suggested a few whiskies had been imbibed already.

'She's here for the wedding. Or rather was.' Delilah was the first to volunteer any information.

'Was she now, how about that then.'

'She said she used to stay on the island when she was younger.'

'If we are talking about the same Rose Derby, and I ken we are, she used to stay in this very bed and breakfast. Sweet little girl she was, but deadly.' George Naismith chuckled at his stew, dipping a large hunk of bread into the middle of the bowl.

'Deadly?' Rob said. 'At ten-years-old?'

'Aye, that's when they are their worst! You think they don't know what they're doing at that age but they do. One minute you're telling them there's no way they can have a dog, the next bam, they've a pony in the back yard and you brought it for them!'

I laughed at this. Having a daughter myself I knew just what George meant. 'That's most little girls when it comes to their fathers,' I said.

'Not me,' said Delilah. There was a sad look in her eyes as she said this. I knew only too well Delilah's past and I knew she hadn't had a father present, to wrap around her little finger.

'Aye, it is Mr Hetherington, but Rose … Rose, she was different. Used to run rings round that Liliya. Only person I've ever seen manage it.'

'She told me it was the other way around,' Delilah said.

'Aye, of course she did, she's hardly going to tell ye what she really did now is she?' George Naismith took another bite of the huge hunk of bread, slathered in stew. Wiping his mouth with a napkin, he seemed to consider his next comment.

'Did she tell ye about the bees?'

'The bees? No,' Delilah replied for all three of us.

'She caught a swarm of bees. No idea how, but she managed it. Chased Liliya all around the fields at Castle

Albrecht with them. When they caught her, Rose said she was just returning them to the farm. Liliya couldn't sleep for a week from the stings. Rose had none. Explain that?'

I took a sip of my whisky and looked across at Rob. From the look on his face he was thinking the same thing as me; not just animal cruelty but cruelty to a friend. Interesting traits in a schoolteacher. No wonder Liliya fought back in the only way she knew how and no wonder she wasn't going to give her the satisfaction of admitting to knowing her. Far better to let her childhood nemesis look like a fool in front of the guests. We savoured our whisky and George Naismith ate the rest of his stew. I had more than a few questions. Did Edward know about this past? Did Rufus know? And finally, had Rose Derby really left the island for good?

20.

Dearth

This is a period in time where weather conditions are not good for foraging bees. This can mean an excess of rain or a drought.

Delilah, Rob and I were out walking the dogs on the cliff top. Penny had declined the offer to join us with Douglas, as she said she had far too much work to do on the wedding cake. Given the short notice Liliya and her mother had given her, for the feat of wedding cake creation, I was sure this was not an excuse. Delilah and Rob were discussing the events of the day before and after a night of broken sleep, I had retreated into myself for some quiet contemplation.

What had once been, to me at least, two unrelated accidental deaths, now seemed to be inextricably linked. The question was how? I'd been awake most of the night trying to figure it out. Overnight the summer rain had beaten a gentle rhythm on the window of the bed and breakfast, relieving none of the humidity in the air that had contributed to my lack of sleep. Prince had not had the same problem. He'd slept soundly all night at the end of the bed and I was thankful Bertie was here to help him work off some energy. My tired bones would not take a Spaniel's excessive bouncing this morning.

Now, last night's rain was as if imagined as the sun shone violently. The island bathed in it and the heather reached high. A plethora of butterflies, winged beetles and, of course, the bees, drifted in front of us as we disturbed the undergrowth of the moorland. Looking out to sea from the top of the cliff, the blue-green, rippling water glistened and twinkled beneath us. So this was the last place Robin Everall had been. Standing here with his notebook cataloguing the insects and the flowers they supped on. What had he seen? Was it the murderer? Was it someone standing over the body? Perhaps not the murderer but someone worried enough silence him; yet another angle to this case. Were the two victims killed by two different people?

Reaching the bench that afforded one of the most magnificent views out across the sea to the mainland, we sat and rested. Delilah and Rob continued their conversation. Talk had turned to the two honey farms. Rob was sure this was where the answer lay. My mind was a sticky spider web of motives and suspects. I was supposed to be meeting Rufus in the pub later to go over the order of the service, but with my mind so distracted I wondered if I was up to the task.

I imagined a line-up and began to order the thoughts in my brain. Suspects to include were anyone with a Russian connection. This could connect them to the first victim our unfortunate ship wrecked Russian and his pocket watch. There were a fair few people that fitted into this category on the island. The majority of the Dame's employees for a start. Or what about Rose Derby with her Romany links? And then there were those I hardly dare consider: Matilda Darensky, Liliya Darensky, and last but by no means least Dame Albrecht De Vries. She'd taken a back seat in my mind up until this point but a woman with a belief in feudal rights, an inbred arrogance and an air of such formidable authority, would surely be capable of murder. So if these were our suspects, and there were at least thirty in this group, what connected them to the second victim: Robin Everall? A student on the organic honey farm, the only connections were the Dame's honey farm employees. They must come across each other regularly on such a small island. Is there some kind of rivalry? A West Side story, shark and jets, montage played out in my head and I chuckled to myself at the ridiculous scenario I had just concocted.

'You're very quiet, Blake,' Delilah said. She was sitting between Rob and I, once again wearing that ridiculous souvenir cap, and I realised she'd been watching me. 'What's going on in there?' she said tapping her temple.

'Not a lot,' I replied.

'I doubt that,' Rob joined in. 'A seething mass of intrigue and speculation that brain of yours Blake. Come on, we've told you our theories, what's yours?'

'Have you?'

'Yes, we've spent the last half-hour talking about it!' Delilah huffed. 'I think Bertie listens more than you do sometimes.'

This was an insult. No doubt about it, Bertie never listened! 'Indulge me I said,' and smiled.

'Delilah reckons it's something to do with Rose Derby,' Rob said.

'I've seen women like that in action before,' Delilah confirmed. 'Dangerous.'

'In what way?' I asked.

'Isn't that obvious? With a temper like that there's no telling what she'd do if pushed.'

So Delilah had gone from defending Rose to agreeing with George Naismiths' diagnosis of the Miss Derby's psyche. 'OK, so what's she got to do with our victims?' I asked.

Delilah leaned closer and listed the points on her fingers. 'I don't think the guy on the beach is Russian at all. I think the pocket watch was planted.'

'Interesting,' I nodded. I hadn't considered this before.

'Rose was staying on a neighbouring island with Edward, right?'

'Yes,' I replied.

'I think Rose planted the pocket watch there to implicate Liliya or her mother. Robin was just in the wrong place at the wrong time, poor sod. I think he saw her and tried to blackmail her, hence the lobster dinner.'

I raised my eyebrows at the mention of Robin Everall's last supper.

'Paid for with ill-gotten gains. She followed him home,

cracked him over the head and pushed him down the well.'
Delilah clapped her hands together and her eyes confirmed
her excitement.

'OK, but why did she kill the fellow on the beach?'

'Exactly Blake, that's what I keep telling her,' Rob
interjected.

'It's simple really, he wasn't murdered.'

'Really? So what about the wound?'

'Well that could have been made afterwards. Couldn't it
Rob?'

'Well … I suppose the time the body spent in the water
might have confused things.'

'There!' Delilah held a hand out to indicate the solution
was in Rob's tentative statement. 'Wrong place wrong time
again see. He was a victim of the shipwreck, a stowaway if
you like and Rose saw her chance to frame Liliya. Some
sort of twisted revenge or something.'

'There's just one thing though,' I said

'What's that?'

'Well if Rose was staying on another island to avoid
this one, what was she doing over here on a beach,
stumbling over convenient dead bodies to frame her
childhood nemesis?'

Delilah's shoulders sagged and she frowned. I felt bad
to have taken the wind out of her sails so quickly but there
were more holes in her story than the shipwreck itself. I
could see she wasn't beaten though. Her brain was
frantically trying to fill the holes before I found more.

'What do you think then Blake?' Rob said.

'My theories are just as fanciful.' I was trying to make Delilah feel better.

'Fanciful?' Delilah looked at me, incensed.

'OK, perhaps you'd prefer the word theoretical,' I smiled.

'Yes, I think I would. How do you know Rose doesn't know the man on the beach? We only have her word that she doesn't. Perhaps she had a serious case of premeditation? Perhaps she just pretended not to want to stay on the island?' Came the reply. I smiled. 'So come on what's your theory?' she finished, sitting back in her chair and folding her arms.

'Well, I do think it's more than probable that the man on the beach is Russian. You don't just carry around antiques like that on a day-to-day basis, not unless they're family heirlooms.'

'It could have been stolen?' Delilah offered.

'Yes, but wouldn't it have been reported and therefore be on record somewhere?' I looked at Rob.

'Yes, but we've only checked UK records. We haven't heard back from the Russian police yet.'

'Well then, why the Russian pullover? If he wasn't Russian, was he pretending to be?' I echoed Delilah's theory of a murderer with pretences. 'As far as I can see,' I continued, 'the connections we have keep coming back to Russia.'

'I hope you're not being discriminatory Blake?' Delilah

smirked.

'No, I am not! I'm just looking at the facts. Half the Dame's honey farm is made up of Russian, Polish or Czech workers. Liliya, Matilda and the Dame, all have Russian connections. This links them all to the man on the beach.'

'So which one is it?' Delilah turned on the seat to face me. The dogs had worn themselves out and returned to the bench to sit underneath it in the shade.

'That I don't know. There are easily thirty suspects there.'

'I'll say.' Delilah sat back on the bench, arms folded, thinking. 'Aha!' she said, lurching forward again, 'but what about Robin Everall? He's not Russian or Polish, or Czech!'

'No he's not, but like you say, perhaps he was just in the wrong place at the wrong time. It leaves us with two big questions. Who killed the person on the beach and did Robin Everall see them? Still no further forward!'

All three of us looked out to sea watching a small flotilla of sailing boats on the horizon. The sun had risen further still in the sky and I wagered it must be nearly time for me to meet Rufus in the pub, but I wasn't done here yet. I hadn't heard what Rob thought yet.

'Rob thinks it's to do with the honey farms,' Delilah said, reading my mind.

'Most of the time these things are fairly simple,' Rob said, from the other end of the bench.

'I suppose they are to whoever's doing it.' I agreed.

'The biggest conflict on this island is between those two honey farms,' Rob continued. 'All the other stuff is normal domestic rubbish. Childhood arguments and grudges don't often inspire murder. In my experience, profit and loss does.'

'True,' I said, remembering some of the very public arguments that occurred when I worked in London. Stockbrokers shouting down their phones, delivery drivers arguing about parking tickets, suppliers insisting invoices hadn't been paid when they had. It all came down to one thing: profit and loss.

'The Dame has made it very clear, she's not happy about Layland's farm. From what I've observed she's the sort of woman who demands her rights. She's not used to earning them, and her rights are to be the oligarch on this island.'

Oligarch was an ironic choice of word, but I couldn't help agreeing with Rob. The Dame certainly got what she wanted. In the case of Liliya for example, she had gained the daughter she wanted and exploited the girl's mother, however benevolent the offer appeared. She employed immigrants potentially because they were cheaper labour but was this any different to Geoff Layland and his work experience students? Could we really believe the Dame was capable of murder simply because she was a hard-headed, aristocratic businesswoman?

I stood up from the bench. 'I better be getting back,' I said. 'Rufus wants to go over the order of service with me.

I'm meeting him in the pub for lunch.'

'That sounds like a good idea,' Delilah said, standing too and then seeing the look of concern on my face. 'Don't worry we won't interrupt, Rob and I can get our own table,' she laughed.

'Sorry,' I felt bad again. I would ordinarily have welcomed their company over lunch but Rufus wanted to concentrate on the wedding and I had a feeling the conversation would not stay on topic if they were to join us.

'Isn't that Penny, down there?' Delilah raised her hand to shade her eyes, pointing with the other hand at a figure on the beach where I'd found the body that first morning on the island. Standing a bit further back from the cliff edge on the small tumuli occupied by the bench, as we were, you had a pretty good view of the beach. In fact, I was fairly sure, you'd have been able to see the body from here.

'I think it is,' Rob said, now shading his eyes from the glare of the sun. It certainly looked like Penny. A navy blue puffer jacket, jeans and black wellies didn't necessarily give her away but the mass of auburn curls did. She had her back to us, head down, hands in pockets and no Douglas.

'She looks like she's looking for something,' Delilah said. 'Come on we should go and help.' Delilah started to walk towards the cliff edge and the path down to the beach. Bertie trotted after her, but Prince hung back with Rob and me.

'Hang on, Blake, isn't that where you found the body?' Rob said.

'I think it is. Yes. You can see the tree, sticking out from the cliff, that obscures your view when you're closer.'

'And this is where you found that notebook?' Rob said pointing to the bench.

'Yes!' I said,

'Then Robin Everall did see something!'

'Of course he did,' Delilah shouted over her shoulder. 'There's no other explanation.'

'Delilah I think we should leave Penny to it,' Rob called back.

Delilah and Bertie stopped and turned around in unison. 'Why?'

'Don't you think it's a little odd?' I said.

'What? She's lost something. We should go and help.'

'What if she doesn't want us to know what she's lost?' Rob replied.

'What are you on about?' Delilah started to walk back towards us.

'She didn't want to come for a walk with us this morning because she had the wedding cake to work on, right?'

'Y… Y… es,' said Delilah.

'Well I don't know much about baking,' Rob concluded, 'but combing the beach, right where a dead man was found, doesn't look much like *Great British Bake Off* to me!'

21.
Dwindling

Normally associated with the spring, dwindling is used to refer to the death of old bees.

'I think you're getting a bit carried away Rob,' Delilah said, as we reached the old oak door of The Fisherman's Rest. The argument had been going on since the cliff top. 'Even if she was looking for something connected with the Russian it would have been washed away long ago.'

'Not necessarily, she might have …,' Rob began.

'I hope you three aren't going to talk about murder for the whole of lunch,' Rufus said from the bar. 'Pint?' He looked at me questioningly.

'These two won't be joining us,' I said, thankful. I had grown tired of the bickering for one morning and the lack of sleep was kicking in, making me grouchy. 'We need to talk about your wedding for a change.'

'Don't worry, don't worry you won't know we're here,' said Delilah, smiling at Rufus. 'Come on Rob we'll sit over here.' They sat towards the back of the pub, an area, as an unspoken rule of the island, reserved for locals. They were risking affronted looks, tuts and cold shoulders.

'Well, let me buy you both a drink at least.' Rufus offered now feeling guilty.

'It's fine, really,' Rob said, holding up a hand.

'I insist!'

Drinks were ordered and we took our tables at opposite ends of the pub.

'I'm glad you've finally seen sense,' Rufus said as we took our seat. We'd both ordered soup of the day: leek and potato, one of my favourites.

'In what respect,' I said.

'With these murders. I'd really rather you didn't get involved and Delilah only drags you into these things.'

'Rufus, my priority is my role as your best man. It always has been. I'm sorry if you thought it wasn't.'

Rufus' cheeks reddened. 'Of course not old chap, I was just saying.'

'Let's have a look at the orders of service. The ceremony will be in the chapel at the castle?' I felt I needed to check. There was another church on the island but in keeping with the Albrecht De Vries family traditions the whole day was to be at the castle. I couldn't be sure though. Matilda may have decided, at the last minute, to spite the Dame further by shunning her chapel.

'Yes.' Rufus replied smiling at last. 'The vicar from the local church has agreed to conduct the ceremony. Matilda really wanted to be married in the chapel. It really is a wonderful place Blake, I should give you a proper tour.'

'I should like that.'

'I'm not sure why we haven't got round to it already; my fault entirely. There's an amazing crypt below the chapel that I know Delilah would love to see.'

'I'm sure she would.' I smiled at the thought of Delilah eulogising over the history of those who resided in the crypt. Gruesome but right up her street. Rufus was right; an olive branch perhaps for my loyal, if sometimes annoying, friends.

'They had to put some steel supports down there last year when a crack appeared in the ceiling due to subsidence. That's the problem with old buildings.'

'I hope we don't all disappear through the floor,' I said.

'We'll be fine. As you know it's only a very small wedding. I want this to be about family. Discovering I had two sons earlier this year has made me realise a few things. I love the idea that I have a family to pass the Blackwood estate to and that includes Liliya. She really is a lovely girl, Blake. I know she behaves abominably sometimes but she really has been through a lot.'

'So you say,' was all I could think to reply. In my opinion a person's past may go some way to explaining their bad behaviour but it does not excuse it. 'So are you having traditional hymns? I don't suppose there's an organ in the chapel.'

'Matilda's hired a harpist from a neighbouring island; she's going to play. She wants some traditional hymns, she was brought up an orthodox Christian so there's no escaping them but I've asked that we have a little light relief while we sign the register. I've asked the harpist to play *Fields Of Gold*, and thankfully Matilda's agreed.'

'She runs rings around you Rufus.' I grinned at him as I

took a sip of beer. The soup arrived which prevented any defence of Matilda. There was no point in Rufus trying. Matilda had him right where she wanted him and nothing was going to sway him otherwise.

We began to eat our soup and I looked down at the order of service Rufus had laid on the table. Wagner for Matilda's entrance, *Lord of All Hopefulness* to start followed by the ceremony then, *All Things Bright and Beautiful*, a signing of the register with the harpist playing *Fields Of Gold* and finally, I was pleased to see one of my favourite hymns, *Lord Of the Dance*.

'Is anyone doing any readings?' I asked looking up from my lunch.

'Oh yes, Edward's going to read a poem. It's really rather lovely. I do feel for him though.'

'Because of Rose?'

Rufus nodded. 'It seems to me he's had a lucky escape though. Matilda told me what she did to Liliya when they were younger, terrorised her.'

'George Naismith said.'

'Who?'

'The Naismiths. They run the bed and breakfast where I'm staying.'

'That makes sense. Not much secret or sacred on this island. Rife with rumour and that's before you've even mentioned the Beast of Salderk.'

'Ah yes the infamous beast,' I chuckled.

'Maybe that had something to do with that poor lad

down the well. Perhaps he saw it, got scared and jumped down there. Not murder at all, just killed by people's overactive imagination!' Rufus and I laughed together at this. Schadenfreude I know but it was hard not to laugh at the image.

Bowls cleaned, we were ready for desert and Robbie from behind the bar appeared on cue. Or at least that's what I thought.

'I'm sorry to interrupt Lord Blackwood, but Mrs Darensky is on the phone. She says it's urgent.'

'Oh. I better go and see what's up,' Rufus said, getting up from the table. 'I'm awfully sorry Blake. It's probably a flower, dress or cake crisis, that's normally the problem.' He followed Robbie behind the bar to take the call.

The noise of the fisherman chatting at the bar combined with the dishwasher meant I couldn't hear what was being said, but I could see Rufus' face. His mouth became tight, drawing a straight line across his face. A frown creased his brow as he pinched the bridge of his nose. I'd seen this before and from where I sat it didn't look like a normal wedding emergency phone call. Rufus was upset.

Replacing the handset, Rufus hurried back to the table. He didn't sit down; instead he lifted his coat from the back of the chair.

'Is everything all right?' I said.

'No,' came the unsurprising reply.

'Can I help?'

'I don't know.' Rufus stood with his hands on the back of the chair, one foot pointing towards the door, one towards me.

'Well let me try,' I said getting up. 'You can tell me what's up on the way.' I could sense his urgency.

We left without saying goodbye to Delilah or Rob. I knew I we would be in trouble for that later. As we started the walk back to the castle, Rufus remained silent.

'What's happened then?' I said

Rufus stopped on the dry mud path that led away from the pub and across the moor. 'Matilda's found a body.'

'A body?'

Rufus started walking again and I followed. 'Yes. There's no need to sound so surprised it probably followed you here.'

I stayed silent, there was little else I could say to that.

'Sorry, it's just too much for her. She's hysterical, saying it's all her fault,' he continued.

'But she only found the body, right?'

Rufus stopped. He was a couple of feet ahead of me in his haste. He rounded on me pointing at me, 'She's not a bloody murderer, Blake. Of course she only found it!'

'Come on Rufus, I'm trying to help, I need to know what happened. Do you want me to go back and get Rob?'

'NO!' he shouted and then a little quieter, 'No, please don't involve him; the detectives from the mainland are up at the castle with Matilda. I just want to get there and see what's going on. I don't want them putting ideas in her head or getting her to make some kind of confession. She's in a terrible state.'

'If she didn't do it, she wouldn't confess surely?' I said gently.

'I don't know. I don't know what to think. I just know she's found a body and she needs me.'

'Of course, come on let's go,' I said, starting along the path again. Rufus had a temper on him, but it only ever raised its head when it came to people he loved. Not for the first time I could see Rufus loved Matilda.

'She says she found him in an apple crusher.'

'Apple crusher?'

'The big concrete thing to the side of the terrace. It's full of flowers now, but there's a huge wheel that runs around a gutter on the outside. It used to be used to crush apples but someone saw another purpose for it and replaced a head for an apple.'

'Ah, that's what it is.' I hadn't paid it much attention before. I had thought it was just a large flower trough. Now Rufus described its use it was obvious. 'What a way to go. Who was it?'

'They don't know yet, too much of a mess.'

'That must have been awful for her.'

'I can't imagine. I was only saying the other day that thing looked dangerous. You'd have to have some strength to do that or at least work out. Matilda won't do any sport in case she breaks a nail. There's no way this is Matilda's fault. I've no idea what she's talking about.'

'Speaking from experience, the discovery of a body can raise all sorts of emotions.' I said.

'I glad you're coming too, Blake. Perhaps you can help make some sense of all this. You're good at this sort of thing.'

I thought it best not to reply. We continued the walk from the pub to the castle in silence; Rufus contemplating the scene that awaited him and how he was going to comfort his distraught fiancée. Myself wondering who on earth had been killed and why.

Given the frequency of staff and visitors on the terrace at the castle I was surprised the murder, if that's what it was, had gone undetected. It was broad daylight. The more I thought about it the more it had to be murder. How do you crush yourself in such a thing? If someone had somehow managed it, an accident perhaps, what on earth were they doing moving the wheel on what was now a garden ornament? Was this about profit and loss too? After all there were plenty of other motives for murder, love being one of them. I'd read it in books and seen it on the television. Crimes of passion were often opportunistic, spur of the moment. Was that what this was? Could the profit and loss at stake here be emotional rather than financial?

I hoped upon hopes that this death really was somehow a freak accident, but I knew in my heart, this was one hope too far.

22.

Adulterated Honey

This is any honey that contains any ingredient other than honey. These ingredients are not shown on the product label.

The police had, understandably, cordoned off the terrace at the back of the castle and a small white tent had been erected over the apple crusher. Rob had gone to speak to the police officer in charge, a Detective Maitland, but he had had little joy. They were keeping this one close to their chests until they knew what was going on. They thanked him very much for his offer of assistance but and I quote, *'considering your relationship with the Darenskys and the Albrecht De Vries, I think it's best you leave this one to us, Sergeant.'* Visibly irritated at not being able to get information, Rob had returned to the drawing-room of the castle where we now all gathered.

'And they wouldn't tell you anything?' Rufus said.

'Nope, I don't blame them. I'd be the same,' Rob replied. 'After all just because I have a warrant card doesn't mean I have a right to know what's going on in their investigation.'

'Well I have a right!' Matilda shouted. On our arrival the police had simply directed us into the drawing-room where the Dame, Matilda and Liliya were already gathered.

They gave no further information other than they wanted us to stay in the drawing-room and someone would be in to speak to us all individually.

'They did say there were more police coming from the mainland. Considering this is the third one ...,' Rob said.

Matilda started to sob quietly. Rufus was sat next to his fiancée and put an arm around her to try and comfort her. 'I think we could do with some tea,' he said and taking the hint I moved across the room to pull the bell for the maid. She appeared promptly.

'Would Sir like some brandy too?' The maid asked, faced creased with concern.

'Good idea,' Rufus replied and she left the room again. 'Good sort that one. I always said I'd never have staff again, but they're jolly useful in these situations.'

'Do sit down, you're making the place look untidy.' The Dame remarked from the high back chair near the fireplace. She'd been sitting there in silence since we walked in. Delilah, Rob and I were standing in front of the sofa where Rufus, Matilda and Liliya sat. There were various empty chairs, about the drawing-room. Delilah took a similar high back chair to the Dame's, which was to the right of the sofa. I took my seat on an old rocking chair near the window. Rob sat on the footstool opposite the sofa.

'Do you think you could tell us what happened, Matilda?' Rob said, as the maid returned with the tea and brandy.

Matilda pulled herself up straight, wiped away her tears, cleared her throat and went to answer.

'I'm not sure this is appropriate, Rob. Matilda's very upset,' Rufus said scowling at the unauthorised sergeant.

'It's fine Rufus. Perhaps it will help if I tell someone I know. Those policemen out there are so impersonal,' she said, waving a hand in the direction of the terrace. 'I think, what I have to say, I should prefer to tell Rob.'

'What you have to say?' Rufus asked.

'Yes. I …' Matilda looked around the room, taking in the expectant faces and the maid busying herself with the tea. 'I think I'd like to tell the sergeant on my own, please,' she said looking at the Dame and Liliya.

To his credit Rufus didn't argue. He stood from the chair. 'OK, but I'll be just outside if you need me.'

'No, you and Blake must stay,' Matilda corrected him.

'Oh,' Rufus said and sat back down looking a little happier but still confused.

'I think that's our cue to leave ladies,' Delilah said standing up and looking across at Liliya who was screwing up her face.

'Are you sure I shouldn't be here too, Matilda,' the Dame said, equally as puzzled as she was put out.

'Yes mum, you need us surely?' Liliya leant forward and put a hand on Matilda's forearm.

'No.' Matilda's reply was short and without explanation. She did not look at either of the women. It was clear she wanted them gone.

The Dame stood up abruptly, brushed down the front of her blouse, took her book from the table beside her chair and marched towards the door. 'Come along we can sit in the garden-room and try to enjoy what's left of the sun, although I'm not sure I'll be able to look out at the terrace. Still, let's be British about it.' She swept out of the room, her linen trouser suit rustling gently as she went. Delilah, Liliya and Bertie all followed, obediently, leaving Rob, Rufus and myself with Matilda. I wasn't entirely sure why I had been given leave to stay but if that's what Matilda wanted.

The door closed behind the three retreating ladies. Matilda sat up straight, pulling on the hem of her skirt.

'I have a confession,' she said not looking at any of us.

'Matilda, I really think …,' Rufus started.

'No you need to hear this,' she cut in.

I was far enough away from Rob, Rufus and Matilda to observe the body language. Stiff and formal, awkward but not guilty, Matilda was not confessing to murder. She was placing a barrier between herself and her confessors.

'Rufus, this is going to be hard for you to hear, but you need to. That's why I wanted Blake here too.' She looked up at where I sat in the window and gave a weak smile. I confidently returned it.

'Is this really necessary, I'm sure we can sort it out amongst ourselves,' Rufus tried again.

'No!' Matilda was firm as she placed a hand on Rufus' knee to silence him. 'You all need to be here, you're all involved.' The tears started to fall silently again and Matilda tried to wipe them away but more fell in their place.

'Just take your time, Matilda,' Rob said and patiently waited as she gathered her emotions and began again.

'You know I have a past,' she said, looking up at Rufus, 'but you don't know everything.'

'I don't need to,' Rufus replied putting an arm back around Matilda's shoulder.

'No, you need to know this; you see this is all my fault. If I'd just spoken up perhaps ….'

'Perhaps what?' Rufus said.

'Perhaps that poor boy wouldn't have ended up down that well and that awful sight outside wouldn't be there.' She dabbed away some more tears and blew her nose. Eventually she looked up at Rob and, chin raised, staring him straight in the eye she said, 'I know who the man on the beach was.'

Rob didn't reply, he held eye contact and waited.

'His name was Alexander Constantine.'

'Are you sure?'

'Yes. That was his pocket watch, it was a family heirloom. The police showed me his photo later and I ….'

'You never told me they'd spoken to you again,' Rufus said.

'Well they did, I didn't want to worry you, I thought I had it under control. I used to know him but I hadn't seen him for more than twenty years. They said it was accidental not murder, I didn't see the harm in telling a white lie.'

Rob coughed. 'So who is he?'

Matilda pulled her shoulders back and wiped her nose with her hanky, sniffing. 'Liliya's father.'

The silence hung between us. Rufus pulled his arm away from around Matilda, replacing it as quickly as it had been removed when he realised the implications of his action. I attempted to look as neutral as possible in the face of such a revelation. Rob, well, Rob was a policeman, a professional in these situations.

'I see,' was his reply, 'and does she know?'

'No! I would never have told her. You see it's not that simple. There's more.'

There was always more. Never in the history of families was a man just someone's estranged father.

Matilda continued, 'I was young when I left home. I had no money, I had to get food and I had to live. Alexander was charming. He looked after me, kept me off the streets, took me in as a sort of housekeeper in an apartment he owned in Moscow.'

None of us spoke. We respectfully listened. It occurred to me that moving to England to be a housekeeper wasn't such a change in her circumstance after all. Perhaps it had been as convenient for Matilda as it had the Dame? I watched Rufus' face as the next part of the story unravelled. His hands moved from Matilda's shoulders once more, his body involuntarily creating distance between them. His ears were listening but his brain was struggling to comprehend.

'He was a rich man. He took me to the best restaurants and theatres, places I would never have gone without him. Alexander held a position with the royal family. I never really knew how he was related to them but he treated me well. I was comfortably provided for and for a while I wanted for nothing, that was until I fell pregnant with Liliya. Then he wanted nothing to do with me. He told me he had a wife and he wanted me to get rid of the baby. I wouldn't and he turned me out of the flat. I was devastated. I never saw him again. That was until Walter Simmons showed me the pocket watch.' Matilda sniffed and dabbed her nose with her handkerchief. 'I never told Liliya.'

The tears were still falling, silently. They made dark spots on Matilda's dress. For once in my life I found myself not making a judgment but instead wanting to tell her it was OK, she wasn't to blame. I couldn't explain the overwhelming paternal instinct I had at that point, for this woman. I was completely still as I watched Rufus and Rob.

'Do you know any more about Alexander's family?' Rob said.

'No. I remember him saying he was a distant cousin of the royals but I don't think he ever lived with them. He never tried to find me again and I never tried to find him. I have no idea what he was doing here. My instinct was to protect Liliya. I don't want her to know. And the Dame! If the Dame knew ….'

'Did you speak to him when he came to the island?'

'No! I had no idea he was here.' Matilda's eyes widened.

'I think that's enough,' Rufus said, as he leant forward awkwardly, to try to comfort Matilda, his body fighting with his brain once more. I had no idea how I would take what I'd just heard if I was him. I knew there was more to Matilda and Liliya but to think the man I had found was Liliya's father; this was beyond my imaginations.

'Liliya mustn't ever know,' she said between sobs.

'The police will want to speak to you and Liliya,' Rob said.

'Can't you try and explain. Tell them Liliya knows nothing,' Rufus said.

'I'll try.'

'I couldn't bear it if Liliya turned against me. I'm supposed to be getting married in a week!' Matilda was almost wailing.

'Shush, Matilda, it's OK darling, we'll sort it all out. It'll all be OK,' Rufus soothed.

'You'll have to tell the police what you've told me,' Rob said.

Matilda nodded silently. There was a knock at the door and I got up to answer it. Opening it I saw what could only be two police officers. Grey suits, equally grey ties and highly polished shoes, they were not the usual residents of Salderk.

'Could we have a word with err … Mrs Darensky,' one of the detectives said, looking down at his notepad.

'Come in.' I opened the door wide. The officer

frowned when he saw the scene. 'We could do this later if it's better.'

Matilda turned to look at them. 'No, now is fine,' she said. Her eyes were red, cheeks flushed and her hair ruffled put she was still dignity personified. 'Come in,' she indicated the empty chairs.

'We'll leave you to it,' Rob said. I knew he meant me when he said '*we*' and I got up and moved towards the door.

'Don't go too far, we'll need to speak to you too,' the police officer said.

'Rob will you stay,' Matilda said before he got much further. 'That's OK isn't it?' she asked the officer.

'If that's what you'd like Mrs Darensky,' he replied rubbing his temple with one hand and retrieving a pen from his pocket with the other. 'Are you sure you wouldn't like a female officer present too or perhaps your daughter?'

'No, I'm fine,' Matilda replied as I was leaving the room.

I took hold of the handle and went to close the door when I heard Rufus ask, 'Do they know who it is yet?'

I pulled the door to but did not close it. In normal circumstances I would not condone but sometimes eavesdropping could gain you a lot of information and after the confession I had just been privy to I was intrigued as to whether or not the body in the apple crusher was another Russian connection.

'Yes. The driving licence in his wallet identifies him as

Geoff Layland.'

I closed the door silently and went to find the others in the garden-room. Geoff Layland was definitely not Russian but it was another connection to the honey farm; this time the owner! Intriguing. Russian royalty, murky pasts, warring honey farms, what else was this case going to turn up?

23.

The Honey Bee

Also known as *Apis mellifera*, meaning *honey-bearing*, the Western or European bee has been the subject of concern due to its decline.

In the garden-room the sun shone bright, in stark contrast to the grisly scene outside. A little white tent had been erected over the apple crusher, shielding the scene from prying eyes. With less than a week to go I wondered how the wedding was ever going to emerge from beneath the shadow these deaths had cast. Weddings invariably included a marquee, however not one of this ilk.

Entering the room I saw Delilah sitting with a book she'd selected from the extensive bookshelves. I couldn't see what it was but I was surprised to see her reading rather than gossiping; a favoured pastime of hers. I was perhaps cruel in this observation but Delilah does like to gather information as the honeybee gathers pollen.

The silence opposite her from the Dame and Liliya indicated conversation had not been on the cards. The Dame was also reading. Wilkie Collins was her choice and Liliya was occupying herself with a game of solitaire. It was rare to see this game played, these days, with real cards on a table, since the advent of mobiles and apps, but on an island where mobiles didn't work, I was pleased to see that little traditions were kept alive.

Liliya was wearing a large floppy seventies sunhat. Straw wide brimmed in its natural colour, she'd customized it with a long silk green scarf that acted as a hatband and now fell across one shoulder. A small pearl brooch held the scarf in place on the hat and I was reminded of my last-ditch attempts to garner summer trade at my old hat shop. I had been left with a large box of plain hats and several metres of ribbon. It was all about charity shop chic these days and no one had been interested in a new straw hat. Delilah had eventually helped me to sell the last few hats on ebay last summer.

The garden-room itself was mainly glass with a small three-foot wall around the base making it more of a conservatory. Two large palms stood in either corner reaching up to the glass roof. About a foot from the top was a row of stained glass, which threw a rainbow on the tiled floor, the reflections dancing around your feet. The furniture was sturdy wicker with Laura Ashley style upholstered cushions. I took my place in the sole empty chair available. The only noise was a far off sound of clunking coming from the old pipes as someone, somewhere in the castle, staff perhaps, as they ran the hot water.

'Winning?' I said to Liliya.

'No,' she replied not looking up from the cards. 'I never do.'

'Hello Blake,' Delilah said. 'What's going on then?' She

placed the book open face down on the little glass coffee table, dangerously close to Liliya's card game. It was entitled *Apiary for the Modern Woman*. I wasn't entirely sure what to make of that but the curled edges and tarnished pages told me it was far from modern. I winced as the spine creaked. Old books are like old friends: you should never take them for granted.

'The police are interviewing Matilda.'

'Is she OK?' Liliya looked up eyes widened in concern.

'Yes. Rufus and Rob are with her.'

'Good,' the Dame said, without moving her eyes from her book. *The Dead Secret* was an apt choice. 'Damn silly, if you ask me.'

I coughed. 'Someone has been murdered,' I said

'And don't I know it!' the Dame replied, looking up at me accusingly. 'Making a damn mess of the lawn they are. How on earth could they think Matilda has anything to do with that?'

'They have to cover all eventualities I suppose,' I replied.

'Indeed! But there was a time when the police knew their place. They had a respect for people like us. Fancy thinking Matilda could murder anyone.'

'Do they know who it is out there?' Delilah asked changing the subject.

'Really, dear, how terribly ghoulish.' The Dame went back to reading her book.

I thought for a moment before replying, weighing up

the pros and cons. What I had heard wasn't strictly official but they had told Rob, Rufus and Matilda so it would be public soon enough. 'Geoff Layland,' I said eyeing Liliya. She did not move her gaze from the cards.

'The honey farm owner?' Liliya said.

'Yes,' I replied.

'Are you sure?' The Dame joined us again.

'Yes. That's what the police said.'

'What on earth was he doing on my land?'

'I think he came to see mummy about favours.' Liliya still didn't look up from the cards.

'What possible favour could he do her?'

'No, *the* favours.' Liliya looked up at the Dame, 'for the wedding. She wants to give the guests a piece of honeycomb as a gift.'

'Really? How peculiar. It'll be full of rubbish, they'll be picking the legs of bees out of it,' the Dame smirked.

'I thought bees kept a very tidy house' Delilah tapped the spine of the book in front of her, 'this book says ….'

'Young lady, has no one ever told you not to contradict your elders?' The Dame gave Delilah a fearsome look that I did not envy, 'and will you please have a care with that book.'

Well at least there was one thing we agreed on.

'Hello, what's going on out there?' Came a voice from the doorway. 'No one will tell me anything.'

'Edward!' Liliya got up from her seat, almost running the short distance to the doorway flinging her arms around the unsuspecting Edward in a fashion I've only ever seen in old black and white movies. 'It's awful, simply awful,' her voiced was muffled by Edward's shoulder.

'Liliya dear do come and sit back down and stop being so dramatic. Edward there's room for you on the couch.' The Dame nodded at the small two-seater Liliya had been sitting on. With two people on it, the chair looked considerably smaller.

'So who's going to tell me what's going on?'

Delilah was busying herself with the book once more, reluctant to speak again after her scolding. I really didn't feel it was my place to announce the news. Liliya was now pawing Edward's arm. 'Where've you been?' she said.

'To try and find Rose.' Edward moved his arm slightly to discourage Liliya's tactile advances.

'Oh,' Liliya frowned.

'You really should forget her,' the Dame said, 'she's just trouble.'

'I had to do something, I felt responsible. I brought her here.'

'Did you find her?' Liliya folded her arms and sat back in the seat.

'No. I had to come back or I'd have missed the last ferry,' Edward sighed.

'There's been another murder,' Delilah burst out, unable to contain herself any longer. The Dame looked up from her book again with this time a slightly more tempered look, but fearsome nonetheless. 'Well, Edward wanted to know,' Delilah said quietly.

Edward looked across at me, 'Another one?'

'Yes.' Why did everyone look to me when the word murder was mentioned? A chap could get quite paranoid.

'Who?'

'Geoff Layland,' Liliya gave a sulky reply.

'Wasn't he coming over here today to talk about the favours?' Edward asked.

'Yes, and it's simply awful.' Liliya took hold of Edwards arm again and gave him her best, distressed-damsel look.

'Liliya!' The Dame growled

Liliya folded her arms, 'Well it is!'

'For Geoff Layland maybe, I will concede being murdered isn't top of one's list of things to do but with a wedding a week away it really is a terrible inconvenience.' The Dame's words were final and she returned to her book again.

'Oh no!' Liliya lurched forward again, one hand on Edward's bicep and the other held to her mouth.

'What now?' The Dame thumped her book down on her lap.

'Does Penny know?' Liliya said.

'Oh goodness, I'd forgotten about her,' Delilah said. 'I'll see if Rob can let her know.' Delilah got up to leave the room.

'I think they'll still be with Matilda,' I said.

'I'll just wait outside the door then.' Delilah gave an innocent smile in direct contrast to the almost imperceptible wink that came my way as she left the garden-room. Listening at doors was not beyond Delilah by any means and I sensed she wanted to be out of the room, away from the Dame and investigating once more. I stayed where I was reluctant to encourage her.

Liliya watched her go. 'You'd think she'd known Penny all her life the way she carries on,' she huffed. 'It should be me that tells her, not her or Rob.'

'You need to stay here,' Edward said firmly. 'I should think your mother will need you once the police have finished questioning her, isn't that right Rosalyn?' He looked towards the Dame.

'Quite,' she said, not looking up from her book.

Liliya stroked Edward's bicep. 'You're so perceptive Edward, you must get it from your father,' she simpered.

Edward coughed and shuffled in his seat but the look on his face suggested he was actually enjoying the attention. I admired the Dame's ability to ignore the scene and feeling uncomfortable I stood up to peruse the bookcase to the left of us, allowing me to legitimately turn my back on the fawning Liliya. It was about now I would have loved to have been able to disappear into my shed on the allotment and complete one of the commissions I had waiting for me on my return. Perhaps one of the Ascot commissions or the little cloche hat I'd promised my niece for her birthday.

'Do you play sport? You're awfully fit.' I heard Liliya continue as if we'd never been talking about the murder.

'I row,' Edward said. 'I don't do as much as I'd like to

but I go to Henley each year.'

Ah, Henley, I thought, retreating to my safe place. A world of boaters, Breton caps and large brim sunhats but it was no good. I was brought back to Liliya, as her green silk scarf adorned sunhat appeared on the head of one of my imagined Henley visitors.

'Really? I'd love to come and watch.'

'You'd be very welcome.'

The entrance of one of the detectives saved us from witnessing any further grotesque flirtation.

'Miss Darensky, would you mind coming into the drawing-room, I think your mother could do with your support.'

'Of course.' Liliya stood up and took a step around the coffee table and towards the door. Turning she said, 'Edward, you should come too, Rufus might need you,' she smiled.

'Edward Turnball?' The detective looked down at a list of names he had in his notebook.

'Yes.'

'We need to speak to you too,' the detective replied. 'Is there another room we could use, Dame Albrecht?'

'Edward wasn't even here,' the Dame replied.

'No I wasn't; I've been over to the mainland for most of the day.'

'I see. Even so we need a statement from you if we could.'

'If you must.' the Dame got up leaving the book on the

chair, ironically open and spine up. 'I'll show you to the study, you can talk there.'

'Thank you madam.' The detective, Edward, Liliya and the Dame left the room, leaving me with the books and my dreams of hats.

I considered the situation: a body outside, detectives and a potential suspect inside. The murder had occurred in broad daylight, somebody must have seen something. So where had everyone been?

Rob, Delilah and I had been out on the moor. Rufus had been in the pub, at lunchtime at least, to meet me. Could he have done it? I laughed out loud at the thought. Why would he sabotage his own wedding? I hadn't asked where had he been that morning. He could have been anywhere.

What about Matilda, Liliya and the Dame? Had they all been here at the castle? Matilda must have been here in time for her appointment with Geoff. Could she be the perpetrator? Doth the lady protest too much? But again why?

Liliya knew about the meeting and might have been here at the castle at the time? Her relationship with Geoff was a long time ago; surely she wouldn't have left it years before exacting revenge. Besides the breakdown of the relationship was down to the Dame not Geoff.

Was it the Dame then? Had she finally had enough of Geoff Layland disrupting her business and family life? Surely she wouldn't bloody her own hands?

That left Edward. He also seemed to have been aware of the meeting between Matilda and Geoff, but he'd been on the mainland. And then a thought struck me. His alibi was the ferryman but was the water between the island and the mainland narrow enough to row? He'd said he was a rower and it may be possible for someone who was fit enough. But then again what was his motive? Did he secretly lust after his stepsister and saw Geoff as competition? No, that wasn't right either; Geoff was with Penny. What about Penny? What had she been looking for on the beach?

It seemed to me there were ample suspects in this case but no solid motive and now we had three bodies. I went back to the beginning. What linked Layland's death to the other two? They couldn't all be separate events, surely? It had to be the honey farm, that's what it kept coming back to. However, now we knew who the Russian was, it meant he wasn't an illegal immigrant come to work on the farm. He was in fact royalty. That threw a spanner in the honey farm theory.

I picked up the book Delilah had been reading and sat back down in the chair. This was indeed a tangled web. I began to read. I needed to take my mind away from the drama outside, maybe and then I'd finally get some answers.

24.

Buckfast Hybrid

Brother Adam, at Buckfast Abbey in England, created the Buckfast Hybrid. It was bred for its hardiness, ability to resist disease and its good nature, preferring not to swarm and instead build strong combs of honey.

'So what was our Russian doing on the beach,' Delilah said. We were sitting on, what was fast becoming our favourite bench on the cliff top overlooking the Singing Caves. The sun was high in the sky and the wind blew wisps of Delilah's hair into a halo and as she spoke she battled to keep it still.

Rufus had requested some space for himself and his fiancée and so Delilah, Rob and I were avoiding the castle for a while to let the dust settle. The latest wedding crisis was that they might run out of champagne; a concern voiced by Liliya. A stark contrast to yesterday's brutal revelations. I'd promised Rufus I would go to the mainland on the mid-morning ferry to collect some extra bottles; anything to help what was fast becoming a very stressful time for my old friend.

Bertie and Prince were galloping around in the heather and shrubs and I had no doubt a good brushing of Prince's fur would be required on returning to the bed and breakfast. Not a task either Prince or I relished. If he had it his way he'd be one big ball of knotted fur.

There was, unsurprisingly, no sign of Penny and Douglas. The mainland detectives had been the ones to inform Penny of her fiancé's death. Delilah had been annoyed: *'I am dying to ask her about Geoff, there must be something interesting in his past.'* She'd said. Rob had given her a look: half exasperation, half policeman. It said leave it! Delilah, for once, had. Sometimes Delilah's zeal for investigation got in the way of sympathy. Her ability to detach herself from the events always surprised me. I put it down to her archaeological background. Digging up the past often brought with it a reminder of our mortality. There must be a point where you become philosophical about the whole subject of life and death. The only time I'd ever seen Delilah truly upset about the possible demise of someone was when it concerned Bertie.

'I'm not sure I believe the whole immigrant story.' Delilah scooped her hair back over her ears. 'They'd have found something else on the boat, his belongings or something. Someone would have known he was there.'

Rob and I looked at each other. We were both eating large slabs of flapjack that had been handed to us as we left the Naismiths' that morning. We had more than enough for the three of us, but Delilah was abstaining. Delilah turned to pull something out of her coat pocket and caught the look on Rob's face.

'You know something!' Delilah waved her Salderk cap

at him, that she'd just pulled out of her pocket and the wind almost whipped it away. It was a shame it hadn't. I stretched my legs out in front of me and a flash of pink colour reminded me that I was wearing equally ridiculous on my feet. For a moment I wondered if I'd entered a twilight zone. What was this place doing to us?

He took a large bite of his flapjack to postpone his answer. Delilah was busy pushing her hair into the cap and securing it firmly on her head when Rob went to take another bite.

'Ar, Ah.' Delilah took hold of the flapjack as it made its way to Rob's mouth. 'Come on spill.'

'Delilah,' I interjected, 'I'm not sure Rob's in a position to tell us anything. The police have probably told you not to talk about it, haven't they?' I offered him a lifeline.

'Yes, that's right,' Rob said, as I handed him a second piece of flapjack.

'Don't give me that. The amount of times you've told Blake things you shouldn't.' Delilah started eating the confiscated flapjack and waited. Rob did not relent he was now very deliberately, clearing crumbs from his fleece. 'Come on it's only me. Who am I going to tell?'

Rob gave Delilah a sideways glance. 'It's not really my secret to tell,' he said and looked at me.

'So there is a secret!' Delilah was pointing the flapjack at him now. 'And you know it too.' She screwed her face up at me.

Bertie ran up to the bench with the hope of gaining

some fallen crumbs from the flapjack Delilah was waving around.

'Don't worry, Bertie, I'll get it out of them.' Delilah leant down to scratch Bertie behind the ear.

She wasn't giving up; we were going to have to give her something. 'I can't tell you either Delilah, I'm sorry. I can say though that you are right the man was not an illegal immigrant. He is Russian and what he was doing on the beach is still a complete mystery,' I said, finally.

This was all true and there was no harm in giving Delilah the bare facts. We knew he was Russian royalty of some description so presumably not an illegal immigrant, he was definitely Russian, Matilda told us this, but no one knew what he was doing on the beach, not even Matilda. Now his identity was revealed it was possible that this might be ascertained but I doubted the police would share this with either Rob or me.

'You know bees round on their queen when they've had enough of her,' Delilah said, looking at me.

'I'm not sure what you mean?' I said.

'Well, the Dame rules with an iron rod as far as I can see and that's going to get a bit tedious eventually. Especially in this day and age.' Was Delilah was still smarting from the Dame's comments yesterday?

'What's that got to do with the Russian on the beach?' Rob asked.

Delilah took another bite of the flapjack deliberately making Rob wait for his answer. She wiped her mouth with a napkin and leant down to give Bertie a piece of the bounty.

'I think you're right about this being about the honey farms. I think the Russian was an employee of the Dame, not an illegal one but he was coming to work on the farm. What if he was a spy?'

Rob almost spat flapjack. 'A spy!'

'Yes, you know industrial espionage. Maybe he'd been working there for weeks and the Dame's bribing her staff into saying they'd never seen him before. What if he'd met the student on the cliff to exchange information!' She took a bite of her flapjack and sat back in the chair arms folded awaiting her congratulations for cracking the case.

'He was not a spy!' Rob said and then trying to change the subject. 'When do you have to catch that ferry, Blake?'

I too was keen to change the subject. I did not want Matilda and Rufus' secret revealed. Rufus had been through enough. 'Eleven.' I replied looking at my watch. It was nine-thirty.

'Come on, Blake, who was he?'

'Delilah, I really think you should leave it. The police know and that's what matters,' I said.

Delilah sat back and folding her arms, she looked out to sea.

'Look you might be right,' I said trying to placate her.

'So he is a spy!'

'No, no, don't be ridiculous.'

'Hmph.'

'I meant I think you're right about this being about the honey farms.'

'Profit and loss,' said Rob, joining in. 'That's what it's all about.'

A figure walking towards us, caught my interest, and I turned to see who it was. I was surprised to see Penny walking Douglas. She looked far from the red eyed, washed out distraught fiancée I expected. Although who am I to say how she should react.

'Penny!' Delilah stood up from the bench. 'How are you?' Her words were caught on the wind and Penny only just heard them.

'Delilah, er hi. I'm fine thank ye.' She approached the bench where we were sitting but her body language said she did not want to sit.

'Why don't you join us?' Delilah said watching Bertie and Princes' excitement as they greeted Douglas.

'That's very kind of ye, but I'm just not in the mood, ye ken.'

'I do,' I smiled.

'Well I best be getting on.' She didn't wait for a reply and she was soon making her way along the cliff again and disappeared out of sight. Douglas was more reluctant to leave and stayed a while before a shrill whistle from Penny called him away.

Delilah sat back down. 'Poor girl, I wish there was something I could do.'

'There is,' Rob said. 'Leave her be.'

'She's a friend Rob, it's the least I can do is offer some comfort.'

'And, you did'

'But if we knew a bit more about Geoff, we might be able to help.'

'People grieve in different ways, leave her be.'

'OK, OK, I suppose you're right,' Delilah said. There was another whimper from Bertie who had returned to the bench. Delilah stood up, reaching into her pocket again. 'I suppose you want this?' she said, pulling an old soggy tennis ball from her pocket and throwing it away into the expanse of the moorland. Bertie and Prince raced off after it, followed by Delilah, at a faster pace than I could ever muster when playing the same game with Prince.

Rob and I turned on the bench and lent on the back of it as we watched Delilah playing with the dogs.

'Do you really think this is all to do with the honey farms?' Rob said.

'It's the only thing that really makes sense at the moment.'

'It's the conclusion I came to. And what do you reckon to Matilda's revelation?'

'I'm not sure. There are several things that connect a Russian to the honey farm, just not necessarily a royal Russian.'

'That's the confusing bit isn't it?' Rob rubbed his temple.

'It kept me awake last night, I hate it when I can't make

sense of something.'

Rob laughed. 'The curse of the enquiring mind eh, Blake?'

'Absolutely! The only person that really knew who the man on the beach was, is Matilda and I really can't see her killing someone when she's in the middle of planning a wedding.'

'I don't know. I've seen some women do some crazy things before their weddings. You'd be surprised what goes on behind closed doors. They call them bridezillas for a reason.'

'Bridezillas?' I laughed, 'No. I can't really see that. Matilda gets her way regardless she doesn't need to be a bridezilla.' I stood up to make my way over to Delilah and head back to the bed and breakfast. I had a ferry to catch. 'The only thing that I can think of is that somehow the Dame knew about Matilda's past. Somehow she must have known about the royal Russian. She's another that gets her way whatever.'

'Hmmm.'

'The problem is we can't ask either of them anything without betraying Rufus' confidence.'

'Ah, but there are some people who can legitimately ask,' Rob smiled.

'Oh?'

'The police!'

'True, but they're not going to tell us, are they?'

'They might tell me, if I ask really nicely.' Rob pulled

his coat from the back of the chair.

'But as a member of the wedding party, they might not,' I sighed.

'True, but leave it with me, I'll see what I can do. In the meantime you concentrate on being best man. You never know what you might find out next.' Rob looked up at me. I could see in his mind working over the facts.

'Come on,' I said, 'we'd better not leave Delilah on her own for too long.'

Rob laughed. 'That's very true,' he said standing up.

There were a couple of walkers far away on the other side of the beach below, to the right of us, and I watched them as we walked across to join Delilah. We had almost reached them when the peace was shattered by a rhythmical drumming sound coming from the direction of the sea. Turning around the source of the noise was revealed.

A yellow helicopter loomed closer, moving quickly over our heads and across the island. As it went past, I looked up and could see the green and white chequered stripe across the side of it that made it clear this was an air ambulance. It flew low enough to painfully vibrate eardrums and we shaded our eyes as we watched it head towards the other side of the island.

'That's going to land soon,' said Rob.

'Was that an ambulance?' Delilah had now joined.

'What on earth could have happened now?' I said as the helicopter disappeared from sight.

'Come on!' Delilah - never one to miss out - was heading towards where the helicopter was last seen.

'We'd better go too,' Rob said. 'There's no point trying to tell her it's none of our business.'

We set off, following Delilah. A feeling in the pit of my stomach told me that, contrary to Rob's statement, this was very much our business. I couldn't get a sense of where the helicopter had landed in relation to us but I knew it had gone west and there was little else in that direction other than the Dame's estate.

25.
The Queen's Court

The queen bee is unable to look after herself and is surrounded by attendants to care for her every need from feeding to cleaning.

The thunderous drumming had stopped within five minutes of the helicopter disappearing from our view. We'd arrived at the castle in time to see the blades start up again and whisk Lord Rufus Blackwood to hospital, his fiancée by his side: suspected heart attack was all the Dame would say.

'I told them they should postpone the wedding, but Rufus isn't having any of it. He says no one's putting a stop to this wedding no matter how hard they try. I told mummy, I said, nothing's worth this much stress. We all know they love each other.' Liliya was sitting on one of the wicker seats in the garden-room. Elbows on knees she was clutching a tissue and Edward sat beside her with a reassuring hand on the small of her back. Edward had clearly completely given up looking for Rose and instead now attended to comforting his stepsister. The sun had gone in and the room felt cold.

'I admire Blackwood's bull headedness in the face of adversity.' The Dame was sat on the chair opposite the bookcase, Wilkie Collins in hand, I wondered if she'd moved at all over the last twenty-four hours. 'He's quite right. We're going to be British about this. The wedding will go ahead!'

'With Rufus in hospital?' I couldn't help myself. I was incredulous. Surely with the wedding only three days away and Rufus hospitalised, we couldn't expect it to go ahead surely?

'Oh pff, it'll be nothing, he'll be home in no time you'll see. Stress! It does all sorts to the body. It used to happen to my late husband all the time. Chest pain here, twinge in the arm there. Attention seeking!'

'Babushka!' Liliya was admonishing in her tone. The only person that could get away with talking to the Dame in this way, I was glad she was the one to speak up.

'Not that I'm saying that Rufus is you understand.' The Dame creased the spine of her book open. 'No, he's shown me he's made of stern stuff, he'll be back before the weekend, you'll see.' She waved a finger as she finished.

I shivered involuntarily. It wasn't just the cold of the garden-room that made me do so; it was the thought of poor Rufus in hospital. Having spent a couple of weeks in intensive care, myself earlier this year, I would not wish hospital on anyone. The nurses were, of course, lovely and I owed them my life but hospitals are such lonely, suffocating places. They reminded me of death. We'd had quite enough of that over the last two weeks. I had wanted to go to the hospital straight away, to see my friend was all right but the next boat to the mainland wouldn't be until tomorrow. I would have to wait for a phone call from Matilda. I shivered again.

'Are you cold Mr Hetherington?' The Dame demanded. In a pale green chiffon trouser suit her rouged cheeks suggested she was far from cold. 'Shall we go into the drawing-room? I'll get the staff to set a fire.'

'That's really not necessary,' I said. The long sleeved shirt and cords I was wearing, were more clothes than most in the room; all were dressed for the height of summer. I hoped I wasn't coming down with something. I had thought the cold wind on the cliffs were blowing away any possible ailments not inviting them in, but perhaps I had caught a chill.

'I insist, I'll call Finlay and we'll get some brandy and tea brought up. He can set a small fire. This castle does get cold, rain or shine, it's so big you see.' She gave a breezy smile and getting up, placed a bookmark to mark her page and led us all into the drawing-room.

Finlay furnished us with suitable refreshment and a very nice homemade Battenberg cake. I sat there drinking tea in the luxurious surroundings of the castle drawing-room, watching the fire. I felt helpless. I was Rufus' best man! I should have been there, to relieve some of the stress. At the very least I should be doing something useful now, but what? It should never have got to this point I should have done something. I gave a start in my chair as I realised I had completely forgotten about my mission to retrieve more champagne. I sat back relinquishing responsibility to the events of the day. Maybe they wouldn't need extra champagne at this rate.

The tiny tent could just be seen from the corner of the drawing-room where I sat; a reminder of yesterday's events, only yesterday seemed like years ago. Everything was so ridiculous and insignificant in the face of my friend's jeopardy. I was reminded that death did not need to be brought about by anything so violent as murder. Only a few years my senior, it could easily be myself in that helicopter. My daughter's words were never truer, *'You're not getting any younger dad, you need to stop letting that Delilah drag you around, getting involved in things that are not your concern.'*

She was of course right but on this occasion, Delilah was not dragging me around and it was my concern. Somehow my oldest friend had become the very epicentre of a murder investigation and was now in very real danger of becoming an inadvertent victim. Guilt and helplessness, the two feelings I hated the most. They reminded me of Eleanor's passing. There was only one thing for it. I had to get to the bottom of this before any more harm came to the ones I cared about.

Tearing my gaze from the fire, I looked up at the gathered company. The Dame had returned to her book after instructing Finlay to tell them as soon as word, of Rufus' condition, reached us. Edward and Liliya sat side by side on the chaise longue. They talked in hushed tones. I couldn't tell about what. The room was large enough for conversations to be held in almost complete privacy if not

245

for the fact that you could still be observed. Were they talking about Rufus? The wedding? The murders? Who knew? I thought once more about the origins of the Darenskys. Not knowing her father and now discovering he was dead, washed up on a shore less than five miles away must be awful for Liliya. I couldn't begin to imagine what it was like.

What was Liliya's father doing here? Matilda said he hadn't contacted her. He couldn't have contacted Liliya she didn't know about him. He must have been here to talk to Matilda, surely she knew more than she was letting on. She'd already been guilty of some serious omissions, where Rufus was concerned. Had she killed her ex-lover, hoping to be rid of him? Hoping she could still secure the Blackwood fortune? I hated thinking this way about Rufus' fiancée but it just kept coming back to Matilda.

I switched my train of thought and forced myself to think of other suspects. I was brought back to the Dame once more. A determined matriarch who was unlikely to let anything stand in her way. Did she know the Russian had been Liliya's father? Had she been concerned the wedding may not go ahead if the truth were known about Matilda's past? Yet, just now, she had seemed very sure the wedding would go ahead regardless.

What about Robin Everall? If the Dame killed him because he witnessed the murder on the beach, where did Geoff Layland fit in? Had his interference with the catering tipped the Dame over the edge once more? What's one more murder when you've already committed two?

As I watched the Dame read, the frown lines on her forehead formed stern disapproval, the crow's feet now signified years of quiet suspicion, the hands not so dainty anymore but in fact very capable weapons. I began to warm to my theory but there were still a couple of things that didn't quite tie up. If she'd wanted to hide Matilda's past, then she had failed. By killing a third person, Matilda had felt forced to confess the very thing the Dame might have been trying to conceal. If the Dame had killed Geoff Layland, then there must be a different motive for this murder. Perhaps the deaths were completely unrelated and we were actually looking for two murderers? Certainly a complication when it came to proving anything about any of the deaths.

Finally, the Dame did not strike me as the sort to get her own hands dirty, however capable she may be. So whom would she have conscripted? If I was to continue with this theory then that's what I should focus on. Who was the Dame's accomplice?

Delilah and Rob's conversation entered my subconscious and I turned around in my seat towards the window where they were standing. I caught Liliya's eye as I did. She'd seen me looking at the Dame and she smirked, perhaps assuming I had more charming thoughts about the lady than the ones I had. I blushed, unable to control the heat as it crept up my neck and into my face. I knew no amount of protest would convince her that I did not have designs on her octogenarian grandmother. In fact, saying anything would only serve to draw attention to the fact that I had been watching the Dame in the first place.

'Walter Simmons knows most of the gossip, maybe he'll be able to help us a bit more with this third murder,' Rob was saying, just loud enough for the rest of the room to hear.

'He is a gossip dear. I wouldn't believe most of it. He likes to think he knows. He rarely does,' the Dame said, without looking up from her book. 'I'd leave it to the police. They'll sort it out.'

Rob turned to look at the Dame who was still looking at her book. I wondered what else she observed under the pretence of reading.

'Mr Hetherington, do help yourself to more tea.' She looked up and across to where I sat. Her smile was benign and gave little away. 'You shouldn't worry yourself about Rufus, he'll be fine you'll see.'

A shrill ring from the hallway made us all jump. The telephone rarely rang in the castle, in fact I was yet to hear a telephone ring anywhere on the island. I had thought, for a while, that none of them worked. It stopped abruptly and as a voice answered. Finlay entered shortly and announced, 'Telephone for you madam.' The Dame left us and I looked across at Rob.

'Does Walter know what's happened up here then?' I asked. As soon as I said it, I realised what my answer would be.

'Huh. Most people on the island will know what's happened up here,' said Liliya

'I haven't spoken to him for a couple of days now,' Rob picked up the conversation, 'but I reckon he'll know what's going on between those two honey farms.'

'You think it's something to do with the honey farms?' Liliya sniffed and dabbed her eyes once more.

'It's the only thing that makes sense,' Rob said, shrugging.

I was looking at the carpet, tracing the pattern in my mind as I thought once more about the possibility of the Dame being, if not the murderer, at the very least an accessory. To employ someone to murder at her behest would require trust on her part and stupidity or greed on the part of the murderer. Stupidity and greed were two traits rumoured to be found in Walter Simmons, but did she trust him? Was Walter feeding Rob duff information in order to move him away from the truth? It would certainly make sense, but then why did the Dame tell Rob not to trust Walter? Was it a double bluff? My imagination was running away from me.

'Blake …? Blake!' Rob caught my attention again. 'What do you think?'

'Yes, *Mystery Milliner*, Mr Hetherington, what do you think?' said Liliya.

The door opened and the Dame entered. 'Rufus will be home tomorrow!' she said clapping her hands together.

'Oh good,' Delilah said. She'd always had a kind heart

and despite her fascination with the macabre I knew it affected her when people left with no clue as to when they would return; a side effect of her mother's desertion on more than one occasion.

'Are they quite sure he's well enough?' I asked. I did not wish Rufus an extended stay in hospital but neither did I wish him to come home too early and risk a relapse.

'Stress! That's what they are saying. No sign of a heart attack.' The Dame was still standing in the doorway. 'They are going to keep him in overnight for observation, Matilda will get a hotel on the mainland and they will both return tomorrow.'

'And the wedding?' Liliya asked.

'Matilda is determined to see it happen. I agree with her. So much effort already, it would be a shame to see it go to waste. She's asked you to check on the progress of the cake tomorrow morning, Liliya, can you do that?'

'Yes, of course, but if Rufus is suffering this much stress, is it right to go ahead? You didn't bully her did you babushka?' Liliya's voice had an infantile lilt to it; an attempt to wheedle the truth from her guardian.

'Certainly not Liliya! Things can't always be the way we want them. We have to make the best of things. Your mother knows that. This wedding is happening and that's the end of it.'

26.

Forager

These are bees that travel out from the hive to find natural sources of nectar and pollen.

It was very early the next morning that Edward found me out on the cliff with Prince. I had chosen to forgo the usual company of Delilah, Rob and Bertie. I needed time to collect my thoughts. I'd rarely had a moment to myself over the last two weeks and every now and then the creative mind needs to retreat into itself. An early morning walk along the cliff top replaced my shed. I knew I would have to suffer Delilah's wrath on my return. She would consider me to be off detecting without her. I was not. Or was I?

The early morning sun was warm on my face and the skylarks serenaded me from high above. A lazy rippling green sea was dotted with gulls and a gentle breeze pushed around the tufts of grass on the cliff top. I could see large bumblebees moving, like little apostrophes, amongst the heather. This was a truly calming place to be.

It was as I sat on the bench taking in the world, contemplating the particulars of the three murders and trying to decide whether or not I really did think the Dame capable of orchestrating this whole affair, when a familiar voice called to me from behind.

'Good morning Mr Hetherington, I hope I'm not interrupting, but I really would like to talk to you. I'm worried about my father.'

Turning around I was met by Edward's furrowed brow, dark eyes and flushed cheeks. How he knew where to find me and at what time I had no idea but he'd obviously gone to some effort. 'Of course,' I replied. I moved along the bench to make room for him.

He perched on the edge of the seat; hands clasped together, shoulders hunched.

'Mr Hetherington, I ….'

'Please call me Blake,' I said, 'What can I do?'

'Well ….'

I looked back out to sea. The gulls and guillemots were putting on a fantastic diving display. Like hot knives through butter they dove in and out of the ambling waves, collecting their breakfast.

'The thing is ….' Edward took a sideways look at me. I turned back to give him my full attention. 'I'm really worried about Rufus. He's not getting any younger.' Edward looked at his feet as he said this aware of my own age and obviously not wishing to offend. 'The stress this wedding is putting him under is just too much and now, to have Matilda accused of murder!'

'She's been accused of murder?' I asked. As far as I knew no one had been arrested by the police, they were still investigating.

'Well, not exactly, more an implication, but Rufus really didn't like the way they spoke to her after she found Geoff Layland. She was very upset.'

'It's not an easy situation to be in, I'm sure.' I watched as Prince searched the heather for interesting smells, occasionally scraping at something with his paw.

'They were asking her all sorts of questions about the Russian on the beach, they think she's related to him somehow. Rufus isn't saying anything but it does worry me. I know very little about her.' Edward shrugged. 'Then again I know very little about Rufus.'

I gathered my best poker face. 'Do you think she did it?'

'NO!' Edward almost shouted and then a little quieter, 'Or at least I'd like to think she didn't. Rufus has had enough upset, he really doesn't need this, he just wants us all to be a family.' Edward turned on the bench to face me, biting his lip. 'You know, Blake, it's almost like he feels he has to make up for lost time. It's not just the Dame that wants the wedding to go ahead. Rufus is adamant!'

'You've tried to persuade him then?'

'Yes, but he's not having it. Says as long as we are all here, the wedding will happen.' Edward twisted his hands together. 'Matilda's made him rest up today. I was thinking, maybe you could go and see him, you know, as his best man.'

'Is he out of hospital?' I said.

'Yes, they discharged him late last night when he

refused to stay. Although if he carries on like he is, I'm sure it won't be long before he's back there. If you could show him there's nothing to prove, that he can just as easily get married after these murders have been tidied away, it might take some of the pressure off him.'

An interesting turn of phrase, *'tidied away'*. Edward seemed less concerned about murder and more concerned about the effect they were having on Rufus' health. There was a level of detachment in the way he spoke about them, which was almost psychopathic; no emotion just fact. I began to feel uncomfortable. How had he known where to find me? Was he a watcher? Did he observe and pick his moment?

On the other hand, when it came to his father Rufus, there was ample emotion. But what was I thinking? It was nothing more than an unfortunate turn of phrase. Edward's only possible motive for murder was to preserve his father's reputation and how on earth could he have known it was in jeopardy? No one knew of Matilda's past, not even Rufus! If Edward did know somehow and wanted the whole scandal to come out, surely it would have been better to keep the Russian alive? Did I really imagine that a second hand bookshop owner who'd only known his father five minutes would kill a random Russian sailor for no particular reason? Then something else occurred to me.

I took a deep breath in. 'Edward, is it that you don't think the wedding should go ahead now or that you don't think it should go ahead at all?'

Edward picked at the quick on his index finger and sighed. 'You have to admit it's a bit suspicious,' he replied.

'How?' Of course I knew what he meant but I wanted to hear it from him.

As he listed his points he moved his hands from side to side as if juggling the evidence. 'Well on the one hand, if Matilda says she has nothing to do with the Russian on the beach, then she doesn't. On the other it's a huge coincidence that he's Russian and so is she. No one else on the island is, not one of the Dame's workers, they're all Polish or Slovakian.'

I nodded and he continued.

'I know Rufus loves her very much, but I know better than anyone, love can be blind, Rose is evidence of that. I always knew she had a temper but I refused to believe the things Liliya said. She told me Rose had chased her one day with a swarm of bees she'd caught. I did find Rose you know.'

I raised an eyebrow.

'She didn't deny any of it,' Edward said. 'That takes some planning, catching a swarm of bees. You've got to have a cold sense of justice that's for sure. So what if Rufus is making a huge mistake? Like I did! And then there's the Dame. She's fiercely defending the marriage. Why? It makes no difference to her.'

'I see.'

'It's a mess.' Edward rested his elbows on his knees, hands knotted in his hair.

'Isn't every family?' I laughed trying to lighten the mood. I was interested that I wasn't the only person that had noticed the Dame's determination in the matter of Rufus and Matilda's wedding.

'What did the police say to you the other day at the castle?' I said at last, wondering what had triggered Edward's line of thought.

'They asked me again if I knew the man who was found on the beach. I don't so I'm not much help there. They asked me how long I'd known Matilda and what relation I was to Liliya. They asked about Rose and where she had gone. They want to question her too because Liliya told them about the argument. They asked lots of questions about where Rose and I had been when the first two murders happened. God knows what Liliya said. I can't believe it's anything to do with Rose. She's got a temper, but murder? I'd like to think I wasn't that wrong. I think Liliya suspects that her mother or grandmother know the dead Russian and she's trying to take the heat off them.'

'What makes you think that?'

'Just something she said.'

'What was that?'

'Well … it was a look more than anything. It was yesterday when we were all in the drawing-room waiting to hear from the hospital. Liliya overheard Rob and Delilah talking about a Russian pocket watch. It was found on the body of the first victim. Liliya and I were talking about the cake and she was wondering how Penny was getting on with it, given what had happened to Geoff. She was saying it was a lot to ask of Penny when she just stopped talking and started listening to Delilah and Rob. She was chewing her nails. I've haven't seen Liliya look nervous, only confident, arrogant even, but I think she was.'

'And you think it was about the pocket watch?'

'Yes. I asked her if she was OK. She snapped out of it and insisted she was fine. She said it was just finally sinking in, everything that had happened over the last two weeks. I wanted to believe her, but it just wasn't quite right.'

'So what makes you think she thinks her mother or grandmother knows the Russian?'

'It was something she said yesterday when the police were here. *'If only he hadn't turned up'*, that's what she said, *'mum and I were happy'*. I asked her what she meant and she laughed. Said she was talking about Rufus, that men always complicated things and her mother was too young to be marrying Rufus and looking after him, but I'm sure she was talking about the Russian.'

The guillemots had started to gather again on the cliffs and the sun had now taken its place in the sky ready for the day's journey. I wondered if this was a sentiment Liliya had ever voiced to her mother or the Dame. Perhaps this was why the Dame wanted the wedding to go ahead. Was Liliya trying to sabotage it? And then I remembered it was her that had first suggested postponing it in the drawing-room yesterday.

'It's all getting a bit complicated, isn't it?' I said finally.

Edward looked at me. 'Isn't every family?' he smiled.

I smiled back, hearing my own words repeated. 'I can see why you're worried,' I said. 'When people who don't really know each other are thrown together in a stressful situation, it makes it very difficult to trust each other.'

'It's more than that Blake. These murders are what's complicating everything, the other stuff, well that's just families, like you say. I just think everyone needs to take a step back and breathe. Get to know each other. There's plenty of time for Rufus and Matilda to marry, when all of this is sorted out.'

I nodded. 'I'll try and speak to Rufus, but I'm not sure he'll listen to me. If he has any idea you or Liliya don't want this marriage to go ahead, I suspect he will do everything he can to see it does. I know my friend and he's not used to losing.'

'Right.' Edward looked out to sea and frowned. 'Could I ask just one more thing, Blake?'

'Of course.'

'I know you've done it before.'

'Done what?'

'Solved a mystery.'

'Huh!'

'Seriously, you have the brain for it. Dad says you do, he trusts you, you're his oldest friend.'

I smiled. It was the first time I'd heard him refer to Rufus as *dad*.

He continued, 'If we could just lift the cloud caste by

these murders, from the wedding, then perhaps things would look a bit different. I'll help in any way I can.' Edward gave me the sort of look Prince gives me when he wants the food I have on my plate.

'I can't promise anything Edward, I'm supposed to be here for Rufus and he's explicitly told me he doesn't want me getting involved.'

'Well this is helping Rufus. He's under so much pressure ….'

'I know.' I put a hand up to Edward's shoulder. 'I'll see what I can do but I'm not promising anything.'

'The mainland police don't seem to be doing much,' Edward replied.

'I think you'll find they are,' I said, 'they just have to be methodical about things, not blunder around with misplaced assumptions like me.'

'Rufus says your assumptions are often bang on.'

I smiled. 'And sometimes they're not,' I said. 'Come on let's head back to the castle. I want to see Rufus now he's back.'

Turning away from the cliff, I called Prince and we started our trek across the moorland to the castle. Delilah would have to forgive me for not returning to the bed and breakfast. Especially when I imparted this new information. There were so many more questions. Why did Edward really think Matilda shouldn't marry Rufus? Was Rufus really the *he* who *turned up* or was it someone else? Surely Liliya wouldn't just come straight out and admit her disapproval of the marriage, to Rufus' son? Unless she thought by telling Edward he would tell Rufus and would somehow stop the wedding? And why was Liliya cosying up to Edward? The one thing I was absolutely sure of was that Liliya was manipulating the situation somehow. I just couldn't see how or why.

27.
Fermenting Honey

This is honey that has more than a fifth of water. Due to the excess water, the chemicals breakdown and create a yeast.

The castle was empty apart from Rufus, the staff and myself. The Dame and Matilda had taken advantage of my arrival to go and make the final arrangements for the flowers in the chapel with Aurora. Liliya had gone to the cake shop to check on the progress of the cake. Edward, unable to relax, had decided to go to Dame's Honey Farm and see if he could find anything out. As he pointed out, he was Rufus' son and near enough relative of the Dame's he might stand a better chance of getting some answers. His plan was to ask some innocent questions about honey production with the hope he may find out something of interest. He'd persuaded me to meet him in The Fisherman's Rest for lunch to compare notes. Rob and Delilah would also be there. There had been a message from Delilah when I arrived at the castle, summoning me to meet them there for lunch. This would make for a table rife with speculation on current events, but this was not what I was here to talk to Rufus about. I had come with the intention, as I had promised to Edward, of persuading

Rufus to take things easy and to perhaps postpone the wedding. I felt like a cad even contemplating it but I feared Edward was right. This wedding may be the death of Rufus.

We were sat in Rufus' bedroom. Rufus was sitting up in bed and I was pouring the tea that had been placed on the chest of drawers at the end of the bed. A few minutes after the tea arrived and the dismissal of the footman, without me saying a word, Rufus had stated his concern.

'What if she did it, Blake?' Rufus' face was grey and tired. Thin age lines had become a map of his recent trials. He looked far from well.

'Do you honestly think she could?' I replied, stirring sugar into Rufus' tea. The revelation of Matilda's shady past and connection with the Russian on the beach had affected Rufus much more than I had realised.

'I can hardly believe some of the things she's admitted to. A mistress to Russian royalty! Liliya an illegitimate child! I'm no saint but at least I've owned up to my past. She knows very well the baggage I come with. I feel deceived.'

'It was a long time ago.'

'Would *you* marry her?' Rufus' eyes were glassy with tears. I'd never seen him so upset. I knew what this admission meant to him, he was a proud man.

'We all have a past, Rufus, you know that as well as I do.'

'I'm not sure I can deal with it. I thought I could but ….' He pinched the bridge of his nose and took a deep breath.

'She did admit it to you. At least she's being honest,' I said. I was beginning to sound as if I'd come here to persuade him to carry on with the marriage, not the opposite.

'What else has she omitted to tell me?' Rufus thumped his fist ineffectually on the duck down duvet. It emitted a puff of air.

'Have you considered postponing the wedding?' Now was as good a time as any to suggest it.

'Considered! Of course I've considered it. But how can I?'

'I know, as your best man, I'm supposed to guide you through the cold feet but I don't think anyone would blame you for postponing, given the circumstances.'

'No, only Matilda, Liliya and of course the Dame!'

I nodded as an image of The Witches Of Eastwick popped into my head.

'It's three days away and it's like nothing's happened. Woe betide anyone that gets in their way. They're a formidable force!' Rufus rested his head back on the tower of pillows behind him.

'Women generally are,' I sympathised. Running my hand through my wind swept hair to tidy it I tried a logical argument. 'If you really think she might have something to do with the murders do you think you should be marrying her?'

'The truth is Blake my head's in overdrive. Matilda's so

set on this marriage going ahead at the weekend, her stubborn determination makes me wonder if she *could* kill to get what she wants. Maybe she thought she'd get away with it? People would think the Russian was washed up with the shipwreck and that would be that.'

'So what about the other two?' I said.

'It obviously got complicated. She was probably trying to silence them and then guilt got the better of her.' He threw his hands up in the air. 'You see Blake? I'm even thinking like you now!'

I passed him his freshly made tea and, taking a cup for myself, I sat on a chair beside the bead and we drank in silence. There was little I could say. If Rufus thought she had done it, he should a) speak to the police and b) cancel the wedding.

Rufus cleared his throat. 'The worst thing is Blake, I'm her alibi.'

'How is that worse?' I replied.

'I lied.'

'Oh.'

He coughed and pushed himself up in bed. 'You may as well know, Matilda and I sleep in separate rooms. It works for us. I'm a terrible snorer and she's a light sleeper.'

'I see.'

'The thing is her alibi for the time of the Russian's death would be that she was in bed with me. Well she wasn't was she.'

'Who else knows you lied, anyone?'

'I think Liliya knows, the Dame of course and her staff.'

Liliya struck me as the sort of person who would use secrets against their owners and waste no opportunity to hold something over them, but the possibility of her casting doubt on her mother's alibi seemed a little far-fetched. The same went for the Dame, and her staff were unlikely to do anything that might result in unemployment. 'None of them have mentioned it then?' I asked.

'No, but they all know we don't sleep in the same room. In hindsight it was a stupid thing to say.'

I did not to voice my concern about the possibility of blackmail. If no one had tried it yet, perhaps they wouldn't. None of the Dame's staff, the Dame or Liliya, had anything to gain from blackmail. If someone did, on the other hand …. 'And her alibi for the other two murders?'

'She was out for dinner with Liliya, when Everall was killed, so I can't vouch for her then and she found Layland who, as the police said, probably had been dead more than half-an-hour. The Dame's her alibi for that. She says they were talking in her room.'

'So you only lied about one alibi,' I said, trying to get the facts straight.

'Yes but don't you see. If I'm willing to lie then maybe Liliya was too. Maybe Matilda wasn't in the pub all night and maybe the Dame was lying too?'

'Isn't it a bit convoluted. Three people would have to independently lie,' I said.

'Three people who love Matilda very much.'

I nodded, conceding his point. 'It's just possible though that she's telling the truth,' I said.

'Yes. That's what my heart wants to believe.' Rufus rubbed his eyes with the back of his hands. He really did look pale.

My next thought made me jump in my chair. 'Hang on! How on earth did someone Matilda's size move that apple crusher? Look, I really think you should talk to Matilda. Tell her you're worried,' I said. With this last thought, all my fears about the possibility of Matilda being the prime suspect faded away. She couldn't possibly have moved something that size.

'But if I said anything, I'd be accusing her. The woman I love and who I am supposed to be marrying in *three* days.'

'And you won't postpone the wedding?'

'I fail to see how I can. They are bound to come up with some reason why I shouldn't and if I even suggest it, it would devastate Matilda. She'd never forgive me. And what if I'm wrong, what if she's completely innocent?'

I stood up. 'I think you need to rest, Rufus. We'll worry about this later.' I wanted Rufus to recuperate and this conversation was starting to go around in circles.

Rufus took hold of my forearm. 'Look, I know I gave you a hard time, Blake, but please, get to the bottom of this will you?' His hand flopped back down on the duvet.

'I'm going to try. I'm meeting Delilah and Rob for lunch, perhaps they will have some ideas.' I didn't mention

Edward. I didn't want to cause Rufus any further worry.

'Good! The old team eh?' he chuckled. It was good to see him smile, if only ironically.

'Between you and me Rufus, I really don't think Matilda's a murderer,' I said, putting a reassuring hand on my old friend's pyjama clad shoulder. 'There's no way she could have moved that apple crusher and if she couldn't, neither could Liliya or the Dame. I think you're safe.' Smiling, I took a step towards the door. 'It also occurs to me that she didn't have to admit to knowing the Russian, she could have carried on denying everything. He had no ID, the police were getting nowhere.'

'I hope you're right.' Rufus' eyelids began to droop.

I left the room quietly. I hoped Rufus could get some rest. It was awful to see my friend in such a state. I had to solve these murders if only for his benefit. The police were taking far too long over it. I knew there were procedures to follow, I'd seen Rob frustrated by them enough times, but Rufus needed results.

***

Leaving the house, I let the footman know that Rufus was sleeping. I collected Prince from beside the front door where he'd been waiting patiently, happy to sit on the gravel by the porch taking in the August sunshine.

I began my walk back across the island to The Fisherman's Rest. It was only ten thirty, the morning felt longer than usual on account of my early rise. I'd be very early to the pub for lunch. Walter Simmons opened at eleven so I'd be able to sit and wait for the others. It would be an opportunity for me to collect my thoughts.

At the moment, Matilda's alibis were occupying me. My overriding thought was that false alibis didn't just suit the person who needed the alibi, they also suited the person giving it. I did not suspect for one minute Rufus was involved. Earlier in the year I had thought he was involved in some unfortunate events in Tuesbury, but I'd quickly dismissed this idea and I had felt guilty ever since. I could not possibly suspect him this time.

Liliya on the other hand; she was a girl that was more than capable of deceit, as I had noted on more than one occasion. What was her alibi for the Russian's murder and for that of Geoff Layland? Then again, if I didn't think Liliya's mother could move an apple crusher, then how could Liliya? Could they have done it together?

Walter Simmons rarely missed a trick. Arriving early at the pub would give me a chance to ask him about that evening and Matilda and Liliya's presence in The Fisherman's Rest. Perhaps they were providing alibis for each other?

Finally, the Dame. As the matriarch in this case, she's always there with a handy answer and or alibi. If they were talking in the Dame's room then Matilda was also the Dame's alibi. Did the Dame feel guilt of taking Matilda's role as mother and replacing it with the role of servant? Was that what was driving her forward so vehemently to ensure Matilda took her place as Lady Blackwood? I'd seen first-hand the result of a determined woman ensuring a wronged loved one got what they were entitled to. She might not be able to move the apple crusher herself but the idea that she had employed someone to carry out the murders was still, for me, a favoured one: a formidable, omnipotent, feudal force, forging on, with money, influence and staff. The more I thought on it, the more the Dame became capable of murder.

28.
Smoker

A smoker is a tool, normally made out of metal, is used to generate smoke to control aggressive behaviour of the bees during hive inspections.

I arrived at The Fisherman's Rest just as Walter was opening up.

'Mr Hetherington, haven't seen ye in this early for a while. Not since the beach! How's the investigation going?'

'I suspect you know more about that than me Mr Simmons,' I said.

He shrugged and held the door open for Prince and me to enter. There was no sign of anyone else in the pub, not even Robbie. The fishermen wouldn't be in for another hour; they were still out emptying their nets. The old stone walls of the pub made the room cold so I chose a stool at the bar where the sunlight pierced the windows.

'What can I get you?' Walter settled himself behind the bar.

'Just a coffee please, for the moment,' I said. Prince lay with his back to the bar, his head resting on his paws ready for a doze. A haze of dust particles, translucent in the sun, hung around him where he'd shaken himself before sitting. 'How are your house guests?' I asked.

'You mean the police officers?' Walter had to raise his

voice over the noise of the coffee machine and I gave a look over my shoulder, concerned the persons in question might have been in the pub somewhere even though I could see no one. There were plenty of nooks and crannies in this pub for the stealthy eavesdropper. I squinted as I looked back at Walter and the sun caught my eyes.

He laughed, placing my coffee on the bar. 'Don't worry, Mr Hetherington, they're all out for the day now. Back up that honey farm no doubt. Questions, questions, questions, but little action as far as I can see.'

'Can I get you anything?' I said handing over a £10 note for my coffee.

'I don't mind if I do.' Walter lifted down a pint glass and filled it with the Salderk Bitter. The sun wasn't quite over the yardarm but it was bathing the bar. Perhaps that was Walter's indicator that drink was acceptable. That's if he had an indicator.

'What do you think they should be doing?' I asked.

'Well, catching the beggar, of course.'

'And have you any idea who that might be?'

'I've got my thoughts. Heard a few things, ye ken?' Walter lent an elbow on the bar, pint in hand. 'How about you?'

'Me?' I took a sip of my coffee. 'Well now, Mr Simmons, I'm just here for my friend's wedding.' I placed the cup back on the saucer and unwrapped the complimentary chocolate before it melted against the cup.

Walter looked at me and stood up straight. 'I find it

hard to believe you don't find some of this interesting,' he said. 'Ye found the first body!'

I was beginning to warm up and I removed my Barbour, placing it on a hook under the ledge of the bar. Prince moved his head to sniff the pocket for Bonio, a search to no avail.

'But was it murder?' I said. I couldn't resist winding Walter up just a little.

'Still smarting about that?' he smirked. Far from the stupid man, people on this island would have you believe, Simmons was an observer, an amateur psychologist if you like. Perhaps he didn't even know it himself but, as I'd got to know him and heard Rob talk about him, I was discovering Walter was often on the money when it came to people. 'What about those De Vries and Darenskys?' he said, turning to the till to put the money for the beer and the coffee through.

He'd caught me off guard and he saw it as he turned back to give me my change. 'What about them?' I replied.

'Lot of power up there, ye ken? The Dame owned this island once upon a time. She says she's given the land and businesses back to us but actions speak louder than words.'

'Oh?' I took another mouthful of coffee.

'She never let Geoff Layland have a fair run at that honey farm. Stopped him profiting at every opportunity. Made it difficult for anyone to support him.'

'Really?'

'Yup. She owns the lease to this place and several other

businesses in the area. Told me if I used Layland's honey in my pub's kitchen she'd terminate my lease.'

'Really?' I was reluctant to interrupt or offer my own thoughts. I wanted an unadulterated opinion from Walter.

'Yup. More coffee?' He could see my cup was empty and lifted the filter jug from the coffee machine to refill my cup.

'Thank you,' I replied.

'The daughter's no better.' He placed the jug back on the machine.

'But the Dame doesn't have any children?'

'Hell she doesn't. Rumour is Liliya's the late Lord's daughter. No one's sure who her mother is.'

'Matilda is surely?' The two of them were similar in so many ways, even in looks there could be no doubt and I knew from what Matilda had told me the Lord was not Liliya's father, the Russian was. Why would she admit all the other stuff about her past if he wasn't? Or was it a double bluff?

'Got you thinking has it, Mr Hetherington?' Walter was looking at me as he drank his pint. 'The point is, ye never really ken what's going on in those families. They don't want you te ken and they have thick hides. Denae care what the plebs say, as long as they're making money from ye.'

I felt a need to defend the castle's inhabitants given my friend was about to join their family. 'Surely they invest in businesses on the island, provide employment and even buy the local produce?'

'Not as much as ye'd think with the money they have. Do a lot of their shopping online. From the mainland. They hardly ever come out to eat, got staff for that,' he sneered.

'Matilda and Liliya were in the pub not that long ago,' I said.

'Aye, on the night young Everall was killed. Bit suspicious don't you think? Not in here for months and then they pop up like the proverbial bad penny on the night they need an alibi.'

There was no denying it, Walter was to the point. I took a sip of fresh coffee and contemplated what to say next. 'They were here the whole time then?'

'So ye are interested?' Walter said, leaning forward across the bar. I made no reply. 'Well, they ate a three course meal and I served them drinks, but I couldn't keep my eyes on them the whole time. They were in here for four hours, that's a long time for dinner, ye ken?'

'I assume you've told the police your concerns?'

'Mr Hetherington! You don't suspect them surely?'

'No,' I lied, 'but you do.' I took another sip of coffee and looked at the clock. The others would be here soon.

He smiled, stood up from the bar and started to polish a beer glass. 'Pure speculation. It can get a bit boring on this island some days. Something like this happens and you've got plenty of time to think.'

'But what would be their motive?'

'Money, what else?'

'Money? How? You've just said they've got plenty of it!'

'The farm's money to the Dame; people with a lot of money always want more.'

'So you think the police have got it right?'

'What?'

'Well you said they were at the honey farm interviewing again.'

'Happen they have got it right, but I've got a feeling there's more to it. I've known that family a long time, they hold grudges ….'

I didn't have time to ask any more, as the door to the pub opened and the merry band of fishermen made their entrance, gabbling in their odd mix of English and Gaelic. Pulling up bar stools, they sat themselves down and Walter set to work pouring beer and shandies.

I finished the rest of my coffee and waited for the others to arrive. I held out little hope that Walter would say much more in front of the fisherman. He was a gossip, but a careful one.

'Hello.' A female voice was directed at me. I looked up from my coffee to discover the voice was actually talking to Prince. It was Ruby the only woman fisherman in the group and she now bent down to scratch Prince's ears. The attention was gratefully received and he licked her work-worn hands, perhaps tasting the salty fish from the day's catch on them.

'Got six fresh lobsters for you Walter,' Rog said, lifting a writhing bag across the bar to the waiting barman.

'Excellent!' Walter replied, 'staying for lunch, Mr Hetherington?' he asked indicating the bag.

'I am!' With only a few more days until the wedding I would soon be leaving Salderk. If I couldn't solve these murders, I could at least savour the fresh produce the island offered.

'I'll save you one,' Walter smiled. 'Rest are for the freezer I reckon.'

'Just a half, I think, might be better,' I replied patting my burgeoning stomach. Despite continually eating since arriving on the island, and the consequential tightening of my trousers, I was wholly unable to resist fresh lobster.

'Lovely dog.' Ruby stood up again, took her shandy from the bar and gulped half of it down. 'Thirsty work, fishing,' she said, seeing me watching her. She was a bright-eyed girl, probably in her early twenties. Her frame was difficult to gauge under the baggy oilskins and wellie boots but her face was delicate and her blonde hair was pulled back tight from her face. 'You here for much longer?' she said.

'Trying to get rid of me?' I teased.

'Oh no, no tha's nae what I meant.' She blushed and turned to the bar taking her pint in both hands and twisting it.

I laughed. 'I'm just here for Lord Blackwood and Mrs Darenskys' wedding and then I'm off.'

'Solved these murders yet?' she said, concentrating on her shandy.

'Not my job,' I said. I was getting used to this question. It appeared everyone on the island had me down as an amateur detective.

'Not what I heard.' She turned, to look at me again, eyes sparkling. She was teasing me this time. I smiled, she was only giving as good as she got. 'You found the first body?' she half whispered.

'I did,' I echoed her tone.

'Oh come on, ye must know something.' She took a gulp of shandy again.

'Nope, nothing,' I shrugged.

'You know what I reckon?'

'No.'

'I reckon that Russian was a Prince come to find his bride,' she laughed.

'Ruby, stop making up stories.' Rog, one of the older fishermen, appeared behind her.

'O' Da, I'm just joking, Mr Hetherington knows that, dean't ye?'

I nodded, although, if Matilda was to be believed, the theory was a little close to the truth. 'What makes you say that?' I asked.

'Oh ye ken, this and that.'

'Ruby!' her father warned her again.

'Leave me alone, I'm talking to the gentleman,' she frowned at him over her shoulder. He turned back to the other fishermen. Looking back at me, Ruby began again. 'Call me an old romantic, but when I saw his picture in the paper, I thought, now there's royalty. Ye just know class when ye see it. And then that pocket watch ….'

I wondered how she knew about that. 'The pocket watch?' I encouraged her.

'Yeah, the one you and Walter found.'

So, Walter was the source of that information. 'That was an antique,' I replied. 'That could have been anyone's before it washed up on the beach.'

'Oh no, he's class, you can tell, right regal nose.' She ran a finger along the bridge of her nose and then finished the last of her shandy, pushing her glass forward for Walter to refill. 'Da, you want another yet,' she called to her father.

The door opened and Edward appeared. He saw me at the bar and walked straight towards me.

'Blake! Shall we get a table?' he said pointing at the table in front of the inglenook furthest away from the fishermen and the bar.

'Drink?' I said as I saw out the corner of my eye, Walter watching us.

'Yes please, lime and soda will do for me, thanks,' he nodded at Walter.

'And I'll have a half of the Buzzing Brown, please Walter.'

'I'll bring them over,' Walter said, with a nod of his head.

Lifting my coat from the hook and beckoning Prince to

come with us we sat at the chosen table. Prince dragged himself away from Ruby who was still petting him in between her conversation with the other members of the crew.

'Pumping the locals for info?' Edward said with a half-smile.

'Not really, but I have found that if you sit somewhere long enough, someone will speak to you and it's generally of interest. It's amazing what people give away without realising.' I hung my coat on the back of the chair and Prince took up his usual position under the table.

'Gentlemen.' Walter arrived with the drinks. 'Can I get you a menu?'

'Yes, thank you,' I replied. 'Four please, Delilah and Rob are joining us,' I finished by way of explanation and Walter returned to the bar to collect the menus.

'Oh?' Edward replied.

'Is that OK? I couldn't say no, it would have looked odd.'

'Of course. No problem. Rob's a policeman, he might be able to add something else to this mess.'

I wasn't quite sure whether Edward meant this as a positive thing or not, but before I could reply Walter returned with the menus. 'I'll be back in a bit, although I already know what you're having, Mr Hetherington,' he said, smiling.

'Fresh lobsters, just in,' I nodded in the direction of the Fishermen.

'Great! Don't suppose there's enough for me too.' Edward looked at Walter.

'I'm sure there is,' Walter replied. Considering how many lobsters had disappeared out the back, there were more than enough.

"nother pint please Walter,' came a voice from the bar.

'So what did you get out of the locals?' Edward asked, once Walter was safely behind the bar again.

'Walter's a proletariat with a severe dislike for the aristocracy and Ruby is an old romantic.' I took a sip of my beer.

'Ruby?'

'The young girl in the oilskins.'

'Ah. I bet she's a looker out of those oilskins,' Edward said. I raised my eyebrows at him over my pint glass as I drank. 'Don't worry, Blake, I'm not my father.'

I almost spat my beer out. 'That's a bit harsh Edward.'

'He did play the field in his day. I wouldn't be here if he hadn't.' Edward was philosophical in his reply. 'Right, let's get down to business.' Edward rubbed his hands together and shuffled on his chair pushing it towards the table. 'I've had quite an eventful morning! How about you tell me what you've found out from those guys over there and I'll tell you what I discovered at the honey farm?'

The chatter at the bar was interrupted as the pub door opened again and Rob, Delilah and Bertie arrived just in time to join our conversation. They came straight over to our table, wasting no time.

'Edward, Blake,' Rob said.

'Where've you been?' Delilah demanded, standing over us.

'Well take a seat and we'll tell you.' I said.

29.
Queen Cage

This is a special compartment in which queens are transported to a new hive. They normally have with them several worker bees and are sealed in with a sugar plug.

Delilah huffed as she plonked herself down in the seat beside me.

'Shall we order some food?' I said.

'I want to know what you've been up to.' Delilah tried again

'Good idea, I'm starving,' Rob joined in with the Delilah baiting. He was a brave man.

I looked across at the bar and nodded at Walter who'd been watching us assemble at the table. He was unable to resist more than a few minutes before coming to take our order.

'Gentleman. Lady,' he smiled at Delilah. 'What can I get you?'

'You know I'll have half a lobster please. Could I have it with some garlic butter and a side salad,' I said.

'No problem.'

The door opened behind him and who I assumed to be the chef entered in checked trousers, followed by a reluctant Robbie. The chef was flushed, possibly from a brisk walk, and she was reprimanding Robbie, which led me to conclude she was his mother.

'Ah, the chef's here, good.' Walter looked relieved. I was too. 'And for you Miss Delibes?' Walter turned to Delilah. 'Lobster's fresh.'

'Just a bacon and brie baguette for me please.'

'Me too,' said Rob.

'I'll have the other half of that lobster,' Edward grinned. 'In garlic butter, same as Blake's please.'

'Can I get you any drinks?' Walter asked.

'A pint of orange and lemonade for me,' said Rob.

'And a coffee for me,' was Delilah's reply. I could see the pain on her face, as the order took far too long.

'Good!' Walter stabbed his order pad with his pen, in a violent full stop. 'Shouldn't be too long, once we've got the kitchen going,' and he hurried off to organise his staff.

Delilah was sitting, arms folded, eyes blazing.

'OK, OK, Prince and I went out for a walk without you, there's no crime in that surely?' I shrugged.

'There is if you've been investigating!'

'Investigating what?'

'You know damn well what, Blake Hetherington, now stop winding me up!'

Bertie barked from under the table and Walter arrived with the drinks. 'Oo, in trouble, Mr Hetherington?' Walter said eyeing Delilah with a smirk.

'When am I not?' I replied. 'Between this one and my daughter I'm always in the dog house.'

We laughed. Delilah did not. Walter returned to the bar and I looked at Edward. I hadn't had a chance to ask him if I could share his concerns about the Darenskys. The last thing I wanted was to betray his confidence.

'What?' Delilah said looking at me and then at Edward.

'It's OK, you can tell Delilah,' Edward said, running a napkin around his glass to remove the beads of condensation.

I looked across at the bar. Walter was busy pulling more pints for the fishermen. They must have strong constitutions. It was surprising they could sail straight or hold onto their stomachs the next morning after what they put away in an afternoon. Despite his interest in our gathering, I doubted Walter could hear our conversation over the din at the bar and the pub was gradually beginning to fill up with lunchtime customers. Walkers, locals and what looked like some potholers, ropes slung over their packs, all taking advantage of a sunny midweek August lunchtime. I'd never been able to see the fascination with dangling yourself by a rope into small dark spaces. The picture of Robin Everall's face, down the well, burst back into my mind. My face gave away my thoughts.

'It can't be that bad,' Delilah said.

I looked at Edward again. I didn't know where to start with this one. Where do you start when you're trying to explain someone suspects their in-laws of murder?

Edward sighed. 'I found Blake on the cliff this morning as I wanted to ask him a favour.'

'OK,' Delilah said, stirring milk and sugar into her coffee.

'I asked Blake to get to the bottom of these murders before they are the death of my father.'

'I thought he was OK?' Delilah was obtuse in her reply.

'He is but ….'

'Oh! You think he's next?' Delilah leaned forward, grinning a little too gleefully.

'God, I hope not!' Edward slumped back in his chair.

'Edward thinks there's a strong connection between the Russian and well …,' I cleared my throat, '… the Darenskys.'

'At last,' Delilah said, 'someone's seeing sense.'

Edward's mouth hung open. 'Sense? I rather hoped I was wrong,' he finally said.

'You normally find the answer to the present in the past,' Delilah replied.

'And what does that mean?' Edward folded his arms and looked pointedly at Delilah for an answer.

'It means I think that the Russian on the beach is something to do with Liliya, Matilda or the Dame's past. He has to be. He wasn't here to work, so what was he here for?'

'How do you know he wasn't here to work?' Edward leant forward and rested his elbows on the table, arms still folded.

'I don't know. It's just a feeling I have. Call it woman's intuition.'

Edward took a sip from his glass, licked his lips and sat back in his chair. 'And suppose you're right?' he replied.

Delilah did her best *I knew it all along face*. 'You know something we don't?'

I immediately felt guilty and looked at Rob. He looked away towards Edward. Although the question was not directed at me, it was becoming hard to keep Matilda's secret when in the last half-hour, two women had pretty much hit the nail on the head with the Russian's connection to the Darenskys. I wondered if Rob felt the same? Thankfully Delilah did not notice the exchange; she was busy watching Edward's face for clues.

'After I left Blake, I went to the honey farm.'

'Laylands' farm?' Rob joined the conversation.

'No the Dame's. I can't help feeling one of those workers must know something.'

'Well, the man on the beach was Russian. As I understand it they don't get on too well with the Polish,' Rob said.

'Turns out our Russian was up at the farm, asking questions. I found a worker willing to talk to me for a price.'

'Really?' Delilah couldn't hide her enthusiasm for this latest bit of information. I relaxed a little, back into my chair and listened. If we all huddled together there was every likelihood Walter would suddenly take an interest in our table again.

'He wanted to know who owned the farm and where

he could find them.'

'They of course told him?'

'Yes. He asked about Liliya.' Edward was frowning. 'When they said she lived at the castle, he thanked them and left.'

'Interesting,' said Rob. 'Do the police know?'

'Yes, he said he'd told a police officer. He asked me not to say anything to the Dame. Said he liked working at the farm, she pays well and he was worried if she thought he'd brought the police or the Russian to their door, she may sack him.'

'Well it fits in with the honey farm theory,' said Rob.

'How?' Delilah asked. 'He was asking about Liliya!'

'It pays to look at things from different angles, Delilah. Maybe he was asking because he knew something about the business. Perhaps this is all about blackmail,' Rob replied.

'Right. Of course.' Delilah oozed sarcasm. She disliked being patronised.

'The problem is,' Edward said. 'If the Russian knew something about the farm and was blackmailing the Dame, I don't see where the other two murders fit in.'

Delilah sat up straight in her chair as if she'd been electrocuted. 'Ooo, what if Robin Everall and Geoff Layland knew too? What if they were all blackmailing the Dame! What if the leak was Liliya? She certainly gets around.' She caught Edward's eye, 'Sorry', she shrugged.

We all paused to take in Edward's information. Delilah

broke the silence with a chink of her coffee cup as she placed it back on the saucer.

'You know it's interesting,' she said, 'the honey farms and the Dame.'

'What is?' Rob said.

'Well the book I was reading the other day, you know Blake, the one on bee keeping.' I nodded and she continued. 'Well, in a hive the workers will do anything to protect their queen.' Delilah took the little milk jug and started to place sugar cubes around it. 'What if this is the Dame,' she said pointing at the jug, 'and this is Liliya, Matilda and the honey farm workers,' she said pointing at the sugar cubes. 'Any one of them will defend the hive if it's threatened.'

'Well that doesn't get us any further forward,' said Rob, 'never mind six little sugar cubes as your suspects. Try this for size.' He dumped the rest of the sugar of the pot and onto the table where they scattered, bumping into cups and glasses.

'Rob!' Delilah shouted. Tutting she started to collect the cubes in the pot once more.

I felt bad for Delilah. 'What if that,' I said pointing at the milk jug, 'is actually Matilda.'

Rob looked at me. I'd said too much.

This time Delilah saw the exchange. 'You two know something don't you?' She narrowed her eyes at us both.

There was an awkward silence. Neither Rob nor I wanted to impart our knowledge. 'Don't tell me if you don't want to, but you know I'll get it out of you eventually.' She was defiant.

'Another drink anyone?' Edward said, sensing the tension, standing from the table and attempting to remove himself from it.

'That would be good, thank you,' I said.

'Come on what is it?' Delilah nudged me as soon as Edward left.

I was puzzled as to why Edward hadn't wanted to know. Perhaps he just hated arguments. Or did he already know? I looked at Rob, he sighed and nodded. I began. 'This is strictly confidential, Delilah,' I said.

'Of course,' she winked.

'No, this is serious.'

'OK. OK. Spill.'

'Matilda has admitted to knowing the Russian on the beach.' I skipped the unsavoury details. 'It's Liliya's father.'

'No!' Delilah sat back in her chair, mouth open.

'She doesn't know,' Rob said.

'Is that right? I mean surely she should know, I mean I'd want to know,' Delilah gabbled.

'Delilah!' I warned. 'This is not our secret to tell.' I finished knowing full well the irony in what I was saying.

'So I'm right!' She was triumphant.

'Right about what?' Edward said returning with a tray of drinks.

Delilah blushed. 'That bees will defend their hive.'

'Of course, I think most people know that.' Edward

put the tray down and handed out the drinks. 'Walter said he was sorry for the delay and our lunches wouldn't be too much longer. You can't rush perfection, or at least that's what she says.'

'We're quite happy here. No rush.' Delilah stirred more sugar into her fresh coffee. 'We saw Liliya coming out of the cake shop earlier,' Delilah said to Edward.

He looked surprised, perhaps unsure how to answer. 'Oh?'

I gave Delilah a look that said, don't you dare. Delilah had given me no reason to distrust her before but I wondered, all too late, whether I should have trusted her with this information. Delilah didn't know who her father was either. This was an emotive subject for Miss Delibes and may prove a secret too far.

'She was collecting the cake,' Delilah continued. 'Huge it is!'

'Well at least that's something to look forward to,' said Edward. 'I just hope we can sort this all out before the big day. With less than seventy-two hours to go we're not really any further forward, other than having thirty plus suspects. I'm not hopeful.'

'We can only do our best, we are, after all, amateurs,' I said.

'I'm sure the police are doing all they can,' Rob said.

'That is funny too,' Delilah said, as if having a conversation with herself.

We all looked at her. 'What?' we said in unison.

'Well, Penny didn't look at all upset.'

'Penny was working?' I said. I felt sure the cake shop would have given her time off, considering.

'Yes, in fact she was positively happy.' Delilah had her audience once more. 'Chatting with Liliya, laughing and joking. Didn't you think Rob?'

'I didn't really take any notice, I was concentrating on my breakfast,' he said.

'Rubbish! You saw, she was happy as Larry. Far from the grieving fiancée.'

'We all grieve in different ways,' Edward said.

'Well, if Rob died I think I'd be a little more cut up. We're not even engaged!'

There was an uncomfortable shuffle from Rob. His face told me that this was not the first time the subject of engagement had been raised.

'Living in sin eh?' Walter appeared at the table with plates of food.

'Quite the modern way these days,' I said trying to cut Rob some slack as he concentrated hard on his sandwich.

The dogs shuffled and snuffled, under the table, sensing the arrival of food and there was a lull in the conversation as we started our meals, all four of us hungry.

I thought about the last half-hours' conversation. The logical place to start was with the first murder: the Russian on the beach. If we discounted the workers on the farm that left us with three very definite suspects: the Dame, Liliya and Matilda. If we made a certain set of assumptions, it resulted in the Dame being prime suspect. These assumptions were: the rival honey farms were at the centre of the case, the Dame disliked her authority being challenged and the Dame wanted to protect her reputation from Matilda's indiscretions. If a second set of conclusions were drawn from that, then Matilda could be our perpetrator. These centred mainly around Matilda wishing to hide her past. The Russian had been asking for Liliya at the honey farm. What if he'd found her? Would Liliya, as Delilah suggested, do anything to defend the hive?

What about our other two victims? If they were connected, the other two victims had to have been because they knew about the first murder. That was the only logical reason. I couldn't believe the tit-for-tat theory George Naismith had proffered.

The dots just didn't want to join up. Would Liliya really kill her friend's fiancé? Surely she'd be more likely to steal him back if revenge was what she wanted? Would the Dame kill again rather than just pay up to keep the witnesses quiet? Did Matilda really have time for all of this in amongst organising her wedding?

I looked across at Edward who was devouring his lobster with gusto. Was it even a queen bee we were looking for? Could it be a sibling wishing to protect another sibling? Did Edward know the true identity of the Russian on the beach? Was he lying about the information from the honey farm worker? Did he in fact already know? Was he really concerned for his father's happiness? Was he just trying to stay close to see what we knew? Perhaps he thought the Russian was a rival for Matilda's affections. Was he so desperate to finally have a family he would kill to protect it?

Instead of solving this case, I just seem to be accumulating more suspects. At the same time I knew we must be on the cusp of solving it. We knew who the Russian was and we could assume why the other two murders were committed. We just had too many suspects with too many motives! Even if we could pin it on one of them, with only assumptions and circumstantial evidence, how were we ever going to solve this?

30.
Festooning

This is the where young bees stuff themselves with honey and hang onto each other.

The following afternoon we gathered at the castle to decorate the hall for the wedding reception. Two footmen joined us, to create swagging around the outside of the hall. I was surprised the Dame had not drafted in extra staff to assist with this task. Rufus, offered her dislike of wasting money on things that *'could well be done by oneself'*, by way of an explanation. A philosophy Rufus whole-heartedly agreed with. That then led me to wonder why she didn't feel she could pour her own tea.

Swagging really wasn't my forte and I was struggling with the swathes of organza as I passed it up to Delilah, who was standing precariously on a ladder, attaching it to the integral picture rail in the hall. I'm used to dealing with fabrics on a smaller scale; swathes of the stuff just become unwieldy and you lose the aesthetics of it. Liliya was at the opposite end of the hall, curling ribbon around tiny pots of honey for the favours. The Dame had hijacked Rob and Edward to help move all the chairs in from the outhouse. Rufus was ordered to sit on one of the chairs that had already been brought in, his instructions were to rest and supervise from afar. Matilda sat next to him making the final changes to the seating plan. The two footmen had begun hanging the swagging at the opposite end of the hall to Delilah and me, and were making their way with impressive efficiency towards us. If they continued at their current pace, with any luck we'd escape the majority of our task.

The ceremony itself would be a very small affair, in comparison to the reception to which the majority of the island was invited. The Dame considered it her duty to entertain the masses as she put it. I had not realised the size of the reception until I was standing, that afternoon, in the long hall awaiting my instructions.

Crystal chandeliers, cavernous bay windows and billowing velvet, floor length curtains, made the hall an impressive sight. The floor was solid oak and creaked under foot, with an eclectic mix of chinoiserie, Axminster and Persian style carpets at various intervals. As you might expect, oil paintings of landscapes and members of the Albrecht De Vries family hanging on the walls. At almost fifty metres long and ten metres wide, the only hall I'd ever seen come close to rivalling this one was St George's at Windsor Castle.

From the top of the ladder, Delilah was telling me about the morning she'd spent with Liliya, Matilda and Penny: a girls' morning. The beautician on the island, who also doubled as a hairdresser, had hosted a pamper-party in the drawing-room at the castle. Needless to say the rest of us had made ourselves scarce.

'So Penny's a bridesmaid?' I asked interrupting Delilah's enthusiasm for her Shellac manicure, whatever that was. I couldn't help interrupting, my brain had been working hard on these murders since the pub yesterday lunchtime and, on hearing Penny's name, I was curious.

'No!' Delilah looked down at me from the ladder, hand on hip. 'Are you listening to me at all?'

I busied myself with the organza. Deep maroon in colour some of the dye was coming off on my hands, giving me a gruesome bloody handed look.

'Penny was invited there by Liliya, you know to cheer her up,' Delilah was undeterred.

I looked across at Liliya at the other end of the hall but she didn't flinch from her task, either deep in concentration or having no hope of hearing unless you raised your voice significantly.

'I didn't think she was down?' I replied remembering yesterday's conversation.

'Well yes, but like Edward said, perhaps I was a bit harsh.'

Delilah admitting she was wrong was not a usual occurrence and I was glad both my feet were firmly on the ground and not up the ladder.

'You've forgiven her then?' I said.

'For what?'

'Snubbing you and Bertie.' I was fairly sure that Delilah's previously churlish attitude towards Penny, had been about her refusal to come out with us to walk the dogs, ever since we'd found Robin Everall's body in the well. One could hardly blame her, but Delilah had definitely felt slighted by her new friend.

'Snubbing? I hardly think she was snubbing us, her fiancé had just been killed.'

Matilda looked up from the sofa and eyed me. I looked back and smiled, I couldn't be sure if she'd heard us talking about the murder or not, so I steered the subject back to the pamper morning.

'So you had a good morning then?'

'Brilliant, just what I needed, manicure, pedicure, facial and a good chat about weddings. Expensive though!'

'Good!' I said trying to untangle my legs from the boa constrictor of organza.

'Good? I don't think so. Archaeologists don't earn much you know.' Delilah lowered her voice and bent down towards me, precariously hanging onto the ladder with one hand. 'It's all right for the others, the Dame paid for theirs, *even Penny's.*'

My face said nothing in return. I hated talking about money. If Delilah couldn't afford it she shouldn't have felt pressured into going but I wasn't about to say that. The mention of Penny again jogged something in my memory.

'We never did find out what she was looking for on the beach,' I said, half to myself.

'Who?'

'Penny.' I handed up another bundle of organza towards Delilah's waiting hands. The footmen were gaining on us. They'd completed one side, compared to our half and were rounding the end of the hall. There was hope.

'Oh, it was a necklace. She'd lost it when she'd been out walking Douglas.'

'Ah.' And then another thought came to me. 'But she walks him on the cliffs doesn't she? I remember her saying the that if she went on the beach, sand got in Douglas' long fur and she could never get it out. It was worse if he went in the water because the salt matted it together.'

'Thank goodness Bertie's got short hair. I can't keep him out of the water.' Delilah shook her arms and rolled her shoulders. 'This is hard work, I'm seizing up here.' She rubbed one of her shoulders and climbed down the ladder. 'Tea?' she said. The Dame had asked the maid to leave a tray of tea and hot water in the hall for people to help themselves.

'Why not,' I said, carefully piling the organza next to the ladder. We walked over to the sideboard where the tea tray sat.

'Tea break already Blake?' Rufus said looking up from Matilda's seating plan as we passed them.

'Can't expect a man to work without tea,' I replied, smiling.

Delilah and I sat on some empty chairs that were placed against the wall next to the sideboard. Rob and Edward were still working hard, appearing occasionally with more tables and chairs. I could see at least fifteen round tables stacked at the far end and a plethora of chairs scattered around the room. There must be enough by now. I could see they were going to need a clean where they'd been stored in one of the outhouses. That would probably be our next task.

'It's an antique apparently,' Delilah said.

'What is?'

'The necklace Penny was looking for.'

I took a sip of tea. 'But wouldn't it have been washed away? The tide was high that day if I remember. When did she lose it?'

'She was hoping it might have got stuck in a rock pool or something. She said she found an earring in one of them the other day; pearl she said.'

'How apt,' I replied. 'Bit of a treasure hunter then?'

'You know she is. She was going to take me out to the Singing Caves where her dad used to take her, remember?'

'Oh yes.'

'She said she'd take me tomorrow if we have time.' Delilah waved a hand at the room.

I watched the footmen working their way along the end wall of the hall. 'These chaps have got it under control,' I said.

'They might get there before us.' Delilah winked at me. It was an odd habit of hers and it had taken me a while to get used to, a young lady winking at me, but it was part of her charm.

'My thoughts exactly.'

'Come on you two, you're getting beaten,' Rufus

shouted from the sofa, jerking his thumb at the footmen.

'You know me Rufus, I've never been a sore loser,' I laughed. We finished up our tea and returned to our task.

'How are we doing people?' Aurora, the elusive wedding planner's voice rang out from the far doorway. It was met with little response. She continued regardless. 'There you are Matilda, I've been looking for you I wanted to speak to you about the flowers.' I wasn't quite sure where else Aurora had been looking but perhaps it was a turn of phrase. 'They can't get hold of the roses you wanted.' She walked towards Matilda and Rufus.

Matilda looked up from their chair. 'And they've only just discovered this have they?' she said.

'Well ... ' Aurora stopped in the middle of the hall, reluctant to come any closer.

'Two days, Aurora. Two days until the wedding, what am I paying you for?'

'Leave it with me.' Aurora retreated quickly from the hall. You could hear a pin drop and Aurora's footsteps could be heard almost running down the corridor and out of the door onto the gravel outside.

Matilda resumed her conversation about the seating plan with Rufus. Delilah came back down the ladder, wincing. 'Oops,' she said.

'Oops indeed. I can see Matilda's point,' I said.

'She is a fiery one,' Delilah whispered. 'She got very cross with the beautician this morning when she was told her toenails weren't long enough for a French manicure.'

'I have no idea what you are talking about,' I said.

'A French manicure is where —— .'

'Delilah, really, do I need to know?' I laughed.

'Fair enough.' She began to climb back up the ladder. Three rungs up, she stopped. 'Come to think of it, so's Liliya.'

'Fiery? Are you sure you don't mean flirty?' I said.

'Well, she lost her temper with Penny. Something about the necklace.'

The sun appeared from behind a cloud and glared at us through the large window we were about to hang swagging above, I looked up at Delilah. 'The necklace?'

'Yes. Liliya gave it to her. She said it was a family heirloom. Matilda was cross too, said Liliya shouldn't be giving away her jewellery like that. Matilda said it was bad enough she lost it hand over foot, never mind giving it to someone else to lose.' Delilah carried on up the ladder and I passed her more organza. She stretched to reach the picture rail and the ladder wobbled violently, so I put the organza down to steady it.

'All right?' I asked.

'Yep, just keep hold of that ladder,' Delilah replied throwing the organza over her shoulder like a sash.

'You OK Mr Hetherington? Miss Delibes?' A voice called from a short distance away. The footmen had caught us up and were starting the second, long wall of the hall.

'Fine thank you,' I replied, relieved to see our trial by organza would soon be at an end. By the time Delilah got the swagging over the window, I had no doubt the footmen would be upon us and we could have another cup of tea.

31.
Bee Venom

It is rare, but a bee's sting can be deadly if the person stung has an anaphylactic reaction to the venom. For the bee the sting is always fatal and they give their life to defend their hive.

A beautiful August day heralded the eve of Rufus' wedding. Out on the moor the heather stretched its limbs outwards, alive with insects, its leaves a silvery grey green in the light. The sun glistened on a calm sea. Even the seabirds were relaxed.

Rufus had been ordered to rest again and Matilda was spending the day with the Dame to resolve last minute preparations. With the promise that I would be back in the afternoon for any emergency best man duties, I had a free pass for the morning.

Across the island, the most southerly beach was host to the Singing Caves. When Delilah had mentioned, yesterday that Penny was taking her there and the likelihood of a free morning, I had asked to join them. I wanted to take another look at these beautiful, long since dormant, volcanic time warps. The three dogs ran ahead disturbing moths, butterflies, beetles and bees as they went. Penny and Delilah gossiped about the forthcoming nuptials. There was not a mention of the murders, except that was, for the maelstrom of thoughts in my head. I was pleased for the chance to flush some of them out with a healthy dose of fresh sea air.

Most of last night was spent running through all the possible scenarios, crashing into the same conclusions and still without an obvious suspect. So far all we had was a dead Russian, loosely linked to royalty, who shortly before he died had been asking after his daughter. In addition there was a dead student and a honey farm owner, who may or may not have seen something. Two days ago I had felt sure the answer lay with the Darenskys and the Albrecht De Vries, but the more the case went on, the more it seemed there were just too many options. Without consistent access to the investigation, even Rob was unlikely to get to the bottom of the case with only twenty-four hours to go. With the more pressing matter of Rufus' wedding I was finally resigned to leaving this one to the police.

The moorland dropped away to reveal the beach below and we shuffled down the steep sandy bank to the beach, the castle behind us gradually disappearing from sight, taking all thoughts of murder with it. I breathed in the fresh sea air.

'Careful just here Blake,' Delilah called back to me a few feet ahead. 'There's a big root sticking out.' The comment reminded of my ungainly descent to the west beach on that fateful first day on the island and I took a moment to steady myself.

'Thanks,' I said and I stepped gingerly over it. Not for the first time, I grateful for my unconventional pink wellies. The girls were way ahead of me, and the dogs further still. There was no way Penny was going to keep Douglas out of the water today, with Bertie and Prince around. The three dogs splashed about in the shallows jumping on their reflections. Penny and Delilah headed straight to the caves. Stopping just in front of the entrance, Delilah pointed up at the rock face.

'The Hebrides are famous for their Paleogene, igneous rock,' Delilah was saying. Penny squinted up at the rock face offering a nod or an mmm, at the correct intervals. I stood just behind them and listened, fascinated by the stories the world around us could tell. 'There weren't a lot of large marine animals around during this time but there were lots of nocturnal mammals. The night was alive during the Paleogene period.' Delilah was warming to her subject waving her hands about frantically to describe the scene. 'It wasn't until towards the end of this period that there was more life in the sea and some of the more familiar life forms we know today.'

'Someone found a dinosaur footprint a few years back,' Penny said.

'Here?' Delilah astonished, looked at Penny.

'Nae here, no, on another of the islands. Lot of fuss there was, about a tiny footprint really. They think it was a baby dinosaur.'

'Interesting.' Delilah turned from the rock, giving her

full attention to Penny.

'I got some newspaper articles you can look at if you want when we get back.'

'I'd like that thanks.'

'Shall I show ye where the fossils are?'

'Yeah, great.' Delilah followed Penny into the cave. As she did she turned to me, 'Coming?'

I followed.

From the outside the caves looked pitch black but once inside the sunlight penetrated easily; shafts of light that cut through the cliff face and out to the other side, to an isolated bay. The gaps weren't big enough for anyone to pass through but big enough to illuminate the caves in the daytime.

A mixture of pebbles, sand and shells made up the floor of the caves and with every other step, seaweed squelched underfoot. The damp walls retained the comforting smell of the sea and crabs scuttled back under the rocks, disturbed by our footfall. There was little wind today and the full effect of the Singing Caves couldn't be heard as it had during my first visit. Instead there was a faint hum when a breeze picked up; a faraway voice beckoning the hapless sailor to sea.

Along the bottom of the rock face there was a myriad of tiny pools filled with anemones, limpets and even starfish. Despite the light that shone into the caves, to see anything up close it was necessary to use a torch, which Penny had brought with her. I could hear the dogs outside.

I hoped Bertie and Prince weren't getting themselves into too much trouble. I could just see them through a crack in the cave wall; the odd flash of fur reassured me they were still on the beach, barking at the sea and any seagull that dared to bait them.

'This is my favourite.' Penny was shining her torch on a faint skeletal outline, barely visible, on the cave wall. A broken comb shape was carved into the rock face. 'Trilobites. Can you imagine them scuttling around the sea floor? And this one here.'

'An ammonite?' Delilah said, reaching forward to touch the outline, circling the shadow on the rock with her index finger. 'They're quite rare here aren't they?'

'Are they? There's loads more down here.' Penny enthusiastically swept her torch round and shone it further into the cave.

As she did I caught sight of some intriguing markings. Little rings on the cave wall and a tiny feathery mark above it. 'What's that?' I asked.

'You've got good eyesight Mr Hetherington,' Penny said, shining her torch to where I was pointing. With only a flash of light from her torch as it whizzed by, I was surprised I'd seen it myself.

'That's a crinoid,' Delilah replied.

'It looks like a plant,' I said.

'It does, but it's an animal. It's very rare to find one this well preserved. Look at all the tiny rings and its feathery arms. Crinoids would sit on the seabed and wait for a meal to come floating by.' Delilah held her hands up, waggling her fingers from side to side to demonstrate the fronds of the crinoid catching its meal.

'Come on let me show ye these ammonites,' Penny said, stepping forward to lead us further into the cave.

As I followed my foot hit something solid but soft. Not a rock or an animal because it didn't move. I thought at first it must be something dead, a bird or a fish but I looked down and in the faint sunlight I could see a black square just by the toe of my foot.

'Wait a minute,' I said. 'Could I borrow the torch a second?'

Stepping back Delilah and Penny joined me again and Penny shone the torch at my foot where I was looking.

It was a passport-sized wallet. It had caught up against one of the rocks and I bent to pick it up with my thumb and forefinger —— I had no gloves. Goodness knows how long it had been there. It was sodden and a small sea snail was making its way across it.

I brushed it off and opened the wallet. There inside was a picture of the Russian on the beach looking decidedly healthier than when I had last seen him. A piece of stray seaweed underlined the name: Alexander Constantine.

'What is it?' Delilah said, taking a step forward unable to contain her curiosity for longer than the thirty seconds it took me to squint at the picture.

'I think we need to go back to the castle with this,' I said.

'With, what? What is it?' Delilah was frustrated.

'A Russian's passport,' I said holding it up to the torch.

'Is it the dead man? Is he who Matilda said he was?' Delilah had blurted it out before assessing the consequences.

We both looked at Penny. Chewing her nails she leant in to look at the passport photo. 'Matilda knew, him?' she said. Given the delay in her response, the tone was definitely that of feigned surprise. I said nothing. Either she knew who he was or she was hiding something else. Either way, the passport had to be handed in.

Delilah was prudent enough not to ask anymore. A bark from the dogs outside broke through the cave wall. 'We'd better get the dogs back,' said Penny.

'Rob's up at the castle,' said Delilah, 'he's helping Edward sort out the mess the police left on the terrace, before tomorrow. Let's take it to him, he'll know who to hand it to.'

My instinct was to go straight to the investigating police officers. Withholding evidence was never a good thing but that meant asking Walter where they were and he would want to know why. I placed the passport in one of the plastic bags I kept in my pocket for dog walking purposes and slipped it inside my coat. At least we knew exactly who the man was now and the first name did match the one given by Matilda. Questions still remained; why did she admit to knowing him before she had to? Was he really Liliya's father? And what did Penny know?

All three of us, dogs in tow, headed back up the sandy slope and across the moor to Castle Albrecht. To my surprise Penny didn't leave us to return home with Douglas and tame his matted fur, instead she accompanied us to the castle, as she had to talk to Liliya about the cake. I thought the cake had been delivered two days ago, but what does a mere man know about the intricate preparation of a wedding cake.

Delilah and I found Rob and Edward on the terrace with the gardener, replanting the apple crusher with trailing lobelia in an attempt to hide the bloodstains. Not a task I would relish. Vigorous trowel work implied the gardener was vexed by his amateur helpers.

I needed to tell Rob about the passport, but I was yet again faced with the prospect of revealing the identity of the Russian and Matilda's secret to two other bystanders, who did not need to know. I was wondering how to broach the subject when raised voices came from inside the castle. From where we were standing the source of the noise was clear. Liliya and Penny were standing in the garden-room facing each other. Penny stood head held high, chin jutted forward towards Liliya, who was wagging a finger at her, other hand on her hip. We were transfixed. The only person unmoved by the scene was the gardener. Only every other word could be heard, resulting in a Morse coded conversation.

'What! … what … doing there?' Liliya was demanding.

'… my fault … nosey … fossils.'

'… not … good … why?' Liliya flung her arms up in the air as Penny drew herself up, preparing for battle.

'… your problem … you said …'

Liliya glanced out of the window and saw us looking at them both. Flinging open the glass garden-room doors, Liliya shouted across the patio.

'Haven't you finished yet?' Her question and ultimately her anger, was directed at the gardener, the only one not looking at her.

'Not long now, Miss Darensky. We want it looking nice for your mother now, don't we?' the gardener replied not looking up and instead reaching for another tray of lobelia.

'Yes!' Liliya shouted. 'We do!'

Penny was looking through the garden-room window at the scene outside. 'Problem?' ventured a brave Delilah.

'No, everything's fine, just a small hitch with the cake,' she replied, voice a little quieter this time. 'If it's OK with you lot, I'll get on,' she said and slamming the doors returned to Penny. The doors bounced back and opened again allowing another snippet of conversation to escape.

'After all I've done for you, you stand there and do nothing, the least you could have done is …' Liliya noticed the doors were still opened and stopped mid-sentence to walk forward and close them, firmly. Delilah, Rob and Edward, turned back to the lobelia. As discreetly as possible, I watched the continuing conversation.

Liliya raised a hand to Penny's cheek, her face now softer and voice no longer audible. I watched as Penny reddened and knocked Liliya's hand away. Liliya said something else a little louder this time but I still could not hear. Penny's face was aghast, mouth open, as she turned and went to leave the garden-room. Liliya tried to take hold of her arm to stop her leaving but just missed. Penny now ran out of the room and Liliya with a brief glance, over her shoulder at the terrace, followed.

Their voices were heard, few moments later, on the other side of the castle, then footsteps on the gravel as they moved away from the house and eventually silence.

'Well, I wonder what that was about,' Delilah said, looking up from the lobelia she was helping the gardener plant. Rob stood up and was stretching out his back.

'Cake's a serious subject,' he said, grimacing, his back cracking alarmingly.

'I wouldn't pay much heed to that lot,' the gardener spoke to us for the first time since we'd got there. 'Sorry sir,' he said, to Edward.

'Don't have to apologise to me,' Edward replied 'Women! Mad the lot of them.'

'Oi.' Delilah flicked a bit of soil from her trowel at him.

'I hope they resolve it by tomorrow,' I said, 'I'm not sure if cake making comes under best man duties but Eleanor used to say I made a good Breeze Block.'

'Then so do I,' said Rob. 'Dentistry is expensive.' We all laughed, all except the gardener who was still engrossed in his task.

Delilah stood up, leaning on the circular disc of the

apple crusher as she did. It moved slightly and the gardener tutted as it crumpled his newly planted lobelia and just missed his hand. 'Careful with that,' he said.

Delilah pulled her hand away. 'It moved,' she said.

'Of course it did,' the gardener grumbled.

'But it looks too heavy! It is heavy!' Delilah said reaching out to push it again.

'This one's a replacement. See.' The gardener pointed to a date stamp on the stone disc: 2000.

'Why's it not fixed?' Delilah asked the obvious question.

'The Dame wanted it to have functionality,' he said. 'For the new millennium.'

Rob pushed the disc with one hand.

'Careful,' the gardener tutted again.

'I suppose it's not very heavy,' Delilah said.

'It's heavy enough to have done for Geoff Layland,' Rob replied. 'If he was unconscious already of course.'

'Look, someone's oiled it,' I said, leaning into the mechanism to see how it worked.

'Of course they have! I do.' The gardener was getting cross. 'Functionality she said and functional it is. You can still crush apples with it, you just don't need a horse to pull the wheel round. You use the crank here,' he said, pointing to the metal handle that was now all too clear. The apple crusher had been under a tent for the majority of my stay and no one had examined it since. We'd all just assumed.

I was amazed. The three of us stood staring at the apple crusher. Anyone could have pushed it over an unconscious Geoff Layland. The question remained, who?

32.

Drumming

In order to encourage bees to move into a new hive, the new hive is set above the occupied one and the beekeeper will knock the sides of the lower hive until the bees ascend.

The morning of the wedding finally dawned. After a brief discussion with Rob the passport was now safely in the hands of the mainland police. A decision was made not to mention it to Matilda or Rufus and we hoped the police would see fit to hold off any further interviewing until after the wedding. After all we'd only confirmed what we already knew; the identity of the Russian on the beach. Matilda and Rufus had already had to cancel their honeymoon. Due to her relationship with the victim Matilda was not allowed to leave the island. I only hoped today would go as smoothly as possible.

At dinner yesterday - a sort of last supper - Liliya had apologised for the argument we had witnessed earlier. Penny had been invited to dinner by Liliya, as a peace offering but she had not turned up. Hardly surprising. Liliya was at pains to reassure us that the problem had been resolved. A problem Matilda seemed unaware of as she regaled us with a description of the cake and what a wonderful job Penny had done. The Dame said nothing, perhaps still smarting at the use of Layland honey over her own.

The tension was tangible in the castle that morning. After everything that had happened over the last few weeks, there was not a soul who was not waiting for the next misfortune. This included myself, engendering guilt, for as the best man I felt it must be my job to remain positive and upbeat.

The ceremony was due to start at one 'o' clock. Delilah, Liliya, Matilda and the Dame, were all getting ready in the bedrooms upstairs whilst the men were downstairs. Our suits were waiting in a small lounge-room off from the drawing-room. A screen had been erected for changing and an hour before the wedding Edward, Rufus, Rob and myself would assemble to change.

Rufus had asked to be alone for a while, which I wasn't entirely happy with but I respected his wishes and Rob, Edward and I had retreated to the library. The Albrecht library was a magnificent room with floor to ceiling bookshelves and a wonderful ladder on runners allowing the avid reader to peruse the shelves at leisure. I was lost in an illustrated, 1920s version of The Tempest published by William Heinemann. A magnificent edition of one of Shakespeare's finest plays. Rob was standing on the ladder perusing a section on angling and game fishing. Edward was sitting in a high back chair with the day's paper. The room was silent, blissfully absent of chitchat.

'Blake, Rufus has gone missing.' Delilah's voice

shattered the peace as she burst into the room.

I tore myself away from a fine drawing of The Tempest itself in full swing. Ethereal faces represented the wind that circled bowed trees and birds straining to fly against it.

'He told Matilda, he'd gone for a walk to get some fresh air,' Delilah continued. She was standing half in and half out of the library doorway. I could see she was wearing a fluffy dressing gown and with full make-up and her hair in curlers, she was a walking cliché. 'He hasn't come back and he should have been by now. We can't find him anywhere. Matilda's worried he's had another heart attack.'

'I'm sure he's fine,' Rob said, from half way up the ladder. 'Leave the man in peace.'

'Rob!' Delilah gave him a fierce look and then fired an equally pleading one in my direction.

I looked at my watch. It was eleven-thirty. I'd lost track of the time. We'd all have to be in the drawing-room in half-an-hour anyway and I was tempted to leave Rufus to his solitude but a gut feeling told me to go and look for him. I stood up from the chair where I was sitting. 'I'll go and look for him.'

'Great, thanks Blake.' Delilah disappeared out of the door as abruptly as she'd appeared.

Rob looked down at me from the ladder and rolled his eyes. 'Poor man, probably just wants a bit of peace and quiet. I know what that feels like.'

'I better check,' I said. 'He's been under a lot of pressure recently.'

'I thought I saw him go into the chapel,' Edward said, looking up from the paper. From the library you could see the entrance to the little chapel where the ceremony would be held.

'Why didn't you say?' Rob voiced my thoughts.

'Well, I know he likes to sit there to think. He's done it most days since he's been here. The last thing he'd want is Delilah bursting in on him.' He looked over the paper at Rob. 'Sorry,' he shrugged.

'No you're right,' Rob said, with a sigh. Perhaps thinking of all the times Delilah had burst in on his moments of peace.

'I'll go and see he's OK. Best man and all that.' I got up to go and find Rufus. I did wonder why Matilda didn't know this would be where her fiancé was, but perhaps Rufus had achieved what many men before him had not – a secret place to retreat from his wife.

Edward replied, 'I'm sure he's just fine.'

For a man who three days ago was worried the stress his father was under would kill him, I was surprised at Edward's relaxed attitude on this day of all days. Regardless, it was my job to rally the troops and if Rufus needed rallying I'd have to do it.

I found Rufus, as Edward had predicted, in silent contemplation sat on the front row of wooden chairs. My shoes clacked on the flagstones but he didn't turn and I did worry for a moment that perhaps he was ill. I hurried a little and as I got nearer I could see his shoulders moving as his hands fidgeted.

'You all right Rufus?' I asked, as gently as possible.

'Jesus, Blake, you gave me the shock of my life,' he said, turning to look at me.

'Sorry,' I replied taking a seat next to him 'and Blake will do, no need to blaspheme. We're in a chapel,' I smiled.

'All very well for you to say, don't you know there's a murderer on the loose?' He folded his arms and sighed.

'Well let's hope they respect the sanctity of the church, hey, old friend?' I tried to lift the mood.

Squeezing his eyes tight shut, Rufus pushed the heels of his hands into them.

'You OK?' I asked, again.

His shoulders sagged and he pulled at his collar. 'I don't know,' he said.

I let him gather his thoughts. I remember, still to this day, how I felt on the morning of my wedding to Eleanor. Would she turn up? Would it work? Would you be able to stand by one person for the rest of your life? And those were just the rational thoughts. I patted Rufus' shoulder, 'Come on, Rufus, it'll be OK.' I wasn't sure whom I was trying to convince. It hadn't been that long ago I'd been trying to persuade him to postpone the wedding, for fear his fiancée was a murderer.

'They still haven't caught him,' Rufus sighed.

'No, but they will,' I said.

Rufus turned to look at me. 'Have you sorted it then?'

'No, but that's not my job is it. My job's to make sure

you get through today.'

A faint banging from the pipework, started underneath us. I ignored it. The castle made a variety of different noises and I'd heard a selection of them during my time here. This was just another. Rufus was far too distracted to even notice.

'I hope I'm doing the right thing,' Rufus said.

'You are. You've promised to marry Matilda and that's what's going to happen. You can't honestly believe she has anything to do with this mess, can you?' I regretted asking the question as soon as it was out.

'I don't know what to think anymore Blake. I know I said I wasn't worried about her past but it's just gnawing away at me. I can't undo it. I know now and that's it.'

'Are you saying you wouldn't be here if you'd known before?' I said.

Rufus shrugged.

'Look Rufus.' I turned to face him squarely. 'I can see how much you love Matilda; the whole world can see it. The way you are with her. She has you wrapped around her finger. She loves you too; she stuck by you after all that nonsense earlier this year. We all have a past, the only thing that sets us apart from it is whether or not we choose to move on.' The banging sound started again, deflating the profoundness of my words.

'You're right, you're always right. Used to annoy the hell out of me when we were younger, but hell, that's why you're my best man!' Rufus got up, straightened his collar and smiled at me. He had a bit of colour back in his cheeks, I had told him what he needed to hear. My job was done.

The banging noise was getting louder and more regular. Just as I was about to say something the door to the chapel opened and Liliya appeared. She peered round the little wooden door and seeing us went to leave, 'I'm sorry,' she said, 'I didn't know you were here.'

'Shouldn't you be helping your mother?' Rufus said, perhaps a little too sternly.

'She wants me to check the flowers are all in place,' she replied.

'Well they are.' Rufus indicated the decorated chapel with a sweep of an arm. 'You can ….' The banging noise from below interrupted him. 'What is that noise?' He frowned.

'It'll be the pipes,' Liliya smiled. 'I'll get the gardener to sort it.'

'The gardener?' Rufus was as puzzled as I.

'Yes, he's good with plumbing, don't worry it'll be sorted before the ceremony,' she smiled and closed the door again behind her.

'Pipes?' Rufus looked at me.

'This is an old place,' I shrugged.

'I've been here almost every day over the last month and not once have I heard that noise. What's more, the crypt's below us and it's just been refurbished on account of subsidence, surely they'd have replaced any old pipes then?'

'Let the gardener sort it, Rufus. Come on it's almost twelve; we should get you in your suit. I think Talisker might be called for as well, what do you reckon?"

Rufus looked at his watch and smiled. 'Come on them, before my feet get cold again.'

We made the short walk back to the castle in silence. I felt uneasy but I couldn't put my finger on why. It wasn't Rufus' doubts; they were normal, especially under the circumstances. I'd expected a minor wobble at some point. No, it was the noise. It had sounded like pipes, granted, but it was a rhythmical sound not like the uneven sounds I'd heard before from faulty plumbing. Hot water pipes made a rhythmical tap as they heated up, but not faulty pipes. Then there was Rufus' terse attitude towards Liliya. Liliya had looked guilty when she entered the chapel. Why? It was her home; she'd have every right to be there. Had she and Rufus fallen out? I didn't feel now was the right time to ask. We rounded the corner of the west wing to enter the main doors and make our way to the gentleman's lounge where the suits were, when I noticed Douglas, Penny's dog, tied to the drainpipe by the main door. There was a water bowl and food beside it. He looked quite content sitting in the sunshine.

'Is Penny here?' I said, as we went into the entrance hall.

'Possibly,' Rufus replied.

'Her dog is.'

'Liliya looks after him sometimes.'

'This morning?'

'Beats me what that girl gets up to,' Rufus replied. 'Penny takes advantage, always asking Liliya for favours. Apparently Liliya gave Penny one of the Dame's necklaces as a gift. Penny lost it. Matilda's furious.'

'I had heard.'

'Liliya's no saint, goodness knows she tries my patience, but I don't trust that Penny. I think she's sniffed money and she's taking advantage of Liliya's need for friendship.'

An interesting observation on Rufus' part. I was reminded of the argument between Liliya and Penny yesterday. There had been a passion in it. Until Rufus had pointed out the dynamic between the two girls I hadn't recognised it. In that argument, Penny held the balance of power, not Liliya. The argument had not been about the cake. If it had been, Penny might have been more gracious, but nothing in her demeanour that afternoon in the garden-room, suggested remorse. It was more indignant, furious, wronged even. I chided myself for not seeing it earlier. I had no time to contemplate it now. We only had an hour before the ceremony.

We entered the gentleman's lounge and Rufus went behind the screen to change. I sat on the chesterfield and waited for my turn. I couldn't help drifting back to my previous thought. Liliya's words now took on a different meaning: *'After all I've done for you'*. If Rufus was right and Penny was taking advantage of Liliya's good nature then perhaps Liliya had finally got fed up. It was Penny that had sought out Liliya, so what had Penny done? When Penny had gone to leave, Liliya had touched her face. Where had I seen that before? Then it hit me. It was so obvious!

'Blake?' Rufus' voice cut across my thoughts. He was peering at me over the screen. 'Are you all right?' I nodded. 'Pass me my cravat, will you?' he said. Passing the cravat over I felt sure I was on to something.

Liliya flirted outrageously with every man that came into sight. But what if it was a mask, a way of keeping the truth at arm's length? What if she was actually in love with Penny?

33.
Mating Dance

The queen bee begins her mating flight followed by a dozen or more males. They fly higher and higher towards the sun until one drone mates with the queen and then explodes.

I was forced to shake any more thoughts of Liliya Darensky and the mystery that surrounded the murders from my brain. We had half-an-hour until the ceremony would commence and Rufus was beginning to pace. I was now primarily concerned for the safety of the, already thread bare Persian rug, on the floor of the gentleman's lounge.

'Should we wait in the chapel?' I suggested, emerging from behind the screen, dressed, with top hat in hand. 'It would take longer to erode the flagstones in there.' The humour went unnoticed.

'Yes, yes we should. I can see people in that way too,' Rufus stood up, tugging at the bottom of his ivory waistcoat.

'Right, don't forget your hat,' I pointed at his top hat sat on the sofa. The nap of the grey felt had been brushed the wrong way on one side and I picked it up before Rufus could get to it, to brush it back the right way. I'd spent hours on these top hats. I wanted them to look the best they could, for myself as much as Rufus. The ivory silk ribbon was also turned under slightly despite my delicate stitching and I smoothed it flat against the hat again.

'Good. Have you got the rings?' Rufus said, watching me fuss over the hat.

I patted my waistcoat pocket. 'Of course!' I handed him the hat, happy it was perfection once more and then checked my own; as I had thought, perfect.

The sun was bright outside and the granite stones of the castle's terrace slabs twinkled. The apple crusher was replanted and washed down, and there was nothing to suggest the horrors it had witnessed a few days ago. The grounds were a peaceful place once more.

Edward was standing by the door to the chapel handing out orders of service.

'About ten so far,' he said, smiling at Rufus. 'You OK, ready to go?'

'Yup, Blake's sorted me out.' Rufus put a hand on Edward's shoulder. 'This is going to be a good day son,' he said. There was a lump in my throat as I remembered the day I walked Jane down the aisle to her waiting groom. It had been a very nineties wedding. A dress covered in duchess satin roses and lace. The edge of her veil had almost obscured my view as we made our way to the altar, but that's what my little girl had wanted and that's what she'd got.

For the first time since we'd got here I wondered what Matilda's ensemble might look like. I was aware of the basic shapes and what hats may be best suited to certain outfits: cloches for shift dresses, pill boxes for fifties style dresses, delicate sinamay numbers for fish tail evening gowns, the list goes on, but as a general rule I stayed away from women's attire, unless it adorned their head.

Matilda had asked me to make her a very chic ivory pillbox hat with sinamay curls and a small lace veil. Made from coconut, sinamay is a very versatile; mesh fabric that's particularly good for summer commissions. I had meticulously handmade and sewn, tiny lilac roses to the edge of the pillbox where it met with the sinamay. She had been so pleased with the finished item she'd hugged me. Not something I'm used to from Matilda Darensky, or anyone for that matter. It had been my pleasure to contribute to Rufus' day in this way and it made me proud to see my creations on display.

I hadn't heard any more of the conversation between Rufus and Edward and I realised I had been standing staring at my shoes. A mark on the toe had caught my eye and I bent down with my handkerchief to wipe it away. *'You'd better get in there then,'* I heard Edward say.

I often retreated to thoughts of hats or even hat watching at large social gatherings; a way of calming the nerves, distancing myself from the chatter. I wasn't entirely sure what I had to be nervous about; there were minimal guests and it was Rufus' wedding day not mine. The police were far away dealing with the murders and we had nothing to fear. But something was nagging at my mind. Was it

Rufus' doubt or just the unsettling effects of the past few weeks? I couldn't pinpoint the source.

Entering the chapel a few people had arrived already. The ceremony, a family affair, included about thirty guests. Some of Rufus' aunts, uncles and cousins, whom I hadn't yet met, and some old school friends, who to Rufus, having spent a lot of time at boarding school, were the equivalent of family. Matilda did not have any extra guests; her family was the Dame and Liliya, so people sat where they wanted, or it would have made for a very lopsided congregation.

We took our place on the front pew, the only reserved seats and waited. I sensed Rufus wanted some quiet time and so I sat beside him and was silent. I soon became lost in my own thoughts.

Weddings were a time for family and I was sad to think that Matilda had so few there to enjoy the day with her. I found myself wondering whether or not she had tried to trace any of her family. Did she know her father or mother? She'd said she was young when she left home, but where was her family now? Had she severed all ties with her past? Until, that is, Alexander Constantine came looking for his daughter. An idle thought drifted in. Was Constantine, Liliya's father or grandfather? I tried to recall the face. It was difficult to tell. He'd had a full beard and his hat hid his face and after being in the water for so long he could easily have looked older than he was. I quickly dismissed this thought. If this had been the case, surely it was better for Matilda to admit to this rather than the indiscretion she had disclosed. If it was a bluff then why not just say it was an old friend and leave it at that, why so much history? No, the answer lay somewhere else. I shook my head and tutted. I was looking for things that weren't there.

'You all right Blake?' Rufus said.

'Yes fine. Sorry Rufus, you know how it is, hard to stop this thing once it's going,' I said, tapping the side of my head.

'I know that feeling,' Rufus sighed and looked at his watch. It was twelve.

'She'll be here,' I said, 'Bride's prerogative to be late.' The vicar appeared from the vestry and came to offer some words of reassurance to Rufus.

I was pleased to note there was no more knocking noise from below the chapel. Liliya must have found the gardener as promised and fixed it. I tried not to think any more about it. I distracted myself from thoughts of murderers by taking in the murderous creations that crowned the heads of the congregations. Very few of them had a bespoke look about them. Most of them department store purchases; some better than others. It was summer and most of the large department stores were filled with Gainsboroughesque affairs made with a cheap sinamay brims and crowns and any number of feathers, ribbons, silk flowers or knots. I, of course, use a much higher quality sinamay, than the ones on display here.

Looking around at the Blackwood cousins, aunts and

uncles I was cheered to see the distinct lack of hatinators; that was until Delilah arrived. Rob was already there, sitting on the back row. I hadn't noticed him appear. He was wearing a smart grey-black suit and his royal purple tie matched Delilah's pretty cocktail dress. For Delilah the dress itself was very reserved. A plain cocktail dress made out of chiffon and taffeta. The hatinator was not so plain. Akin to a flying saucer, it balanced, precariously on the side of her head and from the middle sprouted two anorexic feathers and a collection of fabric and faux pearls that gave the pretence of a rose. I sighed inwardly. Never in the time we'd known each other had she asked me to make her a hat. I didn't know whether to be pleased she hadn't commissioned me to make such a monstrosity, or affronted that she preferred to wear that! She nodded at me as I saw her entering and, with a thumb over her shoulder, indicated that the bride must be hot on her heels. I nudged Rufus.

'Here we go, old chap.' Standing we took our place at the end of the aisle as Liliya entered in a pale lilac knee-length satin dress, gathered at the waist with an ivory sash; beautifully elegant. She held a bouquet of ivory roses and tiny lilac feathers. *The Arrival of the Queen of Sheba* echoed off the stones, creating a blanket of music I did not think possible from such a tiny church organ.

Taking her place, standing next to us Liliya looked tired and fretful. She twisted the rose bouquet in her hands and picked at her cuticles. She barely acknowledged either

Rufus or myself. I had no time to ask her if all was well because the doors opened again. This time Matilda entered with the Dame. The slow walk up the aisle gave Rufus plenty of time to take in his bride.

Her floor length ivory lace wedding dress was painstakingly fitted, showing classic curves in all the right places. The pillbox hat complimented it perfectly. Matilda Darensky was a handsome woman and Rufus was a very lucky man. She was everything a woman should be on her wedding day; composed, radiant and, of course, beautiful. Her waterfall bouquet of roses, wisteria, ivy, and lilac feathers, were exquisite. Everything about her said Lady Blackwood. Far from the Russian slum she had described to us a week ago. All eyes were on Matilda. I had a moment of self-doubt as I checked my waistcoat pocket again for the rings. There was no time for any more doubts on Rufus' part. The bride was here for her groom.

34.

Candy Plug

This is sugar that is placed at one end of a small cage in which the queen is transported. It delays her entry into the hive, as she has to eat through the sugar to eventually be released.

The ceremony went without a hitch, well at least only the intended one. Rufus was visibly relieved and Matilda was beaming. Even Liliya's face had softened and she was beginning to enjoy herself.

After canapés on the terrace we all gathered in the large banqueting hall where the rest of the guests now joined us for a grand sit down meal. The circular tables were decorated with crisps white linen and more ivory roses, this time accompanied by lilac stocks. Little jars of honey waited for everyone at the table and those who had had a few too many glasses of champagne, tucked into the baskets of bread, spreading them with the complimentary honey. There was a general feel of good cheer and celebration.

A long table at the end of the hall held the bridal party. Rufus and Matilda heads bowed together, chatted to each other. To the right of them Liliya was flirting outrageously with Edward and to the left the Dame looked on disapprovingly. Rufus had put me on a table with Delilah and Rob, at my request. I hated the idea of being centre of attention, preferring to observe from one of the round tables rather than being observed on the top table.

Extra staff had been hired for the day and they busied themselves, circling the tables, serving starters and taking drinks orders. Rob, Delilah and I were sitting on a table with a few of Rufus' cousins. Now I looked a little closer I recognised some of them from The Fisherman's Rest, although they looked quite different without walking gear and boots. It was hardly surprising that from a distance, with a nervous groom to occupy me, I hadn't yet realised I'd effectively shared a drink with some of them.

I watched Rufus tuck a stray hair from Matilda's fringe behind her ear. The love that radiated from that table made me glad. I had done my duty as best man and delivered Rufus to the altar. Looking at Matilda now, so happy and content, I found it hard to believe she could be our serial killer. Surely there were easier ways to suppress a secret. Killing three people and then confessing to your past was surely not the most obvious solution.

Facing into the hall, I had a good view of most of the guests from where I sat. Rufus knew me well. I looked around the room as our table waited for their starters. Mr and Mrs Naismith were two tables away. They were holding court over some other locals, although over the general din of one hundred plus people all talking at once, I couldn't pick out the conversation. Mrs Naismith was wearing a very fine felt Derby with a delicate chiffon bow.

Tiny seed beads sparkled in the sunshine that drifted through the large windows. Sitting next to her, clean-shaven with Brylcreemed hair, I'd never seen Mr Naismith looking so manicured. I saw a couple of the girls from the cake shop at the far end of the room, their hatinators and fascinators bobbing up and down as they spoke with rosy cheeked, champagne induced, exuberance.

One of the tables seated the fishermen, normally found at bar in The Fisherman's Rest. I understood they had caught the fish, fresh for the day's feast and, as a result, had gained invitations to what was the island's wedding of the year. Rather comically, they all sat in suits, still wearing their traditional Bretons; escapees from one of Hergé's picture books. Ruby was a rose amongst them all looking lovely in a pale pink silk dress and matching fascinator.

There were a few empty seats here and there. The one at our table should have seated Penny. I assumed the argument with Liliya meant she had stayed away, although there had been no mention that she would and I thought it rather odd she'd forgo the wedding because of it. Then again, Douglas was still outside, I'd seen him on the way to the hall, still happily lying in the sunshine. If she'd fallen out with Liliya to the extent she wouldn't come to the wedding, why was Liliya looking after her dog? I looked around the hall for the cake. A small square table to the left of the top table was empty, suggesting it was missing. Perhaps she was putting some finishing touches to it. It had been commissioned at a very late hour, after all.

The feathers on Delilah's millinery monstrosity tickled my face as I turned back round and I brushed them away. She was reaching under her chair for her handbag.

'Sorry Blake,' she said, rummaging in her bag for a tissue.

'I don't know why you insist on wearing those things,' I replied, eyeing the purple terror with deep suspicion.

'I think it's rather fabby.' Delilah preened the feathers as she spoke. The use of the word *fabby,* only served to add insult to injury in my eyes. 'Was Rufus OK this morning then? No cold feet?' she asked.

I wasn't about to give my friend away. 'Not at all,' I replied.

'Matilda was in a right state.' Delilah lowered her voice and leaned in to avoid anyone overhearing.

'It's a very stressful time,' I replied, in an equal timbre.

'She couldn't find Liliya anywhere. She went walkabouts. That's why we were late. Liliya didn't turn up until almost twelve. Didn't even have her dress on!'

A vision invaded my brain. 'I trust she had something on,' I replied.

'Blake!' Delilah punched me on the arm playfully, her way of responding to my teasing. 'Fancy though, not being there on time for your mother's wedding.'

'Fancy!' I disliked gossip as much as Delilah relished it. Our starters began to arrive and the serving staff made their way around the table delivering delicately stacked beetroot and goats cheese, on a bed of watercress all wobbling violently as they were placed in front of the diner.

'This looks amazing!' Delilah said. 'Oo and the beetroot goes with my hat,' she laughed.

'Indeed it does.' I resented being reminded of the hatinator again.

'Oh lighten up Blake!' Delilah tucked into her starter. On the other side of her Rob was chatting to one of Rufus' cousins. An attractive brunette in her fifties, she was responding to his jokes with the occasional bat of her eyelids and twist of her hair. She was definitely flirting. Whether it was the romance of the occasion or the alcohol, weddings always induced this sort of involuntary behaviour, even from the most staid characters. Looking around the room again, the sea of smiling faces was a complete contrast to the events of the last few weeks.

'Penny's missing a treat,' Delilah said. 'I wonder where she is?'

'I suspect she felt uncomfortable after her argument yesterday,' I replied.

'I did wonder what that was about.' Delilah leant in again and widened her eyes conspiratorially.

'She does seem to flirt a little bit too much with the opposite sex,' I said, my gaze drifting once more to the top table.

'Oh she's just one of those.'

'One of those?'

'Yes you know. If she was a bloke they'd say she was all

mouth and no trousers.'

'I see. I was thinking though ….' I paused halfway through to bundle some watercress onto my fork.

'Come on Blake, I can smell the burning rubber, what's going on in that mind of yours?'

'Well, I wondered, do you think …,' and then I felt foolish, I chickened out. 'No, just ignore me.'

'Come on, out with.' Delilah had finished her starter and had placed her knife and fork neatly on the plate. Folding her arms she looked at me expectantly.

'Well, maybe Liliya doesn't like men at all. Maybe she really is no trousers.'

'What do you mean?' I couldn't tell if Delilah was purposefully misunderstanding or if I was just way off the mark.

'Maybe Liliya's in love with Penny?' There it was, out there. Thinking it was one thing, but saying it was another.

Delilah turned to look at Liliya. She watched as she touched Edward's arm and giggled at a joke he'd made. Her face flirted but the rest of her body betrayed her. Whilst her face was turned towards him, the rest of her body was stiff and upright, facing the table. Under the table her feet were crossed at the ankles. 'You know Blake, you might just be right there,' Delilah said, almost in a trance.

'I don't know. I think I'm making things up.' I wasn't completely convinced. I was sure I was looking for things that weren't there in a desperate attempt to solve this case.

'No. No,' she said, a little too loudly, turning back

towards me. Thankfully, no one except Rob noticed the urgency in her tone and he chose to ignore it. I plucked the last mouthful of beetroot and toasted cheese off my fork and waited. 'No,' she said again. 'You're right, I knew there was something not right about the way she was with Penny at the pamper-party; just a bit too touchy feely. Penny didn't seem to mind so I just thought they had one of those girly friendships, but now you mention it, I think you might be on to something.'

'Delilah, are you sure you're not letting your imagination run away with you? I certainly think mine has.' I had finished my mouthful of food and I wiped my mouth. A neat little beetroot stain marred the crisp white napkin; lipstick on a starched collar.

'Blake, you know you're right or you wouldn't have said it. That's why Liliya paid for Penny at the party! It explains the argument as well don't you see?'

'How?'

'Well, Lilya must have been jealous that Penny went to the beach with me.'

'But I was with you and explain this: why was Penny engaged to Geoff Layland?'

'I don't think Liliya's feelings are reciprocated. Penny was really cut up when Geoff died, she's the sort that keeps her emotions in check, hidden, you know?'

'Not at all like you,' I smiled unable to resist.

Delilah ignored me and continued. 'Penny obviously keeps Liliya hanging around because it's convenient.'

'I can't help feeling there was more to that argument than just a trip to the beach,' I pondered the question out loud.

'Actually, Penny was going to go back to the café but she didn't.' Delilah was off. 'She said she had to talk to Liliya about the cake.'

'I'm pretty sure that argument wasn't about cake,' I interjected. It was no use. Delilah was getting into her story gesticulating wildly and almost knocking the plates in the waitress's hands flying, as she cleared them from the table.

'Penny went in to tell Liliya something right?'

'Right.'

'What if it was about what we found in the cave?'

'Of course! How stupid of me!' Now I was getting excited, I turned in my seat to face Delilah. 'Just because Matilda doesn't think Liliya knows who her father is doesn't mean she doesn't. He came looking for her yes?'

'Yes!'

'What if he found her?'

'What if who found who?' Rob was now interested. The cousin had disappeared, a comfort break perhaps between courses. We now had his full attention.

'Blake thinks Liliya killed the Russian.'

'What?' Rob frowned.

'Now Delilah, that's not quite what I said.' Thankfully the other guests around the table were too busy drinking and eyeing up the next course to pay attention to our conversation, which had got a little too loud.

'But it's the only reasonable explanation.' Delilah spoke a little quieter now, noticing my concern.

All three of us turned to look at Liliya who caught our eye and smiled uncomfortably.

'Penny must have gone to tell Liliya we found the passport,' I said, looking down at the table and adjusting my cutlery; anything to avoid all three of us continuing to look at Liliya.

'So you think Liliya knows Constantine was her father?' Rob said.

'Of course!' Delilah was holding Rob's arm in a fierce grip as the main courses started to arrive.

'And if Penny went to tell her about the passport then she must know too,' I said. 'Yes.' The cogs in my brain were now firing on all cylinders. 'And that must have been what the argument was about! The last thing Liliya wanted was for us to find the passport, because she doesn't know we know who he is!' I jabbed the table with my finger narrowly missing my beef wellington as it arrived in front of me.

'But why would she kill the others?' Rob whispered, trying not to draw any attention to our conversation. 'More to the point why would she kill her father?'

'Don't you see?' I said, getting carried away with the possibilities. 'She hadn't seen her father for years and yet here he was, turning up just weeks before her mother's wedding, he could ruin everything for them, reveal her mother's past. That would mean no more wedding, no more Rufus, no more money and no more Penny! She doesn't know her mother has already told us the truth.'

'That's a hell of a leap Blake,' Rob said.

'Listen Rob, it makes sense,' Delilah said, and turned back to Rob. 'She must have killed Robin Everall because he saw her murder him.'

'What about Geoff?'

'Easy, she's in love with Penny. What's one more murder?' Delilah shrugged, cutting into her beef wellington sending the gravy slopping over the side of her plate.

'You two have lost it,' Rob said, circling his temple with an index finger. 'Too much champagne and an overactive imagination.'

The cousin had returned to the table and began to comment on the beef wellington, drawing Rob back into conversation.

'Don't pay attention to him, he's just annoyed he didn't think of it. I think you're spot on, so what do we do about it?'

'I'm not sure,' I said, still not convinced I hadn't lost it as Rob suggested. I looked at my empty champagne glass and tried to remember how many I'd had. 'We've no real evidence.'

A couple of minutes silence passed as I savoured the glorious fillet steak encompassed in light fluffy puff pastry. It was beautiful, melt in the mouth magic. Beef Wellington was so easy to get wrong but this was perfection. A loud laugh from the top table made me look up. It was Liliya again, happily chatting and laughing with Edward. Rufus and Matilda couldn't stop smiling. Even if I did honestly think Liliya was responsible for three deaths, now was not the right time to do anything about it. I could easily drop the whole subject right then and enjoy the rest of the day.

'It would explain why Penny's not here,' Delilah said.

'How?'

'Well maybe she didn't realise the strength of Liliya's feelings?' Delilah said, taking another mouthful of beef, and then with her mouth still full, her eyes widened. 'Or, or, what if she told Penny she'd killed Geoff, so they could be together?'

'That's a hell of a confession. Why would she do that?' Blake said.

'Picture this. What if Liliya confessed her feelings for Penny? And what if Penny told Liliya she wanted nothing to do with her anymore? What if Liliya got angry and told Penny what she'd done? We do strange things when we're in love.'

I looked up at Lord Rufus Blackwood who'd just married his Russian slum princess. I couldn't help but agree.

'She went after Penny didn't she? We saw her leave the garden-room with her. What if Penny never went home? What if Liliya tried to keep her here?'

'Delilah,' I cautioned.

'She might have killed her too. Why else would Douglas be here and not Penny?'

'Why has she kept Douglas though?' I asked astounded

at this latest suggestion.

'Liliya may be many things but I've seen her with Bertie. She loves dogs, there's no way she'd kill Douglas.'

'This is too far Delilah,' I said, 'I think we just need to calm down and look at this again tomorrow.'

'I still think you're on to something,' Delilah persisted.

I saw Rufus rise from his seat at the top table as Rob turned to Delilah. Rob had been half listening to our conversation and chose the moment Rufus rang his glass for silence to admonish Delilah.

'Give it up Delilah, she's not a lesbian,' Rob said, just as a hush descended on the room. Rob turned back to face the top table as if nothing had happened.

Rufus had the good sense not to draw further attention to the outburst. I looked around. Most of the other guests had finished their meals and the plates were beginning to be cleared. Delilah and I were the slowest to eat at our table on account of the lively conversation.

'I'd like to take this opportunity,' Rufus began, 'to thank you all for coming and to toast my beautiful bride. To Matilda, thank you for completing my life,' he said, raising his glass.

'Matilda!' the guests echoed, standing up, glasses held aloft.

'I've never been one to stand on ceremony and you all know how I feel about Matilda so you'll be pleased to know, I'm forgoing my speech.' Matilda frowned, this was clearly not in the plan but there was nothing she could do about it now. 'Instead, I'll hand you over to Dame Albrecht De Vries who would like to say a few words.' Rufus sat back down to polite clapping and the Dame got up.

As she began, an almighty racket started from outside the house. It was Douglas.

'I'll sort it babushka,' Liliya said, and left the table.

The Dame smiled patiently and continued with her speech. I felt in my pocket for the paper of my own speech, which would be immediately after that of the Dame's.

'I'm going with her,' Delilah said.

'What? Hang on!' I put a hand on her arm to try and stop her but she was intent on her mission.

'Where's she going?' Rob mouthed, as Delilah disappeared after Liliya.

I shrugged aware that the Dame was likely to disprove of anyone interrupting her speech. Rob went to get up and caught a look from the Dame that said sit down. He did.

'And of course, she gave us Liliya …' the Dame was saying, Matilda responding with demure blushes.

There was nothing we could do except sit and wait for the speeches to finish. I had to be there to complete mine. Rufus would never forgive me if I went after Delilah now. Whatever she was up to would have to wait; I just hoped she wouldn't do anything stupid. I couldn't even be sure my wild assumptions were even correct. I hoped they weren't or Delilah was about to confront a murderer.

35.
Bee Blower

This can be gas or electrically powered and blows the bees from the honey supers, to allow collection of the honey.

What was a twenty minute speech about my oldest friend, our childhood pranks, our years apart and finally our re-acquaintance, now became a blur of words as I stood up from the table to take over where the Dame had left off. Not my usual composed self, Rob gave me a look of concern. A good half-an-hour of the Dame's speech had given me time to consider the consequences of Delilah's actions. I couldn't go after Delilah, I couldn't voice my fears to the whole room and I had to complete my speech. Taking a gulp of water I began.

The speech itself was barely coherent and was complete in ten minutes. Rufus, thankfully, didn't seem to notice and the other guests must have put it down to nerves or excess champagne. As I sat back down to polite applause, Rob leant across Delilah's empty chair.

'Is everything OK?'

'Delilah's gone after Liliya,' I said, thankfully heard only by Rob over the applause.

'Why? She's not going to ask her on a date is she?' he chuckled. The applause died down and Rufus stood once more.

'Can I ask you all to raise your glasses in one final toast to the bridesmaid and the best man?' He raised a glass towards our table. It was only now he saw my anxious face and there was a brief moment of recognition, before everyone else was on their feet and cheering.

'She thinks Liliya killed the Russian and that she might have killed Penny.' My whispering was fierce as Rob stood up and turned towards the top table and joined the applause.

'What?' he said, still looking towards the front in an effort not to draw attention to ourselves.

The cake finally made its entrance on a large silver platter and was placed on the small square table ready to be cut. Penny did not appear with it. That was my final excuse for Penny's absence scuppered.

'I think she might be right,' I said, as people began to sit back down.

'Well what are we doing stood here then?' Rob said. We were the only two people still standing, apart from Matilda and Rufus. We looked across at the top table. 'Excuse us!' Rob grabbed my arm and we left the banqueting hall.

Once outside on the gravel at the front of the house we could hear a cheer as the bride and groom cut the cake, and the wedding reception started up again the general hubbub of conversation, the odd chink of a glass or cutlery.

'How long has she been gone?'

I looked at my watch. 'About half-an-hour.'

'Right, you go around to the chapel, check they are not there, I'll go back towards the west wing.' Rob was galvanised into action and I had my orders.

Douglas looked at us and barked. His water bowl upturned he was obviously thirsty but we had more pressing issues.

'What the bloody hell is going on out here,' Rufus' voice boomed from behind us. 'And where's Liliya? Wasn't she supposed to be sorting that dog out?' he said, pointing at Douglas.

'Delilah's disappeared,' I said.

'She's a grown woman Blake, it's her fault if she misses dessert, now come back inside, it's my wedding day.' I couldn't blame him for shouting. Rufus was fed up with the drama of the last few weeks and this was not helping.

'Erm, it's got a bit more complicated than missing dessert,' I replied.

'Look, we don't have time for this. If you and Delilah are right we need to find her now, she could be in real danger.' Rob started to make his way to the other end of the castle.

'What?' Rufus frowned.

'Come on Blake,' Rob shouted back over his shoulder.

'We have to find Delilah and Liliya,' I said to Rufus and turned in the direction of the chapel.

'What? Why? What's Liliya got to do with all of this?'

'I haven't got time to explain, just trust me, it's

important, now go back inside and have some more champagne.' I waved a hand behind me and disappeared around the side of the castle.

I heard his footsteps follow me but looking back I saw he was standing by the corner of the garden-room window, where Douglas had been tied to the cast iron drain pipe, watching. He bent to scratch the dogs' ears and Douglas reciprocated with a lick. Looking behind him, Rufus made his decision and, righting the upturned water dish he filled it from a tap on the wall and turned back to be with his wife.

I was left alone with my thoughts, the crunching of gravel underfoot and then the clack of my shoes across the paving slabs of the terrace. I really hoped we weren't right. I hoped Liliya had gone to get Douglas more water and that Delilah had found her in the kitchen and thought better of asking any impertinent questions. Penny was probably working at the café, maybe never intended to be at the wedding reception, argument or not. Two things about Penny's absence remained unexplained. If she'd never intended to come, why was there a place for her at our table and why had she left Douglas at the castle, on what would be a very busy and important day for the Darensky family?

Walking around the edge of the castle, the walls were vast and imposing. How were we ever going to find them? If Delilah was right and Liliya had killed Penny, what would she have done with her? The last time she'd been seen by any of us was in the garden-room, yesterday. Was she even still within the walls of the estate? Had Liliya put the body in an outhouse until after the wedding? And then it struck me. If Geoff Layland's murder was unrelated to that of the Russian and the student and Liliya had killed Geoff to secure Penny's affections, then after all that effort would she really then kill Penny at the first sign of resistance? With such strength of feeling, surely she'd persevere? But if she'd confessed, as Delilah imagined, in desperation to show the seriousness of her unrequited love, what had she expected Penny to do?

As fantastical and hypothetical as this whole thing seemed, I allowed my brain to run with it for a moment. Maybe Penny threatened to go to the police? It's what any normal person would do if they were told someone had killed for them. Faced with this prospect there's no way Liliya could have just let Penny go. She had two options. Kill her to keep her quiet or keep her here and try to convince her not to go to the police. If Liliya was our murderer then killing was an option that she wouldn't balk at, but this was someone she loved. So, the only option left was that she was keeping Penny somewhere, but where?

The noise of my shoes tapping on the terrace patio stopped as I reached the East wing of the castle and the little chapel ahead of me. My feet fell silent on the grass and it was then I remembered the tapping from the chapel crypt. Liliya had said she had dealt with the problem. There'd been no noise from the pipes during the service and I assumed it was because they had been fixed. I had noted the noise wasn't a noise that faulty pipes usually make. What if the source of the noise was human? That was it. It wasn't faulty pipes; it was like a Morse code. Someone had been tapping the pipes to get our attention. I started to run towards the chapel. Was I too late? Had Liliya's solution to the plumbing problem been finite? I got my answer soon enough.

Approaching the chapel door I could hear voices coming from inside.

'We can sort this out Liliya!' Delilah's voice echoed, allowing me to hear the conversation from the chapel door.

'Oh I'm sorting it!' Came Liliya's reply.

I pushed the chapel door open and tried to look in without making myself known. I couldn't see anything. Pushing the door a bit further, it creaked slightly. I held my breath. Nothing. The conversation continued.

'Not like this,' Delilah's voice again.

Poking my head around the door, I could see the chapel was empty. I stepped forward and slid myself around the door. My shoe clicked on the slabs of the church floor. I inwardly cursed, as there was a pause in the voices.

'What was that? Is there someone else here?' Liliya's voice was high pitched, on the edge of hysteria.

'Liliya, you can't do this,' Delilah ignored the question.

I still couldn't see them. I bent down and silently removed my shoes. In just a pair of black cotton socks, I made my way down the aisle, a very different experience to one only a few hours ago. The slabs were cold against my feet; I placed my shoes on the front pew and at last saw where the voices were coming from.

A door was open to the left of the altar. It was the mirror of the vestry door on the opposite side but this one lead to a staircase and had a faint light glow emanating from below.

'I can do what I like! You can't have her!' Liliya's voice was cracking as she spoke. 'I know you want her, I knew from the moment I saw you with her.'

'We're friends Liliya. For Christs' sake our dogs just happened to get on, this is ridiculous.' Delilah was exasperated and it wasn't helping.

'That's what you say!

'Well ask Penny then.'

I stepped cautiously to the edge of the doorframe and peered in. Luck was on my side. Liliya had her back to me. She was standing at the bottom of a very old wooden staircase. Liliya had hold of Penny who was tied up and gagged. I could see the knot of material behind her head. It explained her lack of a contribution to the negotiation. In Liliya's right hand she held a huge sword, which was pointing at Delilah. I'd seen two of these in at the bottom of the staircase in the castle. I contemplated creeping back out the chapel to retrieve its counterpart and even up the odds. My school fencing days may just come in handy, but Delilah saw me. She made no acknowledgement but I knew

I couldn't leave now; Liliya was highly volatile. As tempting as it was to arm myself in a gentlemanly fashion, this was neither a practical nor a sound plan. Instead I reached across to the altar and took hold of a heavy candlestick standing on a table beside the lectern. I really didn't want to have to use it, let alone against a woman, but with an array of injuries from the last few encounters I'd had with murderers, I wasn't taking any chances.

'Why don't you put the sword down, untie Penny and we can talk about this sensibly,' Delilah tried.

'You can't have her!' Liliya pulled Penny even closer to her and turned the sword towards her hostage.

'Liliya?' Delilah took a step forward, hand outstretched in reassurance.

Liliya was not reassured. She started to retreat back up the steps of the crypt. She still hadn't turned around. I was desperately trying to think of a way to disarm her that wouldn't injure anyone when the door to the chapel gave an almighty creak that could not be covered up. Liliya turned around.

'You! Why couldn't you just keep your nose out of it? You think because you're Rufus' friend you're somehow part of this family, well you're not.' Venom oozed from her words. This was our queen bee!

'It's all right Liliya, I'm not going to do anything.' I put the candlestick down on the pew behind me and stepped back. I was going to have to let her come up the steps with Penny. I didn't dare turn to see who had entered the chapel. I was happy for Liliya to assume it was I that had made the noise, at least that way we stood a chance.

Liliya started to ascend the stairs, dragging Penny with her and waving the sword wildly at me. Penny's eyes were blood shot, her face damp with tears, her eyes wide; she didn't even struggle. I stood back further and held my hands up, showing her I had nothing in them. By surrendering I hoped there might still be a way to salvage this situation.

'Get out of my way,' Liliya yelled.

'You don't have to do this,' Delilah shouted, from behind her.

'Shut up and stay back,' she said, turning back to Delilah. The sword in her hand was getting dangerously close to Penny's face.

For a moment a thought about making a grab for the weapon but it meant pulling on the blade. I would not be able to hold it for one second before the sharp metal cut into my hand. Liliya reached the penultimate step. The candlestick was still within reach of my left hand. It was then I saw Rufus with a second candlestick as he approached the other side of the door, from behind the lectern. Concentrating on the last few steps, Liliya didn't see him and had her back to us.

'We can sort this out,' I tried as Liliya dragged Penny up the last two steps and into the chapel, keeping the sword between them and me. It was last-ditch attempt at negotiation but more than anything a way to try and stop her from turning around. Rufus was now behind her. A sudden scrap of his shoes on the flagstones, gave him away. Penny saw her advantage, kicked out at Liliya and ran up the aisle. Liliya spun round, sword in hand and before I knew what was happening, Rufus had brought the candlestick down on Liliya's head.

A sickening crack signaled contact. Liliya's eyes rolled into the back of her head as she teetered on the edge of the staircase to the crypt. The sword twisted in the air and fell from her hand sliding onto the cold slabs of the church floor. I lurched forward to pull her back but I was too late. Liliya plummeted backwards, ten foot into the crypt, landing in a broken heap at the bottom of the steps. Delilah watched helplessly as Liliya fell, now horrified by what lay at her feet.

I ran down the steps towards Liliya's prone body. Reaching out for her pulse, I felt nothing but twisted sharp bone under the stretched skin of her neck. A trickle of blood fell from her mouth. She was dead. I looked up at Rufus. Penny's shoulders shuddered with sobs as Rufus shielded her from the sight below. Delilah was stunned into silence. I shook my head. Rufus knew what I meant. This was one wedding that was going down in history for all the wrong reasons and the Salderkians would dine out on this story for decades.

36.
Castes

Castes refer to the three different type of bee in the hive: the workers, the drones and the queen.

The reality of the situation hit home fast. Rufus sat Penny down on a pew and removed her gag and ties, then went to call the authorities while Delilah joined Penny on the pew. I stayed in the crypt. Despite Liliya being very definitely dead I didn't feel I could leave. Even after all she'd done it was undignified to just leave her there. The reception came to an abrupt end when the police and medical staff arrived. Matilda and the Dame had to be told and there was no hiding the commotion from the assembled guests. Even the most adept best man could not have shielded his friend from the consequences of such a horrifying split-second decision.

It was the morning after the wedding and we were taking one last walk with Bertie and Prince across the heather topped cliffs of the island, before catching the afternoon ferry back to the mainland. Rufus had left the previous evening, taking a helicopter across with Matilda. Lilliya's body had been transported to a mortuary on the mainland for and autopsy and no doubt Rufus and Matilda had a lot to talk about. Edward had also returned to the mainland this morning to support Rufus. I would have gone too, but there had been no other tickets left on the morning ferry, what with all the journalists coming and going. The island had attracted a plethora of paparazzi as soon as the news hit the mainland.

None of us wanted to stay on the island a moment longer than we had to and had purchased tickets for the next available ferry, which was this afternoon. We'd booked into a hotel on the mainland. The Naismiths had taken it as a slight on their hospitality. Only toast had been on offer at breakfast this morning. Not even a grunt from behind the newspaper. I'm sure the animosity was in part, more to do with my evasion of their questions, depriving them of any juicy gossip in regard to the wedding finale.

Rob, Delilah and I were now sat on the bench that looked out to sea. The guillemots and seagulls carried on as if nothing had happened to disturb the peace of this serene island.

'I still can't believe you went after her like that,' Rob said to Delilah.

'Why not? Someone had to, you were too busy chatting up that cousin and Blake had his speech to do.'

'Hey, that's unfair.' Rob turned and frowned at Delilah. 'She was chatting me up,' he smiled.

'Whatever. Either way you look at it, it was down to me.'

'No it wasn't. I'm the police officer!' Rob leant down to scratch Bertie's ears who had come to join us, and chosen to sit under the bench from where he could watch Prince run from left to right after flies.

'Off duty!' Delilah marked triumphantly.

'Seriously Delilah,' I took my turn. 'You could have been killed.'

'Well I wasn't.'

'It didn't end well though did it?' Rob said.

'I hope you're not suggesting that was my fault?' Delilah looked at her feet.

Rob did not reply. The three of us watched the seabirds collecting their lunch. Delilah sighed and rubbed her temple. It was fair to say she felt some responsibility for the situation that had unfolded yesterday. We were to visit the police station on the mainland, tomorrow to give a full statement.

'She told me everything, you know,' Delilah said, to neither of us in particular. Sitting either side of her we stayed silent, anticipating the need for Delilah to get it off her chest. 'Everything! Her father had come looking for her at the castle. The Russian?' Delilah looked at me. I nodded.

'Well he told her who he was. She was overjoyed at first, but then he told her he had no money. He tried to blackmail Liliya in exchange for his silence. If she gave him the money, he wouldn't tell Rufus exactly what Matilda had been.'

Rob raised an eyebrow, inviting Delilah to continue.

'It was almost as if she had this huge burden and she needed to tell someone. I think it's the only thing that saved Penny and I. Liliya just wanted to talk. She was desperate for Penny to understand. Maybe she thought if I understood, Penny would see too? She told me that Matilda had lived in a slum in Russia. She was young and she'd left home, running from an abusive father and she had no money. She had to get food, had to live and there was only one thing she knew she could do and do well. She'd always had a way with men, so naturally thought nothing of them paying to spend time with her.' Delilah cleared her throat and continued. 'They were rich men, and Alexander, the Russian on the beach, was one of them. He'd held a position with the royal family, treated Matilda well and made sure she was comfortably provided for. Then she fell pregnant with Liliya.'

Delilah put her hands on her knees and stretched her arms, Bertie shuffled under the bench. We of course knew this story but Rob and I continued to listen, knowing that Delilah needed us to.

'Of course Liliya was upset to discover her past. Imagine the roller coaster. Finally meeting your father and then discovering your mother had been a prostitute. She was angry and wanted revenge. How dare this man try to blackmail them, try to ruin what was a very nice life she had and destroy her mother's hopes of happiness with Rufus? She arranged to meet Alexander on the beach later that day by the caves and pay him the money. Little did he know that that would be the last thing he ever did. She took one of the swords from the castle with her and waited for him in the cave. She said killing him was easier than she'd thought. She just left his body in the cave. It was almost too good to be true when the storm and the tide took it out to sea and back onto the beach on the opposite side of the island. The shipwreck was a perfect explanation. When Robin Everall approached her the next day, saying he'd seen her with the sword and the Russian, and then also tried to blackmail her. Well, killing a second time wasn't all that difficult.'

'It never ceases to amaze me how many people find killing easy,' Rob said.

'I think that's just because you see it more often than others,' I said.

Rob laughed. 'I've seen more of it since I met you two. Seriously! What is with Hetherington and Delibes?'

'It's not our fault,' Delilah said.

'Did Liliya say anything about Geoff Layland?' Rob said, a policeman's curiosity getting the better of him.

'Oh yes. I was right about that.' Delilah nudged me. 'After she killed the Russian and Everall, she thought that would be it, she was bound to be caught, but she wasn't. In fact she said she felt invigorated, finally in control of her life. She'd been in love with Penny for some time and finally saw a way to get her attention. Geoff Layland was never good enough for Penny. She said killing him was the easiest of them all.'

'Wow!' said Rob.

'She just didn't care anymore. I think it was the

confession from Alexander that he was her father and her mother's past that tipped her over the edge. Her needs had to come first.'

'You don't say,' Rob said.

Prince trotted up to the bench, bored with insect chasing and sat down looking at my pocket. He knew there were biscuits in there and he'd decided it was snack time. I reached into my pocket. The familiar rustling now enticed Bertie out from under the bench too, to take his place beside Prince. I gave them both a biscuit.

'How's Rufus?' Rob asked me.

'Not good. I haven't spoken to him since last night on the phone. We're going to meet up when I get over there tomorrow,' I replied.

'It was supposed to be the best day of his life,' Rob said.

'I know.'

'I can't see how he can stay with Matilda after this,' Delilah chipped in, always the one to voice what no one else dared.

'Who knows?' I said unwilling to speculate on the state on my friends' very new marriage.

'He killed her daughter!' she said.

I looked at her unsure how to respond.

'Better that than she'd killed you or Blake,' Rob said, firmly.

'Are we going for a pint before we head back?' Delilah asked.

I was in awe of her ability to switch off so easily. 'I don't think so,' I said. 'I've already had to avoid some awkward questions from the Naismiths this morning, I don't fancy running the gauntlet of Walter Simmons, do you?'

'No!' Rob agreed.

'Oh, he's all right,' Delilah tried.

'He's probably concocted a story already about how he knew it was Liliya all along,' Rob said.

'Well he did say he didn't trust them,' I said.

'Yes but who trusts Walter?' Rob replied, laughing.

'Very true.' I fished around in my pocket for another biscuit for the dogs. 'You know in a funny way, I'll miss this island,' I said. I'd grown fond of the Naismiths. Even Walter had his own eccentric charm. I wondered if Penny would recover from her ordeal and stay here or feel the need to distance herself from it all. She was young. She could make a new life for herself on the mainland away from the memories. What would happen to Rufus and Matilda? I supposed I would find out soon enough. All I could do was be there for my friend no matter what the outcome. There would of course be an inquest and an investigation into Liliya's death. I too, like Delilah, couldn't see how a marriage could survive this. The Dame would no doubt carry on regardless. Ever the matriarch, she'd no doubt tell herself it was her duty to restore order. That's what it always came down to in the end: *One's position in society*. We were all fighting for our place in this world, some more than others.

I suddenly felt an overwhelming need to be by my friend's side. The shock-induced numbness, caused by yesterday's events had worn off. The whole situation was still somewhat surreal but I knew whom it would be worst for and that was Rufus. All he'd wanted was a family.

'Come on then,' Rob said, standing from the bench. 'Let's stop navel-gazing. I won't be sorry to see the back of this place, talk about a busman's holiday.'

Delilah stood up and took Rob's hand, setting off across the cliff back towards the bed and breakfast. I stood up and followed them. Our bags were already packed and ready to go, waiting to be collected. I was looking forward to returning to Tuesbury, my cottage *Little Acorns* and settling back into village life. I watched Rob and Delilah a few steps ahead of me in the sunlight, the dogs bounding ahead of them, perhaps sensing the return home and normality. Delilah rested her head on Rob's shoulder as they walked and his arm encircled her, pulling her close. Were there more wedding bells on the horizon? I wasn't sure I could take the excitement.

'Come on Prince,' I said, looking down at my furry friend as he dropped back to join me. 'Let's go home.'

Acknowledgements

My thanks, as always, are due to my friends and family for their support.

Thanks also to my proofreader, and editor, Piers Cardon for his work on this project and his faith in Blake.

Finally a huge thank you to my ever loving and supportive husband who always believes in me, even when I don't.

Thank you for reading 'LIVE AND LET BEE.' If you've enjoyed reading, then further information, on existing and future publications by D S Nelson, is available via:

www.dsnelson.co.uk

You can follow D S Nelson via:

Twitter: **@WriterDSNelson**

Facebook: **www.facebook.com/WriterDSNelson**